"A HALF CASTE"
AND OTHER WRITINGS

THE ASIAN AMERICAN EXPERIENCE

Series Editor

Roger Daniels, University of Cincinnati

*A list of books in the series
appears at the end of this book.*

"A HALF CASTE"
AND OTHER WRITINGS

ONOTO WATANNA

Edited by

LINDA TRINH MOSER

and

ELIZABETH ROONEY

University of Illinois Press

Urbana and Chicago

© 2003 by the Board of Trustees
of the University of Illinois
All rights reserved
Manufactured in the United States of America

1 2 3 4 5 c p 5 4 3 2 1

∞ This book is printed on acid-free paper.

Library of Congress Cataloging-in-Publication Data
Watanna, Onoto, 1875–1954.
"A half caste" and other writings / Onoto Watanna ; edited by
Linda Trinh Moser and Elizabeth Rooney.
p.   cm. — (The Asian American experience)
Includes bibliographical references.
ISBN 0-252-02782-5 (cloth : alk. paper)
ISBN 0-252-07094-1 (pbk. : alk. paper)
1. Asian Americans—Fiction. 2. Eurasians—Fiction. 3. Asian
Americans. 4. Eurasians. 5. Asia. I. Moser, Linda Trinh, 1964– .
II. Rooney, Elizabeth, 1953– III. Title. IV. Series.
PR9199.3.W3689A6   2003
813'.52—dc21   2002006416

For Patrick, Jamie, and Casey with love.
And for Tam Gonsalves and the late
John Denis Gonsalves.

CONTENTS

PART 2: NONFICTION

ACKNOWLEDGMENTS

Help came from many in compiling these stories and essays. We are grateful to the University of Calgary Library and especially to the Special Collections librarian, Apollonia Steele, for invaluable assistance. We thank the staff members of the Toronto Reference Library for their help in uncovering long-forgotten stories and articles. We also thank Southwest Missouri State University for a summer faculty fellowship in 1998, which funded travel to various libraries and provided the necessary time to write and edit. For furnishing administrative assistance, we thank the English department at Southwest Missouri State University. Special thanks goes to the extraordinary Glenda Carnagey and her army of student workers, as well as to graduate assistant Marcia Nichols, who risked her eyesight typing from the sometimes blurry copies we provided her. We are particularly grateful to the English department faculty members at Southwest Missouri State for their support, especially W. D. Blackmon for his constant enthusiasm and Gayle Mercer for her encouragement and friendship. We also owe special gratitude to Ann Lowry, editor at University of Illinois Press, for her advice, patience, and continuing support of this project and to Jane Mohraz, associate editor, for her skill and care and for suggesting the collection's title.

We benefited from many scholars whose research and thoughts on Onoto Watanna helped shape the collection: Jean Lee Cole, Dominika Ferens, Maureen Honey, Noreen Lape, the late Amy Ling, and Annette White-Parks. We are especially indebted to Samina Najmi of Wheaton College, whose knowledge of Watanna and comments on an early version of the collection helped shape the introduction and our choices of what to include, and to Diana Birchall for bringing Watanna alive for us through her meticulous biographical research; Birchall's charm, wit, and generosity made "Winnying" thoroughly enjoyable. We are also grateful for the advice of Kathryn

West at Bellarmine College; her willingness to edit for typos and her continual support are the signs of true collegiality and friendship.

For their generosity and enthusiasm, we thank the many members of the extended Eaton clan, especially the Laferrière, Lewis, Birchall, and Rooney families. We thank Tim and Mary Rooney for their constant support and encouragement. For providing hospitality and inspiration while working on this project, we are most grateful to the Gonsalves and Moser families. Finally, special thanks go to Patrick James, Miles Trieu, and Ryan Trinh Moser for making room in their lives for Onoto Watanna.

INTRODUCTION

Linda Trinh Moser

The short stories and essays collected here for the first time span the novel-producing years of Onoto Watanna (1875–1954), the first novelist of Asian ancestry to be published in the United States. The earliest, an essay entitled "The Half Caste," appeared in 1898, a year before the publication of her first novel, *Miss Numè: A Japanese-American Romance* (1899). The last, "Elspeth," a story, appeared in 1923, two years before Watanna published her last novel, *His Royal Nibs* (1925). Elizabeth Rooney located most of the stories and essays using clues gathered from the boxes of notes, receipts, manuscripts, letters, scrapbooks, and other writings by Watanna left to the University of Calgary (where it is housed in the library's Special Collections) and in her family's possession (Elizabeth is Watanna's great-granddaughter). Of the approximately fifty short works authored by Watanna included or mentioned in her papers, we have selected nineteen—thirteen stories and six essays—divided into two sections: Fiction and Nonfiction. In compiling this collection, we began by omitting stories and essays for which we could not locate original publication information. We have also excluded those works still under copyright protection. From the remaining stories and essays, we selected those that would enable readers to see the scope and versatility of Onoto Watanna's writing. Many of the most notable stories in the collection have nothing to do with the Japanese themes that earned Watanna so much fame and notoriety. Even the ones that do center on Japanese themes offer perspectives that differ from those in her better-known novels. Taken together, these short works encompass a variety of themes, styles, and characterization that demonstrate Watanna's broad scope as a writer.

Onoto Watanna has posed particular challenges to literary scholars who have tried to classify her work. Samina Najmi notes that "feminist and Asian American literary critics often simply ignore Watanna, not knowing what else to do with her."[1] Elaine H. Kim's groundbreaking study, *Asian Ameri-*

can Literature: An Introduction to the Writings and Their Social Context (1982), for example, does not include her, although it mentions her sister Sui Sin Far (1865–1914) and other half-Asian writers, Sadakichi Hartmann (1867–1944) and Han Suyin (1917–).[2] The silence was undoubtedly related to choices Watanna made throughout her career. In contrast to Sui Sin Far's positive and realistic portrayals of Chinese immigrant communities, Watanna's work tends to exoticize rather than explain Asian culture. More troublesome to critics is her self-depiction. Although she was a Chinese Eurasian (her father English, her mother Chinese), Watanna almost never revealed her half-Chinese ancestry publicly, as her sister had done, but instead "passed" as a Japanese Eurasian. Inventing an appropriate biography, she claimed Nagasaki as her birthplace and a Japanese noblewoman for a mother. Even the name Onoto Watanna is a fabrication; it only sounds Japanese.

Onoto Watanna was the pseudonym of Winnifred Eaton, born in Montreal on August 21, 1875. Lillie Winifred, as she was christened, was the eighth child of Grace A. Trefusis (1846–1922) and Edward Eaton (1839–1915), whose children would eventually number fourteen (twelve of whom survived past infancy).[3] The Eatons were married in Shanghai on November 7, 1863. Edward had traveled to China, probably hoping to establish himself in the silk trade between China and England. Although Grace was born in China, she seems to have been educated in England; most likely, she returned to China to do missionary work.

By 1872, the Eatons had immigrated to Canada from England. Edward Eaton intermittently worked as a merchant and clerk but eventually abandoned these occupations to devote himself to painting, a passion that never allowed him to earn enough to support his ever-growing family. The Eaton family was extremely poor; at various times, the older children were taken out of school to help support themselves and their younger siblings. While Watanna's older siblings worked outside the home, she helped care for her young siblings at home. Despite the unevenness of her formal schooling, Watanna received a considerable amount of literary training at home, where she read works by such notables as Dickens, Tennyson, and Kipling.

In 1896, Watanna left home for Kingston, Jamaica, where she worked as a "general writer and reporter" for *Gall's News Letter*. Less than a year after arriving in Jamaica, she moved to Chicago, where she first began using her Japanese-sounding pseudonym. In early 1901, she relocated to New York, where in July she married Bertrand W. Babcock, with whom she had four children: Perry, Bertie (who died in childhood), Doris, and Charley. Divorcing Babcock in 1917, she married Frank Reeve. Although the couple initially set up house in Calgary, where Frank was establishing himself in the oil and cattle business, Winnifred's career beckoned. Without her husband, she moved back to New York and then to Hollywood, where she worked as a chief scenarist until 1931. In January 1932, she permanently returned to Calgary, where she remained until her death in 1954.

As Onoto Watanna, Winnifred Eaton had gained a large and devoted audience in the United States. Although the writer probably began using the Japanese-sounding name to lend credence to her "Japanese" novels, essays, and short stories, she continued to use the name for stories that did not feature Japanese subjects and themes. Works as varied as "Delia Dissents" (1908), featuring an Irish immigrant domestic, and "Margot" (1901), about a violin-playing protégé, were signed Onoto Watanna, suggesting that the pen name had become a successful marketing ploy. Although she also used multiple variations of her legal name to sign her work throughout her career, all the stories and essays included in this collection were published under Onoto Watanna.[4]

Watanna's favorable reputation as a writer was established in the early stages of her career. Her first novel, *Miss Numè of Japan* (1899), was positively reviewed in the *New York Times;* it was followed by thirteen other novels, nine of which take place in Japan.[5] William Dean Howells praised her second novel, *A Japanese Nightingale* (1901), describing it as "a lesson in the art of imitating nature."[6] By far her most successful work, *A Japanese Nightingale* went through several printings and was adapted into a Broadway play. Despite the historical popularity and success of her work, modern literary critics tended to ignore her until very recently. Initially, when mentioned at all, Onoto Watanna's name and work stood for racial, ethnic, or cultural betrayal. Echoing the sentiments of many early critics, Xiao-Huang Yin, for example, described Watanna as a writer who "trades her birthright for recognition and popularity."[7] Despite the negative assessment, Amy Ling found reason to praise her. In a 1983 essay, Ling discussed the feminist aspects of Watanna's novels, noting that "the heroines of her novels . . . are intelligent, independent, and strong-willed."[8] Ling continued this theme in *Between Worlds: Women Writers of Chinese Ancestry* (1990), which provided the first lengthy overview of Watanna's numerous novels, noting that the writer "supported herself and her [four] children entirely by her pen."[9] This later work provided a social context for the professional choices Watanna made, enabling readers to view her Japanese masquerade in positive terms. Noting that "the distinction between Chinese and Japanese Americans was extremely pronounced" when Watanna began her writing career, Ling argued that "passing" as Japanese was a "viable response" to historical racism against those of Chinese ancestry.[10] It allowed Watanna to avoid the animosity Chinese immigrants experienced and to present a biracial Asian identity similar to her actual one, despite its inauthenticity. Ling's groundbreaking interpretation of Watanna's career and literary choices generated a resurgence of interest in Watanna's work, represented by the recent reissues of *Me: A Book of Remembrance* (1997), *Miss Numè of Japan* (1999), and *The Heart of Hyacinth* (2000); *A Japanese Nightingale,* combined with *Madame Butterfly,* is forthcoming. Complementing the reissues of the novels, important studies of Watanna have also begun to appear, most notably Noreen Groover Lape's *West of the Border: The Multicultural Literature of the Western Frontier* (2000), which includes a chapter about Watanna's romance novels; *Onoto Watanna: The Story of Winnifred Eaton* (2001), a biography and critical overview of her work by her granddaughter, Diana Birchall; Dominika Ferens's *Edith and Winnifred Eaton: Chinatown Missions and Japanese Romances* (2002), a comparative study of the two sisters' work; and Jean Lee Cole's *Literary Voices of Winnifred Eaton: Redefining Ethnicity and Authenticity* (2002), a survey of the diverse perspectives found in her novels and screenplays.

The short stories included here rely on the same devices that made Watanna's novels popular: plucky heroines, romance (often cross-racial), and surprising plot twists. In the six stories set in Japan, Watanna performs a careful balancing act, simultaneously conforming to and resisting popular Western images of Asians. This duality becomes apparent in the numerous depictions of relationships between Japanese women and Western men that are reminiscent of *Madame Butterfly* (1898), perhaps still the most famous depiction of Japanese-American romance.[11] Echoing details from the tragic love story, Watanna's fiction brings together impoverished Japanese women (who, like Madame Butterfly, are often orphaned) and Western men sojourning in Japan. The revisions, however, never end in suicide, as *Madame Butterfly* does; Watanna manipulates the established formula in various ways to create successful cross-racial romances. Her Japanese heroines resist the image of Asian women as victims or passive "lotus blossoms," which had been popular since Commodore Matthew C. Perry forced Japan to end over two hundred years of political and economic isolation in 1854.[12] Refusing to rely on male protection, these heroines are self-reliant language instructors, nurses, and performers who support themselves financially, much as Watanna herself did.

The changes Watanna makes challenge an assumption inherent in *Madame Butterfly:* that Asian women are naturally submissive and subservient. Otoyo in "Two Converts," for example, leaves a husband who mistreats her physically and emotionally. She supports herself by teaching English to the Reverend John Redpath. Spousal abuse, however, is not Otoyo's only obstacle; Redpath's prejudices and religious intolerance of divorce encourage her to stay in the abusive marriage. By including Redpath's beliefs as an obstacle to Otoyo's happiness, Watanna calls attention to both gender and cultural bias, thus underscoring the dual oppression suffered by Asian women. Like most of Watanna's other female protagonists, Otoyo is triumphant in the end. The story surprisingly concludes with not only her conversion to Christianity but Redpath's conversion as well. Because the reverend has fallen in love with Otoyo, he is "converted" to the idea of divorce and, more important, the rights of women and racial others.

Just as Watanna's self-reliant female characters differ from Madame Butterfly, her male characters form a sharp contrast to Butterfly's selfish and insensitive American lover, B. F. Pinkerton. Like Masters in "A Contract," most of Watanna's Anglo male characters refuse to leave their Japanese lovers, often becoming engaged to or marrying them against the advice of family and friends. Other variations in her male characters emphasize that regret alone cannot atone for the mistreatment of Asian women by American or European men. The tragic end of *Madame Butterfly* allows Pinkerton the possibility of atonement when he returns to Japan to accept responsibility for his half-Japanese child. Watanna, however, is not so forgiving of male characters who mistreat or abandon their Japanese wives and biracial children. Redemption eludes such characters as Norman Hilton in "A Half Caste" (1899), who, like Pinkerton before him, returns to Japan. Hilton's intention is to claim his half-Japanese daughter, whose mother he deserted nearly sixteen years earlier. Demonstrating regret, he recounts how "he had married a Japanese girl—in Japanese fashion—adding, with unconcealed grim contempt for himself, that of course he had left her in American fashion."[13]

Told that his daughter is dead, Hilton conceives of another way of redeeming his past. He intends to do what he failed to do in the past; he plans on "settling down" and "returning to America" with Kiku, a geisha with whom he has fallen in love. Despite Hilton's remorse and resolve to do right, his attempt to redeem himself fails when Kiku shockingly reveals that she is the daughter he had abandoned years earlier. The potential incest foregrounds connections between the past and present crimes. Given a choice this time, Kiku will not be victimized again. Instead, the previous concealment of her identity, which becomes a way to avenge past wrongs, highlights the problems that arise when fathers desert their families.

"A Half Caste," however, does not merely point out the problems of a particular individual or family. Hilton's present crime is not just his potential to commit incest but also his continual disregard for Kiku's refusal to return his affection. Hilton's presumption that Kiku returns his feelings underscores how Americans misinterpret Japanese thoughts and emotions.

In other stories, Watanna continues to draw a connection between racial stereotypes and the kind of misinterpretation Hilton makes. In "Kirishima-san," Jack Mortimer, an American, articulates the West's presumption that Japanese relationships are based solely on utilitarian needs rather than those of the heart. Likening Kirishima to "the rest of [her] race," he tells her, "You don't even know the meaning of the word 'love,' much less are you capable of understanding it." While the "cold and indifferent" response Kirishima gives to Mortimer's confession of love further supports his stereotypical interpretation, the overall story undermines it by revealing how it conveniently covers up Mortimer's own coldness and indifference. Earlier, Mortimer had denied his feelings for Kirishima to his sister who reproached him by saying, "I hope you have not been foolish enough to fall in love with a Japanese woman, Jack." His response that he was "just having a little fun with her, that's all," which the love-struck Kirishima overhears, provides a better explanation for her seeming indifference than any supposed Japanese cultural practice or genetic predisposition. Falling back on stereotypes that blame the Japanese for their lack of love becomes a convenient way for Mortimer to absolve himself of his own wrongdoing. By calling attention to the ways Americans use racial, cultural, and gender stereotypes to their own advantage, Watanna creates the possibility of dismantling them.

Watanna's nonfiction also reveals efforts to undermine negative attitudes about Japan. The essays' style and thematic scope suggest an attempt to instruct North American audiences about Japanese culture and identity. Like her novels, however, the essays include descriptions of the more exotic and quaint aspects of Japanese life: kimono-clad geishas, blooming cherry trees, miniaturized shrubs, and samurai legends. Yet, as Diana Birchall notes, the essays "are not written in [her] usual lively imaginative style. Strictly research pieces, they were a way to make some money while not letting her background work [for the novels] go to waste."[14] Like her invented Japanese persona, the essays may have helped make Watanna a more marketable writer. If she presented herself as an expert on Japan, her novels might seem more credible. With such titles as "The Japanese Drama and the Actor" (1902), "Every-day Life in Japan" (1904), and "The Marvelous Miniature Trees of Japan" (1904), Watanna explains a variety of cultural details, ranging from the origins of Japanese drama to the duties of a Japanese housewife and the cultivation of bonsai. But they also defy stereotypical thinking by stressing the importance of appreciating another culture on its own terms.

Although Watanna rarely includes direct protest in her "research pieces," she makes a surprising exception in "The Japanese in America" (1907), an essay that explicitly articulates her concern over the treatment of Asians who immigrate to the United States. Watanna's failure to depict in her novels the lives of more Asians in America has probably encouraged the notion that she is not interested in issues related to Asian immigration. *Sunny-San* (1922), the last Japanese novel Watanna would write, is the only one to include a character who moves permanently from Asia to the United States. In earlier novels, Watanna had made references to the American experiences of Japanese characters; however, they stay in the United States only temporarily. *Miss Numè of Japan* (1899) depicts the title character's return to Japan after a brief sojourn in the United States. In *A Japanese Nightingale* (1901), readers learn Yuki will visit the United States with her husband, Jack Bigelow, but she will not reside there permanently. Bigelow insists that they "will come back here [to Japan] again" (225). By limiting Japanese characters in her novels to the roles of temporary visitors to America, Watanna seems to present Asians as aliens unable to assimilate in the West.

Watanna calls attention to Asian immigration to the United States far more often in her essays and short fiction than in her novels. In "The Japanese in America," Watanna clearly undermines the image of Asians as unassimilable aliens, making her most overtly political statement and stand against racism in print. In the essay, Watanna responds to an article (which she quotes at length) written by a *New York Times* correspondent from Oakland, California. Describing Japanese immigrant communities as a military, economic, and moral threat to America, the correspondent reiterates the arguments expressed by members of the West Coast's Asian Exclusion League, which formed in 1905 to prevent immigration from China and Japan; their efforts would lead to legalized limitations on immigration from Japan, laws prohibiting Japanese farmers from owning land, and the Supreme Court's 1922 decision to deny naturalization privileges to Japanese-born U.S. residents.

Mirroring a strategy she used in her short stories, Watanna simultaneously supports and subverts Asian stereotypes throughout the essay. While she is willing to accept some of the correspondent's stereotypical descriptions of the Japanese, she also undercuts them by describing Americans in the same terms. This particular strategy challenges the supposed opposition between Asia and America upon which anti-immigration supporters depended. In response to the charge that the Japanese are "bursting with conceit," Watanna agrees but asserts that Americans are too when she compares American attitudes after the Spanish-American War with those of the Japanese after their 1905 victory against Russia (the first modern-day conflict in which a European country was defeated by an Asian power). The way Watanna depicts her ancestry in the essay also challenges the idea that East and West are mutually exclusive. By describing herself as "Eurasian" and "Irish more than English—Chinese as well as Japanese," Watanna insists on an identity that embodies many cultures and blurs racial and ethnic boundaries. At the same time, she continues to conform to a more accepted version of mixed-Asian identity. While she does reveal her Chinese ancestry, the simultaneous insistence on Japanese heritage also protects her invented identity as Japanese Eurasian, Onoto Watanna.

In the same essay, Watanna undermines a pejorative description of the Japanese as "servants" by placing everyone in that category. She writes, "We are all servants—of various sorts. I serve you, for whom I write. You serve your customers, or your clients. Shall each one of us kick at the one below us?" In other places, she fails to dismiss notions of Japanese difference and instead draws on them for humor. Such is the case in the anecdote about her need to fire Taku, her Japanese employee, because his insistence on bathing nude in the kitchen scandalizes other servants. Although public bathing in Japan is a cultural reality, Watanna's description of how "he would arise politely and bow to [the Irish maid] from his watery retreat" is probably invented. The image suggests that the Japanese would be impervious to American behavioral codes and conveys Western notions about public bathing as a sign of immodesty and immorality. Although the description of Taku's bathing and bowing habits relies on a mixture of ethnographic fact and stereotypical views, Watanna reminds readers that public bathing is only immoral by American, not Japanese, standards, thus reinforcing a need for cultural relativity.

Like "The Japanese in America," several of Watanna's short stories focus on Japanese living in America and comment on the problems and barriers they face because of race. "The Loves of Sakura Jiro and the Three Headed Maid," for example, depicts a Japanese immigrant seeking a job fitting his self-image as "a poet, a dreamer." To this end he turns down the possibility of working long hours for low pay in the business sector and begins work as a magician. As an entertainer, Jiro gains success in American culture, symbolized by his eventual romance with Marva, an Anglo-American woman working as a sideshow "freak," the three-headed maid of the story's title. On the one hand, Sakura Jiro's sideshow act fulfills America's taste for Asian exoticism. On the other, the act reinforces the domestic (as opposed to exotic) aspects of tricks supposedly invented and perfected in the East. Sakura Jiro's greatest trick, described as a "feat" he "has striven during his whole life to perfect," presents an exaggerated image of domesticity. After inhaling natural gas fumes, Sakura blows into a tube, igniting a gas burner on which his assistant places a pan and cooks four pancakes. After distributing the pancakes, Jiro collapses, but his culinary effort has won him Marva's love by proving his fortitude and dedication to his art.

Despite fantastical and humorous elements, the story mirrors a historical reality of early Japanese immigrants whose employment possibilities were limited to the domestic labor mimicked by Sakura's unique method of cooking breakfast. At the same time, it also suggests the innovative ways Japanese immigrants survived unfair and hostile conditions. Jiro's magic turns the tables on Americans who would exploit his labor by exploiting their taste for the "exotic." He also capitalizes on general ignorance about Japan. What his American audiences believed to be exotic is in actuality only a clever manner of making a very common American meal—pancakes.

Sakura Jiro's creative role as a magician also mirrors his creator's literary masquerade as Onoto Watanna, which similarly garnered her fame and fortune. Other characters also adopt exotic disguises in their pursuit of pecuniary success. Jiro's rival in love and fame, Ostero, the Spanish juggler, is really an Irishman named Kelly.

"Miss Lily and Miss Chrysanthemum" (1903) touches on other aspects of Watanna's biography, particularly those related to her mixed-race origins.[15] Lily and Chrysanthemum are half-Asian and half-English sisters living in Chicago. The story allows Watanna not only to explore how mixed-race ancestry affects the sisters' psychological development but also to critique mainstream attitudes about Asian Americans.

Lily, or "Yuri," is described as "supersensitive," a trait that suggests a psychological problem often stereotypically attributed to those who are biracial. Lily's isolation from society, however, is due not to her individual psychology but to society's "strange antipathy" for and "prejudice" against those of Asian ancestry. Watanna earlier explored this personal subject in an essay, "The Half Caste" (1898). Like "Miss Lily and Miss Chrysanthemum," the essay counteracts a reliance on "half caste" stereotypes in its discussion of the effects of mainstream attitudes on individuals of both Asian and Anglo ancestry. "From their earliest childhood," the essay asserts, "whether in this country, Europe or Japan, they are made to feel that they are different from those about them."

The story goes further than the essay in undercutting negative images of mixed-race individuals by focusing not on Lily's disadvantages but on her successes. She does not internalize or compensate for feelings of inferiority as other popular literary depictions of mixed-race Asians often suggest.

Instead, her isolation from American culture encourages both financial and intellectual independence. She becomes the epitome of a self-made "working girl" who supports both herself and her younger sister.

Watanna's interest in the resourcefulness of working women emerges throughout the other short stories. In the autobiographical story "A Neighbor's Garden, My Own and a Dream One" (1908), Watanna depicts challenges faced by women writers: how to balance the demands of motherhood and a career. The dual roles as mother and working woman prevent the narrator of the story from honing her domestic skills. Supporting herself through writing deters her from creating a garden as elaborate as those of her female neighbors who are unemployed. "[W]ith my work as a writer," she says, "I found that the most I could do in life was to produce a book and a baby a year."

Many of the stories dealing with class issues reveal another sharp divergence from Watanna's novels: they feature white women. For "Delia Dissents," Watanna brings back the Irish maid from her 1907 novel, *The Diary of Delia: Being a Veracious Chronicle of the Kitchen, with Some Side-Lights on the Parlour*. Recounted in the Irish brogue of its title character, Watanna reveals her skill at reproducing accents while comically describing how Delia single-handedly prevents a strike of domestic workers, which in turn wins her the love of Larry Mulvaney, a fellow immigrant from Ireland.

Like "Delia Dissents," most of Watanna's stories about working women feature romance and happily-ever-after endings, but they also touch on the problems faced by women trying to juggle domestic and economic interests, much as Watanna herself had to do. In "Eyes That Saw Not" (1902), co-written with Watanna's first husband, Bertrand W. Babcock, Elizabeth risks her future domestic happiness in order to write. When her fiancé, John Swinnerton, discovers she has been elaborating on and rewriting the stories he has dictated to her, he sends her away, accusing her of stealing his work. In "Elspeth" (1923), one of the best-written stories in the entire collection, the domestic life of the widowed Mrs. Maitland also seems to suffer when her long working hours leave Elspeth, her "pretty and temperamental" sixteen-year-old daughter, to her own devices. When Mrs. Maitland describes herself as "this business machine that could only throw to her [daughter] a few snatches of her time," the story seems to support the notion that families suffer when mothers work. This view is strengthened further when Elspeth drops out of school and elopes with Hal Holloway against her mother's wishes; Elspeth's premature entry into adulthood is directly connected to her mother's inability to supervise her.

The story, however, abruptly changes its view on working mothers after Senator T. Beveridge Holloway, Elspeth's wealthy father-in-law, cuts off his son's financial support, accusing both mother and daughter of being a "couple of adventuresses and cheat swindlers, blackmailers." Unlike Senator Holloway, Mrs. Maitland is resolved to support both Elspeth and her new son-in-law, whom she insists must finish college. Instead of harming or destroying the family, Mrs. Maitland's employment ensures her family's economic and emotional happiness. Mrs. Maitland's willingness to work also, in typical Watanna fashion, leads to the possibility of romance. Impressed by her unflappable resolve, her long-admiring male employer invites her on a date, her first since being widowed. Mrs. Maitland's work ethic thus creates the possibility for a more stable and potentially larger family (including a husband for her daughter and perhaps one for herself), ultimately proving that women can be effective simultaneously at home and in business.

The short works of Onoto Watanna are a significant contribution to Asian American letters. While Watanna's representations mirror such works as *Madame Butterfly* by depending on stereotypical images of Asian women, they also foreshadow characters from more recent fiction by Asian Pacific American writers who resist those images. Like the trickster protagonist Wittman Ah Sing from Maxine Hong Kingston's 1989 *Tripmaster Monkey: His Fake Book* (a novel in which Onoto Watanna/Winnifred Eaton makes a brief cameo appearance), Watanna's characters are always capable, clever, inventive, and resourceful. While they may sometimes verge on the trite, her characters never fail to surprise. Nor, for that matter, does Watanna. Her ability to create a cast of characters and themes beyond the scope of her Japanese novels will undoubtedly challenge readers to develop new ways of interpreting her life and work.

Notes

1. Samina Najmi, introduction to *The Heart of Hyacinth,* by Onoto Watanna (1899; reprint, Seattle: University of Washington Press, 2000), xxxiii.

2. Elaine H. Kim, *Asian American Literature: An Introduction to the Writings and Their Social Context* (Philadelphia: Temple University Press, 1982), 283n14.

3. Although a baptismal record spells her name with only one *n,* Eaton usually spelled it with two.

4. Watanna signed her work with a variety of names. For example, she uses Winnie Eaton for two early works: "Sneer Not" (1896), a poem published in *Gall's News Letter;* and "A Poor Devil," which appeared in *Metropolitan Magazine.* Next to a

clipping of the story in a scrapbook, Watanna described it as her first published story (n.d., box 14, Winnifred Eaton Reeve Fonds, Special Collections, University of Calgary Library, Calgary, Alberta, Canada). *Cattle* (1924), her second-to-last novel, was published under Winnifred Eaton; however, in this later period of her writing career, she also used Reeve, her married name. "Other People's Troubles: An Antidote for Your Own," a novel published serially in *Farm and Ranch Review* (1919), was published under Winnifred Reeve. Her last novel, *His Royal Nibs* (1925), features another name variation; signed by Winifred Eaton Reeve, she has dropped the second *n* from her first name.

5. Her novels in order of publication date are *Miss Numè of Japan: A Japanese-American Romance* (Chicago: Rand McNally, 1899; reprint, Baltimore: Johns Hopkins University Press, 1999), *A Japanese Nightingale* (New York: Harper and Brothers, 1901; reprint, New Brunswick N.J.: Rutgers University Press, 2001), *The Wooing of Wisteria* (New York: Harper and Brothers, 1902), *The Heart of Hyacinth* (New York: Harper and Brothers, 1903; reprint, Seattle: University of Washington Press, 2000), *Daughters of Nijo* (New York: Macmillan, 1904), *The Love of Azalea* (New York: Dodd, Mead, 1904), *A Japanese Blossom* (New York: Harper and Brothers, 1906), *The Diary of Delia: Being a Veracious Chronicle of the Kitchen, with Some Side-Lights on the Parlour* (New York: Doubleday, Page, 1907), *Tama* (New York: Harper and Brothers, 1910), *The Honorable Miss Moonlight* (New York: Harper and Brothers, 1912), *Me: A Book of Remembrance* (New York: Century, 1915; reprint, Jackson: University Press of Mississippi, 1997), *Marion: The Story of an Artist's Model* (New York: W. J. Watt, 1916), *Sunny-San* (Toronto: McClelland and Stewart; New York: George H. Doran, 1922), *Cattle* (New York: W. J. Watt, 1924), and *His Royal Nibs* (New York: W. J. Watt, 1925).

6. W[illiam] D[ean] Howells, "A Psychological Counter-Current in Recent Fiction," *North American Review* 173 (December 1901): 881. In this same review, Howells also generously wrote, "It has its little defects, but its directness, and sincerity, and its felicity through the sparing touch make me unwilling to note them. In fact, I have forgotten them" (881).

7. Xiao-Huang Yin, "Between the East and West: Sui Sin Far—the First Chinese-American Woman Writer," *Arizona Quarterly* 7 (Winter 1991): 54.

8. Amy Ling, "Winnifred Eaton: Ethnic Chameleon and Popular Success," *MELUS* 11 (Fall 1984): 11.

9. Amy Ling, *Between Worlds: Women Writers of Chinese Ancestry* (New York: Pergamon, 1990), 29.

10. Ibid, 24.

11. Puccini's adaptation of the story is the best known today. During the height of Watanna's popularity, however, three different versions of *Madame Butterfly* were available to the public. John Luther Long (1861–1927) published the original version as a novel in 1898. David Belasco (1853–1931) adapted Long's story into a one-act play of the same name; it was produced for the first time on March 5, 1900, in New York City's Herald Square Theater. Puccini transformed *Madame Butterfly* into

an opera after seeing Belasco's play in London; it premiered in Milan (1904), London (1905), and New York (1906).

12. On March 31, 1854, the United States and Japan signed the Treaty of Kanagawa, thus ending a policy of seclusion launched by the Japanese in the mid-1600s.

13. All the following quotations from Watanna's short works are in this collection.

14. Diana Birchall, *Onoto Watanna: The Story of Winnifred Eaton* (Urbana: University of Illinois Press, 2001), 56.

15. Samina Najmi cleverly notes that the story also alludes to Eaton's biography by "including [a variation of] her given name, Lillie." Handwritten note to Linda Trinh Moser, November 14, 2000.

PART I

SHORT FICTION

A HALF CASTE

A miscellaneous crowd of men, women and children jostled each other on the wharf, some of them going perilously near the end of it in their eagerness to watch the passengers on the *Empress of India,* which had just arrived.

Norman Hilton stood on deck, his hands thrust deep in his trousers pockets. He seemed in no hurry to leave the boat, but leaned against the guard-rail, watching the surging crowd on the wharf beneath.

"Shall you go ashore to-night?"

He started from the moody dream into which he had drifted; then answered, absently, pushing his cap far back on his head:

"Well, I don't know. Fact is, now the journey is over—I feel—er—just a trifle nervous."

His friend looked at him keenly.

"Second trip for you, I believe?"

"Yes."

"Fifth for me," his companion continued. "Rather be here than anywhere else."

"Why?" Hilton looked at him curiously.

The other laughed, waving his hand lightly toward the city.

"You know my weakness—and, for that matter, your own—women. I like the Japanese style, too—artless, jolly, pretty—er ———. Agree with me?"

"Perhaps."

Hilton put a cigar between his teeth and began smoking it. He broke a silence that fell between them with the information that on his former voyage he had married a Japanese girl—in Japanese fashion—adding, with unconcealed grim contempt for himself, that of course he had left her in American fashion.

"Expect to see her again?"

"No, she is dead!" He paused for a moment, and then added, a trifle hesitatingly: "There was a child. I want it."

"Ah!"

Hilton finished smoking his cigar and threw the stub into the bay.

"I have a hard job before me," he said, nervously, "as I have little or no clew to the child's whereabouts. It was nearly sixteen years ago, you know." He paused again, ruminating, and took a few slow strides across the deck. "I am alone in the world. She is about all the kin I have, in fact. It sounds brutal, I suppose, but during all these years I have made no inquiry about her whatever. I forgot the fact of her birth almost as I forgot the mother's existence. I don't know what possessed me to come now, anyhow. One of my unconquerable impulses, I suppose. You know how they affect me."

His friend made no remark whatever. Hilton had always seemed to him so young a man that it was hard for him to realize for the moment that he was actually the father of a girl of fifteen. He was an extremely handsome man, with a keen, clever face, hair slightly tinged with gray, and fine athletic figure. He dressed well, and had the appearance of a man of the world, one who was in the habit, perhaps, of putting himself always first and best. In his early youth Hilton had gone the pace of most young men of fashion and wealth in a foreign land. Divorced from his American wife scarcely a year after his marriage to her, he had lived alone ever since. His wife had remarried long ago. Now, at the age of forty, Hilton found himself altogether alone in the world, with a strange weariness of his own companionship and an unconquerable longing to have someone with him who actually belonged to him. Then, one day, there came a memory of a little Japanese woman who had once really loved him for himself. Hilton's hard eyes had softened a trifle. He was suddenly keenly alive to the fact that he was a father; that he owed his first duty in life to the one being in the world who belonged to him—his little Japanese daughter, whom he had never seen, for she had been born after he had left Japan. He could not account for the vague yearning and longing for his own child that now suddenly possessed him.

* * *

Okikusan (Miss Chrysanthemum) was in trouble again. This time she had offended her master by refusing to dance for the American who threw his money so lavishly about. He had specially asked that the girl with the red cheeks, large eyes and white skin be asked to dance for him.

The dancing mats were thrown, the music started, and Kiku had thrust forward one little foot and had courtesied to the four corners of the earth.

Then she twirled clear around on the tips of the toes of one little foot, her hand tapering out toward the American. She had started to dance without once glancing at the visitor. By chance her eye happened to fall on him, and with a sudden whim she paused in her steps and subsided to the mats, her little feet drawn under her.

The proprietor of the tea-garden came toward her in amazement.

"What does this mean?" he asked, in a terrible voice of suppressed anger.

"That I will *not* dance for the foreign devil!" she said, defiantly.

Takahashi, the proprietor, looked in trepidation at his customer as she spoke, fearing that he had overheard her, and perhaps understood the language. The American was watching the girl with amused eyes. Then he crossed to where she sat on the ground.

"Why did you stop dancing?" he asked her, in fairly good Japanese.

She answered him in broken English:

"Tha's account I nod lig' to danze for you!" she told him, candidly.

"Why?"

Takahashi answered hastily for her.

"She is mos' rude. I beg your augustness to pardon her. She is the most miserably rude and homely girl in the tea-house. Deign to permit me to furnish you with someone who is more amiable to dance for you. I will dismiss this one."

"And if you do I will never come here again," the American told him, for Kiku-san was the prettiest thing he had ever seen, far prettier than all the other geisha girls. If she would not dance for him he would not insist. In fact, he was content simply to look at her.

Takahashi made some abject apologies for her, volunteering the information that he never could understand the girl's unreasonable dislike for foreigners. Then he left the two together.

The girl still sat on the mat, looking straight out before her, her face unreadable in its cold indifference. Hilton could not understand her. She was so unlike any Japanese girl he had ever met, for they generally were so willing and eager to please. After a time he broke the somewhat strained silence to say, in his soft, drawling fashion:

"Would you not like something—er—to drink? Shall I fetch something for you?"

The question was so absurd that the girl's studied indifference broke down.

"Tha's nod your place to waid on me!" she said, loftily, rising to her feet. "I thing thad you lig something to dring. Yes? Thad I git paid to worg here. I thing I bedder bring you something to dring," she added, stiffly. "Bud I nod lig to waid on you. I prefer vaery much waid on Japanese gents."

There was a sibilant softness to her voice that was bewildering in its charm and sweetness, and her broken English was prettier than anything he had ever heard.

When she brought the hot saké back to him her face was smiling above the dainty tray, and as she knelt at his feet while he drank it, he could see that her former petulant mood was gone, and that she was now using every effort to please and conciliate him.

"Now you look like a Japanese sunbeam," he told her, softly, looking unutterable things at her out of his deep gray eyes.

"Tha's account I 'fraid gitting discharged," she told him, calmly, still smiling. "Mr. Takahashi tell me if I nod vaery kin' to you he goin' to send me long way from here."

"Ah, I see. Then you are only pretending to smile?"

She shrugged her little shoulders.

"Yes," she said, indifferently. "Tha's worg' for geisha girl. Whad you thing we goin' to git paid for? Account we frown? Or account we laugh? I thing that's account we laugh. Thad is my worg. You nod onderstand? *You* worg, I worg, *aeverybody* worg. All different ways. Geisha girl *mus'* be always gay—always dance, laugh, sing; laugh mos' of all—to mek you laugh, too, so that you pay the money, mek us reech. I nod lig vaery much thees worg, but whad kin I do? Thad I nod worgin' I goin' to starve. Tha's bedder I worg foraever. Whad you thing?"

"That you are a philosopher," he told her, smiling, and added: "But what a cynic, too! I didn't expect to find it among Japanese women—cynicism."

The girl smiled a trifle bitterly.

"Oa!" she said, "you nod fin' thad 'mong Japanese—only me! I different from aeverybody else." She set the tray on the ground and sat down at his feet.

Takahashi strolled across the grounds and passed them slowly, giving the girl a quick, stern, almost threatening look, and beaming on the American in a fashion that annoyed him.

Okikusan began to speak to the American, raising her voice so that the words would reach Takahashi.

"Bud I lig you. My! *how* nize I thing you are!"

Hilton stared at her in amazement. The moment Takahashi had passed out of sight, she rose impatiently to her feet.

"Tha's a liar," she said, with quiet scorn. "You thing I mean thad?—that I lig you? I only spik thad for please Takahashi-sama."

The soft outlines of her face had suddenly hardened and surprised him with a look of shrewd understanding, such as he had never seen on a Japanese woman's face before.

"*You* are lig this," she said, making a sweeping gesture with her hands, "so fool conceit. Tha's way all big mans come from the West. They thing my! we so *nize!* Thing, we foolin' with liddle Japanese women thad don' know much."

"How old are you?" Hilton asked her, curiously.

"Twenty-two," she told him.

"You look like a child."

* * *

It was two weeks later. With a restless fascination he could not understand, Hilton went every day to the little tea-house on the hill. Always he sought out Okikusan, and would spend the entire day with her, totally oblivious to almost all else save the girl's beauty and charm. It was her weird shrewdness and cleverness that had first attracted him to her. Formerly he had delighted in the Japanese women because of that artlessness which is so original and refreshing in them. Kiku was anything but artless. She said things that no American girl would say, and that few Japanese girls would understand, and in spite of this she was a charming individual.

And Hilton forgot his mission in Japan, forgot that Japanese women had always been merely the playthings of a moment; that he had tired of life—everything save the delightful, irresistible feelings that had awakened in him. What was it? Hilton was in love, and with a Japanese woman! Years ago he had married one in Japanese fashion, and had left her. She had been a gentle, clinging little woman, with whom he had passed a dreamy, sleepy summer. What could he do with Kiku? She was unlike any Japanese woman he had ever known—unlike any woman he had met. She was the one woman in the world he had loved during all his long, checkered career—a life spent in idle pursuit of his own pleasures.

* * *

Hilton's friend, who had accompanied him on the voyage, was beginning to feel anxious about him, for, in spite of his admission of his own weakness for Japanese women, he was far more alive to and quick to scent real danger than Hilton, who followed his extravagant impulses only, while the cooler man kept a level head in the midst of his pleasures.

"My dear boy," he said to Hilton, "you've got the fever, I believe?"

Hilton laughed weakly.

"Nonsense!"

"You are in love with some Japanese girl!" his friend continued. "You want to look out for them, you know."

Hilton rose to his feet and began pacing the room in long, irregular strides.

"Don't you suppose I am old enough to be proof against such things?"

"Well, I don't know, Hilton, to tell you the truth. You see, Japanese women are different. You're only human, after all. I'd advise you to marry her—for a while, of course, as you did the other one."

"I have an idea," Hilton said, with some hesitancy, "that I am too old for another affair of that kind. I thought of settling down—that is, I intended returning to America, and—er—marrying."

"What are you waiting for, then? The child died, did it not?"

"So they say."

He flung himself restlessly across a couch, staring moodily at the fusuma.

"What do you say to our leaving next week?"

"Good."

"Better keep away from the tea-house in the meanwhile," his friend advised.

Hilton did not answer.

He did not go near the tea-house, however, all the next day. By evening he was seized with a fit of unconquerable restlessness and blues. He was awake the entire night, tossing restlessly from side to side.

He kept up his resolution all the next morning, but about the middle of the afternoon threw it up, and almost rushed across the rice-fields to the little tea-garden.

He found her in a field blazing with a vivid burning glory of natan and azalea-blossoms. She saw him coming toward her, and stooped down among the long grasses to hide from him. The man was intoxicated with his hunger for her, and caught her in his arms with all his pent-up love and passion.

"Kiku," he whispered, "I tried to stay away. I could not. Don't you understand?" He was holding her close to him now, and covering her face with a passion of kisses. "I love you! I love you! I love you!" he began, murmuring in her ear.

The girl's eyes were fixed full on his face. He caught the elfish, searching full gaze, and for a moment released her. She stooped to pick up the scattered blossoms that had fallen.

"Go 'way!" she said, pettishly. "I nod lig you. You mus' *nod* do thad," she continued, as he tried to draw her into his arms again. "Tha's nod ride! Tha's ———"

"It *is* right, Kiku-san," he whispered, "because I love you!" His words hurried over each other. "I am going to take you away with me, Kiku-san—to my home. We will be married. I cannot live without you, and ———"

The girl shivered, and her face grew suddenly white.

"Go 'way!" she repeated, this time with almost an imploring note in her voice. "I don' wanter tell you. I thing it bes' nod. No, I nod tell you—aeverything. Besides, I nod lig you vaery much. Jus' lidle bit now. At first I hate—hate with all my heart! Now I ver' sawry—ver' sawry thad, thad I bin unkin'. Tha's account you unkin', too."

"I unkind!" he repeated, stupidly. "I don't understand, Kiku-san?"

"No, you nod onderstan'," she said, in despair. "What kin I do? Oh, pitiful Kwannon! help me! I thing I tell you. I bin mos' vaery onhappy long time now, because aeverybody hate me. Account I loog lig American. You nod onderstand? No? My fadder"—she paused a moment—"he leave my modder. We vaery onhappy so thad she goin' to die. Then w'en she die I worg, worg hard at the factory, an' here. Nobody lig me account my fadder American, an' I thing account thad I goin' hate all Americans foraever, because my fadder vaery wigged, because he mek my modder suffer! And me? I suffer, too."

A grayness had crept over Hilton's face. He felt suddenly weak and old.

"You still nod onderstand?" she asked. Her hands had fallen from his now, and he had staggered back a few paces.

"Not yet!" he said, faintly.

"Then I tell you," she said, firmly. "I nod lig you because w'en you come here someone thad know my modder w'en she alive point at you and say '*Thad* you' fadder!'"

The silence that was between them now was horrible. It suddenly assumed a savage mockery by the wild singing of a nightingale which flew over their heads and trilled aloud its song of gladness.

The man could not speak. He stood looking out in front of him with a pitiful look of horror, and only half comprehension on his face.

After a while the girl continued:

"Firs' I thing I will tell you. Then I remember my modder and how onhappy she be, and how hard I worg all those years w'ile you have so much rich, an' then I hate you foraever and bury all sawry for you in my heart, an' I hate all mens from the West, foraever so fool of conceit. Tha's a liar thad I say I twenty-two years old. I thing now thad my time come to fool. I thing I revenge my modder? I thing I mek you suffer lig her. You nod onderstan? Always she have pain here!" She clasped her hand over her heart, and then continued, wearily: "Tha's account you tich her to luf you. I nod onderstand that liddle word vaery much. Aeverybody say I nod have aeny heart. All hard daed. Tha's account I luf only my modder, an' she die. An' I also hate you thad you kill that modder."

Through the mists of pain and horror that had overcome him the memory of dead days were coming back to Hilton. He could not think of Kikusan now as his own child—his very own blood—he would not!

"You must be mistaken!" His voice sounded strange, even to his own ears. "My child died—they told me so."

The girl laughed bitterly.

"Tha's bedder I daed. I going away. Aeverybody thinging I daed 'cept me. I know always. You thing I loog lig Japanese girl?"

She suddenly loosened her hair, and it fell down around her in thick, shining brown curls.

"Thad lig Japanese girl?—thad?—thad?—thad? Thad?"

She pushed back the sleeves and showed him the white purity of her arms.

Then she turned and left him with the same still look of despair on his face and the pitiless sun beating on the golden fields.

(*Frank Leslie's Popular Monthly,* September 1899)

TWO CONVERTS

After a hard day, spent in going over his new parish and the mission church and school, the pretty, trim little house on the hill, with its sloping roofs and wide balconies, looked refreshing and restful to the Reverend John Redpath. Everything about it was dainty and exquisite.

His predecessor was leaving the American chairs, tables, and beds behind, but apart from these it was furnished entirely in Japanese fashion.

The Reverend John Redpath was past forty, but he had the guileless conscience of a boy whose ideals are as yet unsmirched by bitter experience. It was with boyish enjoyment and curiosity that he sat down to the queer little repast prepared for him, and to which, of course, he was wholly unaccustomed. His predecessor talked to, or rather at, him during the meal, but John, while apparently listening, was absently noting the quaint pattern of the shoji, the dim light of the andon, and the bamboo mats and tall vases. There was a faint odor about the place that delighted him.

Tiny as the house was, John found that he was now the master of three servants. One was a jinrikiman, one a coolie and gardener, and the last his housekeeper and maid-servant.

In the morning the glorious sunshine of Japan poured its wealth into his room, waking him from a strangely refreshing sleep. He found, after he had bathed in the delightful water, subtly perfumed like everything else, that he was averse to drawing on his heavy shoes and treading on the exquisite matting. The thin partition-walls, the freshness and cleanliness of everything, delighted him.

Immediately after his breakfast, the smiling, round-faced little maid, curtsying and bobbing between the parted shoji, announced that some one awaited him in the zashishi (guest-room), and the minister hastily left the table.

His visitor sat in almost the centre of the room; and as he entered she put her head prone down on her two hands, spread palm downward on the floor. She remained in this apparently cramped position for some time.

"How do you do?" he said, pleasantly. As soon as he spoke, the girl rose to her feet. She was very pretty, despite the demure drooped head, little folded hands, and plain gray kimono, and he felt instinctively that the greater part of her dignity was affected. When he drew forward one of his American chairs, and motioned courteously for her to be seated, she seemed childishly timorous. The chair was so big, and she so small, that she almost disappeared in its depths, her feet reaching only quarter-way to the floor. The minister smiled cheerfully at her, and encouraged thereby, the girl smiled back at him, her face dimpling and her eyes shining, so that she seemed more than ever a child, and very bewitching.

"You wish to see me on business?" queried the minister.

"Yes. I hear you come at Japan to make nice speeches at our most augustly insignificant and honorably ignorant nation. That so?"

She waited a moment for him to say something, but he merely smiled at the way she had put it, and she continued, with a little argumentative air:

"Now what I most anxious to learn is, how you going to make those same great speeches at those ignorant people if you don' can speak Japanese language?"

"Why, I shall have to learn the language, of course," said John.

"Ah," she said, "tha's just exactly what I riding after."

"You what?"

"Riding to—a—a—maybe you don' quite understand. Tha's just liddle bid silly barbarian slang. Excuse me."

"Oh, I see," he said. "Now what is it you—ah—"

"I like to teach you thad same language, so's you can make those beautiful speeches."

"Ah, that's it, is it?"

He sat down opposite her, and drew up his chair.

"You've come to apply for a position as teacher; is that the idea?"

She inclined her head.

"You've had some experience?"

"Ten years," she solemnly prevaricated.

"Good gracious!" said John. "Why, why, you are much older than I thought."

She bowed gravely.

"Well—er—whom do you teach? Have you classes, or—"

"I am visiting teacher. I come unto you to teach."

"Have you many pupils?"

"Most pupils of any teacher in all Tokyo." She produced a very long piece of rice paper, on which she had spread out the names and addresses of twenty or thirty people.

"Of course," said the minister, "I shall have to take lessons of somebody, and if you think that you are efficient for the work—"

"I am augustly sufficient," she said.

"Hm!" said he, and looked at her doubtfully. "Of course I had not decided with whom I should study. You look very young—excessively young, in fact. I don't want to do anything hastily, but if you will call to-morrow, I will—"

"Yes, yes," she said, "I will come sure thing—er—to-morrow; thad day most convenient to you?"

"It will be convenient, I presume."

"Oh, *thank* you," she said, gratefully, and began backing across the room toward the door.

When she had left him, John deliberated over the matter, and after much weighty thought, he decided that it would be better for him to have a man teacher. It would look better. Of course it was too bad to disappoint the little girl—she only looked like a little girl, despite her ten years' experience—but still this would be the wisest course for him to pursue. He had an uncomfortable feeling, however, that when he told her to come the following day, she had understood him to mean that he wished to commence taking lessons, for he could not quite forget how grateful she had looked, the extravagance of her expressions of gratitude.

And the next day she arrived with a large bundle under her arm.

"You see," she informed him, smiling confidently, "I been making purchases for you—books, slates, paper, pencils, ink—that sufficient to study. Now we begin!" And there was nothing left for the minister to do but to begin.

Three weeks later the Reverend John Redpath, by dint of great perseverance, study, and diligent work, was able to say a number of Japanese words—never quite intelligibly, it is true, except when repeated immediately after his teacher, who, despite his apparent stupidity, was the incarnation of patience, and had great hopes that he would surely speak the language "some nice soon day."

It must be said that the minister was very earnest and laborious in his endeavor to learn the language. Arguing that it would be practically useless for him to attempt any sort of work until he had first mastered it, he devoted the greater part of his time to studying. Much of the time so spent was given up to the discussion of trivial matters that bore no relation to the rudiments of how to read and write in the Japanese language, but to John such talks were as essential to his Japanese education as were the studies through the medium of the books. He was learning something new in this way all the time; and, moreover, he had always considered it one of the duties of life to become well acquainted with those near him, and—well, Otoyo was now almost a part of his household.

John made a discovery. Despite the fact that she made her living by giving lessons in the Japanese language to various visiting foreigners, she was not of their religion. In fact, she belonged to that great bulk of "heathen" that the Reverend John had manfully come forth to reclaim.

After that he insisted on double lessons replacing the one received each day by him. Following his lesson, he undertook to teach her the Christian religion, through the medium of the Bible. John soon found that Otoyo as a pupil was altogether different from Otoyo as a teacher. She plied him with questions that staggered him, and which he, poor man, found it almost impossible to answer.

John was not a brainy or a brilliant man, and the girl kept him on his mettle constantly. He had acquired a peculiar fondness for her, and her conversion was near and dear to his heart. Not only was he interested in her future life, but in her present. He tried to teach her new methods of thought and living. He was anxious to know how she spent her time when away from him, who were her relatives, and whether she had lovers. She was reluctant to talk about herself, and he thought her strangely secretive.

One day the Reverend John Redpath received a letter. It was written in elegant Japanese characters, and he took it to Otoyo for translation. She laughed a little, nervously and excitedly, as she read it through. Then she became quite solemn.

"Tha's a letter from my husband," she informed him, calmly.

The Reverend John sat up in his chair and stared at her dimly. He felt almost powerless to move, and when he finally found his voice, it was husky and strange.

"What do you mean?" he demanded.

"Tha's a letter," said Otoyo, slowly, "from my husband, Mr. Shawtaro Hashimoto, to you, the Revelind John Ridpath. You like me read it to you?" Her eyes, bright and guilty, still looked straight into his. They never so much as flickered.

The minister was filled with ungovernable rage toward her. Her deceit smote him.

"How long have you been married?" he inquired, briefly.

She counted on her five pink fingers, standing out straight, plump, and separate. "Ten months," said she.

"And you never told me one word! You—"

"You din ask one word," she said.

"I took it that you would have informed me of such an event. You won my confidence. I do not see how I can trust you again," he said, sternly; and then added, as a bitter after-thought: "After all, it is a matter of total indifference to me whether you are married or unmarried. It is the principle that pains me."

"Revelind John Ridpath," said Otoyo, her eyes all clouded, "I don' tell you that sad tale about me because I din wan' to pain your so gendle heart."

"I don't understand you," he answered her, briefly.

"My marriage most unhappy in all the whole world. My father and mother marrying me unto this gentleman. He just so bad and cruel as all the fiends of that place you tell me about. I hate him! Therefore I just leave him, go live all 'lone and work hard this-a-way."

"It was barbarous to marry you against your wish," said the Reverend John, visibly relenting. "I have heard of this custom of your people. I hope some day to show them how wrong it is. But you have done wrong to leave your husband."

She sighed heavily, hypocritically. "Ah, I thought I would like to learn that Chlistianity religion," she said, and looked down pathetically. She had touched a sore spot, and he winced. He got up from his seat and began pacing the floor restlessly. After a while he came back to her.

"What does he want with me? If he wishes you to return, my duty is plain. Read me the letter, if you please."

"He don' wish me return. He just want to make liddle bid rattle and noise, just to make you know he own me, and thad I just—his—slave."

"Read the letter, please."

It was as follows:

"EXCELLENCY,—I have to request your lordship against the forbidden misconduct of making my wife a Christian. It is my desire that she shall not embrace a religion foreign to all my ancestors. I also honorably request that you must not condescend to teach her other barbarous customs and manners of your West country. I desire my wife to follow only the augustly unworthy and honorable customs of my country. I beg that you will accept my humblest compliments.

SHAWTARO HASHIMOTO"

That was all.

"Of course," said the now irate Reverend John, "I expected opposition in my work. I will brook no dictation, and, Otoyo, we will continue the lessons."

There was an element of combativeness in John Redpath's nature. He was an Englishman. A few days after this first letter there came another one, and a few days after that another, and still another. They were all couched in pretty much the same language. The minister ignored them, though Otoyo informed him that she had answered, acknowledging them all, as this was the correct and proper thing to do in Japan. In fact, she wrote laboriously polite and diplomatic letters from the minister to her husband, signing them boldly with the minister's name.

Meanwhile she had artfully wheedled her way back into the minister's confidence. She had managed to make him believe that her husband was a brute of the worst type. She made up pathetic tales of his bad treatment, how he had beaten and starved her, and kept her from seeing her ancestors (parents and grandparents). The minister was, as I have said, an Englishman, and a brave one. Her tales, told with all the art of which she was mistress, awakened his native chivalry, and, mingled with his unconquerable fondness for her, there arose in him a strong desire to protect her.

Otoyo now showed a ready inclination to embrace the new religion. Matters which hitherto had seemed abstruse and hard for her to understand she now declared were becoming as clear as the Lake Biwa. She professed an inordinate admiration for the rule "Love one another," and lamented the fact that in all the language of Japan, flowery and poetic as it was, there was no such word as "Love." Nor in all the philosophy of Buddhism had the injunction "to love" been once laid upon them.

And the minister, who was an honest and straightforward man, and unused to the arts and wiles of the Orient, took all her questionings to heart, and labored unceasingly to lead her to the light.

But one day a terrible thing happened. Otoyo failed to appear, and for a week the minister saw nothing of her. Filled with anxious forebodings and imaginings as to her fate, he lost his head completely, and acted in a most undignified and unmissionarylike fashion, searching all around the town by day, and coming home late at night, moping and growling like one half demented. The end of the week found him haggard and broken-hearted.

When Otoyo came back, she brought with her quite a large box and a number of bundles, which she carefully carried into the zashishi and there deposited.

At the inquiry of the minister as to what they contained, she informed him placidly that it was her wardrobe. She then undid a scroll of paper, and after glancing over it herself, she handed it, together with another letter from her husband, to the minister.

He gave them back to her. "What is this?" he asked, testily.

"Thad," she pointed to the scroll, "is my divorce. My honorable husband divorcing me. Thad," she pointed to the letter, "is a letter for you from my same honorable husband, Mr. Shawtaro Hashimoto."

She read it:

"EXCELLENCY,—I have repeatedly warned you against my dissatisfaction of making my wife convert as a Christian. You have answered me, politely acknowledging my letters, but you have paid no heed to my requests. I have also warned you against teaching her the barbarian ways of your honorable nation, and this also you have politely acknowledged, but failed to heed. You have now not only converted her at this so abominable religion, and the barbarian ways of the foreigners, but you have stolen her wife-love from me. I have therefore divorced her, and now send her to you herewith."

It is needless to describe the sensations of the Reverend John Redpath. He was too confounded at first for speech. Then he began striding up and down the room, like one nigh crazy. "I will not be the means of separating man and wife. It is preposterous. I'll have the fellow arrested! I—"

"But," said Otoyo, argumentatively, "he don' did nothing that you kin arrest him for. If you go have rattle and fight at the pleece station with him, they going to lock you up for making such disturbance. He don' git hurt."

"Are you defending *him?*" said the minister, turning on her almost fiercely.

"No, Excellency; I just giving you advice. Now pray be calm, like nize good Chlistian minister unto the gospel, and listen at me."

"You listen to me," he said. "I want you to go right back to your husband. There must be a stop put to this—"

"Tha's too late go back," said Otoyo. "I already divorce. I not any longer his wife."

"What are you going to do?"

"Me?" she opened her eyes wide. "What I do! Why, stay at your house—be wife with *you!*"

"What!" he shouted.

She pouted, and then rose up indignantly. "Excellency," she said, "I answering that letter. Tha's p'lite to answer that honorable letter. Tha's also p'lite that you marry with me. Why, evry mans at Japan, even poor low coolie, do such thing if my husband divorcing me for you."

"What did you answer?" he demanded.

She brought out a copy of her reply:

"AUGUSTNESS,—I have received your so p'lite letter, and the wife also enclose. I acknowledge I have convert your wife at that abominable religion, and taught her the honorable barbarian ways of my country. Therefore I must accept the wife enclosed, for which I condescend to thank you."

He looked at her almost stupidly.

"You can't stay here, Otoyo, and it was very wrong to answer like that."

She denied this fiercely. "Tha's right do. You living at Japan. Therefore mus' be like Japanese. Roman do's Roman do!" she misquoted.

"Would a Japanese have answered that way?"

She nodded emphatically. "Just like same thad," she declared.

"And accepted you, and married you!"

She nodded again, violently now.

"Well—I won't!" said the Reverend John Redpath, and turned his back on her.

Otoyo approached him slowly, then she suddenly placed herself directly in front of him, forced her own little hands into his, and compelled his eyes to look into her own, which were imploring.

"You not going to send me out of your house?"

The Reverend John cleared his throat and straightened his shoulders bravely.

"I see only one course to be pursued."

"You desire me leave you, Excellency?"

"Ye-e-es," said the Reverend John, nervously. And then, as she dropped his hands and turned quickly to obey him, he shouted, with startling vehemence, "*No!*"

* * *

A few days later there were two ceremonies performed at the mission-house. At the first the Reverend John Redpath himself officiated. He christened Otoyo, and pronounced her a convert to the Christian religion. In the second his predecessor acted, coming up from his city parish to repeat the Christian marriage service over their heads. He would have been horrified had he known that he had married two converts instead of one—one a convert to Christianity, the other a convert to divorce.

(*Harper's Monthly,* September 1901)

KIRISHIMA-SAN

She had just administered her daily scolding to her pupil, and sat watching him with a look of extreme exasperation and hopelessness on her face.

"*How* you egspeg aever speeg Japanese when you nod try. I tell you all the time thad you mus' *nod* talk at me lig thad, bud you have so much persist I noto onderstan' to tich you."

There was almost a sob in the last words.

The young man, who had been all the time enjoying her anger, and, in fact, generally purposely provoked it, was suddenly covered with contrition.

"Oh! I say, Kirishima-san," he said, taking the book from her, "really I'm a brute. Now go ahead again. I'll be good as a—lamb. I'll speak Japanese in a week."

The girl's face instantly brightened.

"My! *How* good you kin be wen you wanter be." She opened the little book and put her head severely on one side.

"Now how you say gooe morning?"

Jack Mortimer scratched his head, tried to look over her shoulder at the book, then gave it up. Kirishima looked reproachfully at him.

"All day I teach you thad liddle word," she said. "You *oughter* know it vaery mos' well."

"What does it sound like—start it for me."

"Now I tell you *once* more, an' thad you forgit again I thing you forgit foraever an' aever." She paused a moment before interpreting the words for him; then a bright idea seemed to strike her.

"I *tell* you whad," she said, confidently, almost mysteriously; "I kin tell you one grade way thad you naever forgit thad."

"Yes? Well, go ahead."

"You riglegt the grade big States in America?"

"Well, I guess so."

"Whad you call thad State where you tell me all big—pol- pol-li-tishins cum from?"

"Ohio," said Jack solemnly.

"That's ride," said Kirishima-san.

"'*Ohayo*' is 'good morning' in Japanese, an' you say thad jus' lig you say the 'Ohio' in America."

Kirishima-san went home that day with a very bright little face. She had finally managed to teach her big, stupid pupil how to say one Japanese word properly.

Now Jack Mortimer had lived in Japan one whole month, and although he had had almost daily instruction at the hands of Kirishima-san, who had become known among the Americans as an "imminent Japanese teacher," he literally could not learn to speak the language. When Kirishima, who was small, pretty and bewilderingly fascinating in her daintiness and charm, scolded and stormed at him, Jack would tower above and watch her in admiring silence, deliberately trying to appear even more stupid for the sake of seeing her angry; when she coaxed him he was just as bad, but when she broke down in sheer despair and there was a suggestion of tears in her voice, Jack would break down also and would become the most abject, contrite, cringing pupil that ever was.

He knew that the real cause of his bad progress lay in the fact that he was far more interested and intent on studying Kirishima-san herself rather than the Japanese language. Besides, apart from the fact that Kirishima was his teacher, she was also his confidante and friend. Although she always assumed a certain superior sort of dignity which was irresistible to Jack, nevertheless she really did take a great deal of interest, and sympathised with him in all his troubles (most of which he invented just for the sake of gaining her sympathy). She would listen to him very gravely when he bewailed the smallness of his American mail, would sweep and tidy his office for him and often cut the pages of his magazines and papers in the neatest way, while he dwelt on the fact that he was fatherless, motherless, brotherless, and almost sisterless, since his one sister was married—and Jack told Kirishima that was next door to burying herself. Kirishima had five brothers and seven sisters, besides a father and mother. She professed a deep sympathy for the desolate American, and would try in every way possible to keep him from becoming lonely.

"You mus' worg," she told him, wisely. "Now whad you thing thad you goin' nod to git lonely wen you nod worg. I worg vaery hard all day an' all nide. I tich some pipples. Thad's account my fadder have lods of children. So I mus' worg an' help mek the munney."

She told him this confidentially one day. Jack doubled her salary in consequence the next week.

* * *

Jack Mortimer had arrived in Japan with a large party of tourists. It was their intention to spend only a few months in Japan, and as the time was so limited, they spent most of it going from one place to another, seldom staying over a week in any one city. Jack, however, had taken the notion into his head that he could learn the language, and so had advertised in the *Kokumin no Tomi* for a teacher, with a vague idea that he could learn the language in a couple of weeks. This idea came from the fact that a good number of his friends in America, who were considered authorities on the subject of Japan and the Japanese, had written articles for magazines, novels, and sketches on the subject, after having lived only a couple of months on the island. When Kirishima-san had applied for the position Jack had engaged her on the spot, asking for no references whatever. A few days after he rented a little Japanese house of his own, told his party he proposed remaining in Tokyo a few days, and settled down to hard "cramming." The result? At the end of two months his vocabulary consisted of the following: *Kirishima-san* (Miss Azalea). (He corrupted this name to "Shima.") *Nippon* (Japan), *sake* (wine), *ohayo* (good morning), *sayonara* (good night).

He was inordinately proud of this vocabulary, and fired the words at Kirishima at all times without regard generally to their meaning.

Finally his party, which in the meanwhile had travelled nearly all over the little island, returned to Tokyo and called on him in a body.

Now, the day before this a curious thing had happened. Jack had been unusually good during the lesson, trying in every way possible to learn it, and thus please Kirishima, who had not once had occasion to reprove him. He had gone laboriously through a whole list of words without once interrupting her to start some conversation that had no connection with the matter on hand whatever, as was his wont. This unusual docility must have astonished Kirishima. She glanced at him sideways out of her little eyes, and said, as she shook her head: "*How* good you becomin'. I thing I sugceed mek you vaery good boy."

If Kirishima-san had known the proverb about giving some people an inch and they take a mile, she would have applied it to Jack. The moment she showed the least sign of relenting from the stiff, almost solemn attitude she usually assumed when trying to teach him, and gave him the smallest word of approbation, he immediately took advantage of it.

"There, Shima, I have studied a hard lot to-day, haven't I? We'll put the blamed book by now. Learned enough for one day. Let's talk."

Kirishima instantly froze again.

"No," she said severely; "thad you not interrupt don' mek thad you study. No—you nod study. You jus' mekin' believe. What kin you say more in Japanese thad you nod say yistidy?"

Jack rose stubbornly to his feet, and crossed his arms, looking very aggrieved and hurt.

"Look a here," he finally said, as he saw Kirishima was not to be melted, "I've studied hard, desperately hard, to-day. Even you, who always scold and are so hard to please, were astonished. We're going to have a holiday now. May as well close the book," he added, as the girl paused irresolutely.

Kirishima did close the book, and slipped it into her little bag.

"*Vaery* well," she said; "you kin tek holiday. I go home tek holiday, too."

"No, you don't," said Jack, as she marched toward the door. "Now, see here, Shima-san, can't you stay and talk with a fellow for a moment?"

"Now whad you thing," she said with exasperation, "thad I have nodding bedder to do but stay talk with you?" and added with a scornful toss of her little head: "You thing thad I *geisha* girl thad I talk and amuse you foraever?"

Something in this remark made Jack grin copiously. He fancied he detected in it a suggestion of pique, for he had tried to tease her only the previous day by pretending that he was in love with a *geisha* girl.

"No, indeed, I don't think you are a bit like them, Shima. If you were, you'd—" he paused, choosing his words carefully, "you wouldn't freeze a fellow all up."

The girl's eyes were lowered.

"I nod wanter freeze you vaery much," she said; "an' if I freeze thad's nod because I nod thing vaery kind to you. *Geisha* girl only laugh at you an' not freeze, but she nod lig you foraever. Me? I lig you all with my heart;" she hesitated as Jack came nearer to her, and added hurriedly: "Thad's because you my pupil, an' I mus' be kind to you."

But Jack would not take this into account, and when she stepped toward the door to pass out he stood in front of her, his fine fair face illuminated with a smile half of tenderness, half of amusement.

"Can't pass *now*, Shima," he whispered.

"I thing I mus' pass," she said in confusion.

"Not till ———" he stooped down and took her startled face between his hands. "There!" he said, and kissed the small, inviting mouth.

It was with some uneasiness that he noticed she was nearly fifteen minutes late for the lesson the next day. He began pacing the floor in long irregular strides. Then his man had announced his visitors, and the gay party of Americans had come in upon him.

"Well, *what* have you been doing?"

"Why did you not go with us?"

"And, oh, Mr. Mortimer, what a pretty little house!"

"Are you living in it all alone?"

"How funny!"

The ladies covered him with questions.

"Fact is," he told them, "I thought I'd like to study the language some— couldn't very well if I was running all over the country. So I took this place, and"—he straightened himself proudly—"am getting along famously."

"You are?" said a pretty girl shaking her finger at him slyly. "Oh, yes, we've heard all about it—and—the teacher."

Jack Mortimer was only twenty-two years of age. The girl's bantering words and the laughing, knowing eyes of the rest of the party confused him.

"Now, what is she like?" the girl continued, rushing headlong into the subject, as women usually do, without pausing to consider whether it was any of her business or not.

"Like the rest of them," he said hastily, scarce knowing what he was saying himself. "They all look alike, you know."

His inquisitor was an extremely charming girl. On the voyage out Jack had been unusually attentive to her. She shook her head very sagely at him. Perhaps Jack had been wiser had he remained silent and avoided explanation.

"Fact is," he said weakly, "she is—a—a—jolly little thing. Had lots of fun with her. She—a ———"

"In love with her, I suppose," the girl put in shrewdly.

Jack's sister, who was one of the party, was watching his flushed face curiously.

"Well," she put in sharply, "I hope you have not been foolish enough to fall in love with a Japanese woman, Jack."

"Why, how absurd!" he said hurriedly. "Why—er—I'm just having a little fun with her, that's all."

Something fell sharply to the floor in the next room. Jack pushed the *fusu-*

ma aside. Kirishima was kneeling on the ground, picking up the pieces of a broken slate.

"When—er—did you come in?" he asked with a wild sinking at his heart. She raised a perfectly calm, still face to him.

"I have jus' cum," she said, "an' I fall an' braeg my slate."

She did not give him his lesson as usual, and he was unable to detain her as his visitors were still there, and were watching with interested eyes the little Japanese girl as she answered Jack's questions in a quiet, emotionless fashion, scarce looking at his guests, apparently indifferent to their persistent curiosity in her.

Long after his guests had left him Jack Mortimer sat miserably in his office, thinking of Kirishima-san, and his own mad folly in having spoken of her so in that momentary shame he had felt when Miss Newton quizzed him and his sister looked half scornful.

"It is not true after all," he said to himself. "God! how could I have been such a cur? That girl ———"

He suddenly picked up his hat and passed outdoors.

*   *   *

Night was falling in Tokyo. Softly, tenderly, the darkness swept away the exquisite rays of red and yellow that the departing sun had left behind. The streets were almost deserted, and stillness reigned over the city. Jack Mortimer had promised his friends to take them to a picturesque tea house that evening, but instead he was striding toward the hills with a restlessness he could not conquer.

Kirishima's young brother came to the door.

"I want to see your sister."

The boy eyed him suspiciously.

"My seester nod see aeny one. Thad's too lade."

"Tell her," Jack said impatiently, "that—that I wish to see her about some work. I have a new pupil for her. Give her this;" he handed his card to the boy, who took it reluctantly from him.

When Kirishima came into the room she was accompanied by her father, mother, and brother.

"I came over," said Jack, in a panic, "because—er—I've a pupil for you."

"Thad's fonny thad you nod waid till the mornin'," the girl said, icily.

"Well—fact is, they're going away to-night," he said, wildly conscious that he had made an absurd statement.

"Thad's still mos' fonny," the girl said, "thad they go way. How you egspeg I kin tich?"

This question floored Jack.

"I would like to see you alone," he said, in a low, imploring voice.

The girl turned to her brother, and said something in Japanese. He got up and left the room.

"My fadder and modder nod onderstan' spik Americanazan. You can spik to me now," she said.

Jack stood helplessly before her.

"But I—I want to be alone with you, Shima," he repeated, desperately.

The girl looked him full in the face. Her words were slow and distinct.

"Thad's nod ride thad I seein' you alone," she said, cruelly. "I goin' to marry vaery soon now. So thad's nod ride I seein' you alone."

"You are going to marry?" he repeated, dully, and then was silent. He looked at her with uncomprehending eyes in silence. She stood perfectly cold and indifferent, her eyes downcast.

"I will go now," he said, bitterly. "There was no new pupil. I used that as an excuse. I came over simply to tell you that I was a fool. You must have heard the conversation this afternoon. My man said you had been there some time. I wanted to apologise—to tell you I didn't know what I was talking about. However,"—his voice broke a trifle with his pain, for he was consumed with self-pity for the moment—"however, you have had the laugh against me all the time, because *I* am the one that cares now—not you. I did try to make you care for me, and only succeeded in falling in love with you myself. But you are like the rest of your race, I suppose. You don't even know the meaning of the word 'love,' much less are you capable of understanding it."

He had not intended speaking like this to her, but he was carried away with his self-pity. The girl stood perfectly silent, seemingly indifferent.

"It is quide lade now," she finally said. "Thad I goin' to marry I will nod tich you aeny more."

As he passed out miserably into the night she said, very sweetly:

"Sayonara," and repeated mockingly, as she used to do when teaching him, "Goo night."

* * *

Jack Mortimer's Japanese house was in great confusion. Japanese *bric-a-brac,* mingled with American chairs and tables, were distributed everywhere. Out of the chaos he was trying to pack up what things he wanted to take with him, for he had decided to make a trip with his party to Matsushima Bay. Jack had never kept house before, and as he was giving the house up altogether he was at a loss to know what to do with all the American furniture he had purchased. It was a week since he had seen Kirishima. He looked tired and a trifle haggard.

One of his friends sauntered over through the day.

"I'd leave all this truck behind," he advised Jack, as he lit a cigar and found a seat on a half-packed trunk.

"I dare say," said Jack, "but unfortunately, my landlord insists on my taking the "truck," as you call it, away with me. Says the Japanese have no use for American furniture—unpleasant in the houses during earthquakes and other jolly circuses in Japan."

"What the deuce ever induced you to go into housekeeping? Should have thought you'd have found it more comfortable and convenient at one of the hotels."

"I dare say," the other answered, and added spitefully: "Suppose I thought it a better place to study."

His friend laughed.

"Say, Mortimer, what is all this talk about this Japanese teacher? Brown pointed her out to me at the hotel the other day. Said you—you cared for her. Of course it was a joke."

"Yes, I cared for her," the other answered shortly, almost irritably.

His friend surveyed him a moment in amazement, and whistled under his breath. He could not bring his English intelligence to understand how an all round, wholesome American could fall in love with a little Japanese woman, his own acquaintance with them being peculiarly limited.

He changed the subject, delicately making some remark about the oddity of the *fusuma*, but Jack was persistent in a dogged sort of way, and seemed almost to want to talk to some one on the subject.

"It was like this," he said, grimly. "You remember my telling Miss Newton the other day about my fooling with *her*? Well, it was the other way."

"The other way?" His friend was puzzled.

"Yes," Jack continued deliberately. "She was fooling with me. She is to be married in a month or two, I believe."

With a sudden energy and recklessness he began pulling at the things in the room and crushing them into the boxes and trunks. He broke a long silence that fell between them by looking up suddenly and saying: "Never dreamed I should really care for a Japanese woman. I'd have laughed at the idea a few months ago; but, somehow, she was different. She will laugh now, I suppose."

His friend left him. As he passed thoughtfully down the street he came face to face with Kirishima-san. He recognised her almost immediately, for she had had pupils in the hotel where he was staying. She seemed in a hurry, and there was a distressed, anxious look about her little face.

"Where are you going?" he asked her abruptly, pausing in front of her.

"I thing I goin' home," she answered vaguely, hanging her head.

"You're going the wrong direction, then."

"Yaes?" She seemed confused. Suddenly she said quite nervously for a Japanese: "The Americazan—he goin' away, I thing?"

"Yes," the man said, sternly.

"Whad for is he goin' away?" Her voice trembled.

"Because you don't want him to stay," said Jack's friend bluntly.

The girl caught her breath with a sob.

"Yaes, but I want vaery much thad he stay."

The man's face softened. He caught a hint of the girl's charm, and began to understand Jack's infatuation for her. There was something so appealing and alluring in the little drooped head.

"Go and tell him, then," he told her.

Without a word the girl almost ran down the street. She paused before entering Mortimer's house. Then she pushed the door open without even knocking.

Jack was trying to whistle as he packed some Japanese stones and relics that Shima herself had given to him.

"I cum tell you," she said almost breathlessly, "thad I nod lig for you to go 'way."

Jack had risen on her entrance, and now stood irresolutely in front of her.

"What do you mean?"

"I don' to onderstan'," the girl said, pitifully; "but I lig thad you stay in Japan foraever an' aever." She paused, and then added almost tremblingly his name—"Jag."

"Shima!" In an instant he was with her. "Do you mean that?"

"Yaes," she said, tearfully; "bud I suffer vaery much thad you talk with the pritty Americazan lady 'bout fooling with poor liddle me—an'—an' _____"

"I—I was a—a—liar," said Jack.

"Yaes," the girl agreed.

"And a fool," he supplemented.

"Yaes."

Her assent staggered him somewhat. He looked down at the little drooped head a moment.

"When are you going to be married, Shima?" he asked sternly.

"I dunnon," she said, in a forlorn little voice. "I thing I tell lie, too."

Jack was silent a moment watching the girl thoughtfully; then he said very gently: "But it was true, Shima."

"No." She shook her head emphatically. "I only foolin' with you."

"But it is true," he persisted, "because—look up, Shima—because you are going to be married to me."

(*Idler*, November 1901)

MARGOT

A little snapping-eyed artist, with a huge pinafore covering her natty shirt waist and short walking skirt, dropped her palette on the ground and turned to the sleepy, lounging camp with an exclamation that startled them.

"For all the world, look! Here comes Maude Muller in the flesh!"

A young girl of perhaps fourteen or fifteen years climbed the fence which divided the farm lands from the forest, and approached the artists' camp with timid confidence. She laid her pail of fresh milk and butter and eggs on the grass, smilingly inviting them to buy.

"Nectar for the gods!" said one young fellow quaffing a tin cup of the rich milk. "Thanks thee, thou fair maiden, and what may thy name be?"

"Now quit your fooling, Bud!" said the sharp-eyed little woman, with a reproving glance at her irrepressible brother. Then turning to the girl she said with a gracious smile:

"We should like very much to have you bring us these good things every day, if possible. We spend the summer here. Do you live far away?"

The girl shook her head. "Only five miles!"

"Only! And do you walk it?" glancing apprehensively at the little bare feet.

"Why, that's not far! I like it!"

"Take your sun-bonnet off, won't you? Stay just as you are now. Did you ever see such hair!"

"What are you going to do?" said the girl, growing suddenly abashed and conscious of the curious eyes turned upon her.

"Sketch you, my dear child."

After that first encounter the little girl came down to the camp regularly every day. They painted her in every conceivable attitude; sometimes with her wistful eyes peering out large and wondering from the depths of her old sun-bonnet; sometimes with her tawny bronze hair blowing in the winds about her. They copied her little faded cotton gown, worn at the elbows and ragged at the edges, and reproduced with loving exactness her little bare feet and tanned legs. But all their labor could not do justice to the child's mobile face, which reflected a thousand inconstant moods that puzzled the artists. Now it was stormy and discontented, now sad and wistful; now vitally awake with feeling and interest; now sombre and hopeless; always rippling into the sunny glow of a child's sunny soul.

There came a day when the artists waited in vain for Margot, and the landscape lost its charm for them. They had become strongly attached to the queer, brooding, reticent little waif who had come each day among them, listening eagerly to their chatter, and smiling happily when they addressed her, though seldom speaking herself. A delegation of eight started out from camp to find her.

She must have seen them approaching the house, for she ran down to meet them.

"Thou fair but false one," began Bud, but the others cut him off ruthlessly.

Margot led them proudly into the old-fashioned and stuffy room which served as a "parlor." Beyond this room they could see the expanse of a large kitchen and living-room, glowing with comfort and cleanliness.

"Why have you not been down to the camp lately, Margot?"

"Mother got a baby!" announced the girl, with shining, dancing eyes.

The artists relieved themselves with exclamations indicative of amused exasperation. This would mean perhaps the prolonged absence from the camp of Margot, who would doubtless be transformed into a nurse-girl.

"Look here! Where did you get these, Margot?" and one of the artists picked up some sheets of music. The girl flushed proudly.

"They are mine!" she said. "I bought them."

"But for heaven's sake—"

"I play!" she said, with a sharp tone to her voice, as though she expected to be disputed.

"You play! Not these? Why look here—Chopin—Von Bulow—"

The girl went to a corner of the room, and drew from under an old stuffed sofa a dingy violin case. With a new pride in her flushed face and parted lips, she threw her head back, and, tucking the violin under her chin, commenced to play.

The guests sat in amazed silence. She was playing one of Chopin's nocturnes without time or music, but with correct note and with the strangest feeling and expression. It was weird and uncanny, but despite the crudity of its execution they recognized with startled wonder the genius of the player. When she laid the violin down there was absolute silence for a time in the little parlor. Then Kemp Evans, a long-legged Englishman, strode over to her, and laid his hand with nervous excitement on her shoulder.

"Who on earth, Margot, taught you to play like that?"

"Nobody. Only daddy and the hired man teached me the notes. Daddy gave me his old fiddle for keeps last Christmas. I saved up till I had enough to send for the best music to the big stores in New York. They sent me those."

"And you learned without instruction to play them all?"

"I knowed the notes already. They were hard at first, but—I loved them. I like Mr. Von Bulow best. I have read all about him too. I have named our baby for him. Only his name was so long, I just call him 'Von' for short!"

A great change now took place in the life of Margot. Upon the discovery of the child's genius Kemp Evans, who was something of a musician himself as well as an artist, undertook to give the little girl lessons on the violin, whilst his wife, the kindly, bright-eyed little woman who first accosted Margot, endeavored to improve her education. The camp, one and all interested in Margot, contributed in various ways to her education and development. In return, the child patiently posed for them, either alone or with the baby, little Von, in her arms, heroically refusing to take the "rests," on which the artists insisted.

The mellow summer began to lose its light, and the campers with sighs of regret folded their tents and returned once more to the noise and distraction of the city's life.

All through the bleak winter days when the snow clouds descended on the land white and gentle as a benediction, Margot read and studied and practiced with her violin, drawing from its precious strings all the melody of joy and bewilderment and sudden awakening that had come into her life. Restless as a caged nightingale, with a new ambition beating in her little brain and heart, the child could find solace in nothing but the music which had become her very soul. Sometimes with her face pressed against the tiny pane, Margot looked out into the great snowy world that bounded her horizon, and insensibly her face grew luminous with tenderness and hope. And so the heart of the little girl quieted its beating, and her soul found a source of comfort in her music, and the vague but vivid fancies of her imagination. The two successive summers following brought back her friends, and the girl's dreams fluttered into life.

"It is time now," said her benefactors, and a little fund was raised among them. Margot went out from her home of beauty and love to a great peopled city, full of hustling men and women, thrilling with life and hope and feeling, but incomparably lonelier than the silence of her mountain home.

Her artist friends had written to the Conservatory of Music, at which

Margot was to study, requesting them to meet her, and if possible to secure a home for her in some house where other pupils of the Conservatory lived. The officers had complied with the request, and Margot, who had never been beyond a few miles of her mountains had now a tiny room on the top floor of a huge New York boarding house, especially recommended as it permitted its boarders to practice on their sundry musical instruments.

As Margot took her seat at the long table down whose length eleven pairs of girlish critical eyes were turned on her the morning after her arrival, she said "Good morning" with a nervous little smile to the tall blonde who graced the seat next to her. She was rewarded by a cold stare from a pair of glassy blue eyes, and an irrepressible titter shivered around the table. There were amused smiles; heads tilted; one of the girls looked cooly at Margot with a prolonged scrutiny, and then deliberately winked across the table at her neighbor.

All her uncertainty and timidity vanished as by a shock, and she sat up stiff and straight, her hands clenched, her face flushed and her great dark eyes stormy and defiant.

After that awful breakfast, Margot flashed into a comprehension of the difference between herself and those about her, and with the same marvelous quickness with which she had studied in the mountains her music and her books, she now studied the art of dressing after a certain law called fashion, and guarding her speech and actions in such manner that to these tittering fashionables, studying to cultivate and manufacture an imaginary talent, she proved both a sphinx and an irritation. She came and went among them with a silence that was absolute and a dignity and coolness of demeanor that disturbed their equanimity.

One particular Sunday morning, as Gene Manning, one of the boarders, came up from breakfast, he ran, accidentally, against Margot, who was coming down the dark stairway. He apologized for the encounter and paused a moment to exchange a few pleasantries with her, marveling and amused at the girl's painful shyness, for the suddenness of the encounter had surprised her out of her customary reserve, and she blushed and stammered under the young man's quizzing eyes. Meanwhile the tall blonde looked over the banisters and stared at the couple on the stairs. She had been waiting for Manning herself and had grown impatient. Among the students, and particularly to herself, he was considered her personal property. She sauntered slowly into the parlor and with amused contempt mentioned that she had just caught Gene flirting with that freak on the stairs. Wasn't it too droll for anything? When the young man joined them he was greeted by a storm of jeers and laughter. That night a plot was hatched.

Margot was in love! At first it was a rose that had boldly knocked at the door of her heart. She found it on her dressing table one night after an unusually depressing dinner. Someone must have laid it there. The rose was but the forerunner of other slight, though sweet, favors that steadily found their way to her lonely heart. And then one day she discovered his name badly erased from the title page of a volume of love lyrics that had accompanied a little bunch of violets.

After all, the pretty tokens could have come from no one else, for he was the only one in the house with whom she was on terms of even slight intimacy. From the day they had met on the stairs, Manning, with good-natured scorn of the teasing of the girl-students, had made it a point always to stop and speak to Margot. She met his overtures with a gladness that touched the young man.

Margot wore the violets in her hair that night, and she smiled with dreamy happiness as she passed Gene Manning's table. When she took her place in her customary seat at the long table, however, her face grew stiff and cold again, for a cynical smile was reflected on the faces of the students. She ate her dinner in silence, but she lingered in the hall after it was finished. Gene Manning passed her with a cheerful "Good evening," but did not stay to speak to her. She climbed the four flights of stairs wearily, and there was a pitiful and puzzled expression in her face, as she took the flowers from her hair, and began to sob on her violin.

There was a knock at her door and a confused noise outside. Margot laid her violin down quickly and opened the door. There was no one there, but a note had been thrust underneath the door. With trembling hands and beating heart the girl carried it to the light under the gas jet, tore it open and began to read. When she had finished, she sat down on the floor, and with her chin resting on her arms, she stared out at the quiet moon which had stolen over the high buildings and was smiling in on her.

"It is too good to be true," she said dreamily, and then, "Oh, dear God, how good you are to me!"

One of the sheets of the letter fell from her fingers. She picked it up quickly, and with a sudden passion covered it with kisses, then with the letter pressed against her face, she walked back and forth in the tiny room.

She paused at her dressing table and smiled at herself in the mirror, she smiled at her violin and she smiled out into the quiet night, and up at the pageantry of the heavens with its diamond bursts of stars and the sweet moon. The whole world had become changed for her. Suddenly she drew out her little desk and began to write.

When Gene Manning read Margot's letter, he sat staring at it in stupefied amazement before he could fully grasp its meaning. Then he threw his head back and laughed. Only for a moment, however, for the sinister aspect of the situation suddenly struck him, and despite his irritation and chagrin, he grew quite alarmed. So he went directly to her. She must have been waiting for him, for she opened the door at once. She was visibly trembling though her eyes were shining. He dashed into his subject with brutal disregard.

"I have just got your letter. I am awfully sorry, but really there is some absurd mistake somewhere. Someone has been playing a joke on us, you see. I never wrote to you at all, and as for sending you flowers and gifts, why—" He stopped there. He found it impossible to proceed.

The girl was standing as if petrified, her great dark eyes staring at him with a dumb expression of horror and anguish. He stuttered and stammered, and endeavored to say something more, but the stony misery which had settled in a gray shadow on the girl's face robbed him of speech.

"Perhaps I had better go—" he finally said. "I assure you I am sorry to have hurt—awfully sorry. If even I can do anything—You see a fellow doesn't—Good-night!"

He went out quickly, taking with him her letter. Once alone in his room, Margot's face came back to his vision, haunting him with its startled expression of anguish.

"If you can but read my love in these few incoherent helpless words!" she had written in her letter.

The day after the clever invention of the students of the Conservatory and its bitter results, Margot came to the table with an inscrutable face that baffled them. One of the girls said "Good morning" to her, but Margot stared at her with a haughtiness that her blonde neighbor might have been glad to emulate. That day she asked the landlady to remove her seat to another table.

Margot passed Manning in the hall with a studiously averted head, and when he spoke to her she did not reply. He went up to his room and took a crumpled letter out from his pocket, and read it over very slowly and carefully. He smiled and whistled as he dressed.

A few nights later, he made his second pilgrimage to the top flight of the boarding house. At the end of the long, narrow, dark hall was Margot's little room. He approached it almost fearfully, and hesitated outside her closed door, his face indecisive and uncertain. Out upon the silence of the dingy hall a long plaintive note stole, so weirdly strange that instinctively he held his breath in an agony of feeling. Margot was speaking to him on her violin. He stood outside her door, motionless and silent. When the last thrilling note had quivered away, he groped his way down the dark passage into the lighted hall above the banisters and went back into his room. Once more he drew out her passionate letter. "In love I am only a crude little girl without diplomacy or art."

"Poor, crude, little girl!" he said softly.

*   *   *

The great concert hall blazed with light. The audience was opulent and enthusiastic. They sat back in their seats chattering and fanning themselves, discussing the quaint history of the new artist whom they had come to hear and see, this stripling girl from their own mountains. The painful shyness and reserve of the girl which had caused her to ignore blindly the wheedling of those who had elected themselves her patrons and managers and to refuse to be "interviewed" or "reviewed" by anyone and everyone, pleased her audience. They were her admirers before they had even seen or heard her. They expected much.

It was past eight o'clock and the audience was beginning to look speculative. Fifteen minutes passed and they became restive. At eight-thirty they were whispering impatiently and visibly annoyed. Some youths started clapping by way of encouragement, but no response rewarded their efforts.

It was approaching nine o'clock when a nervous man, in evening dress, came to the front of the curtain. He mopped his perspiring brow with his handkerchief and his voice trembled nervously as he addressed the audience.

"Ladies and gentlemen, a most untoward and lamentable accident prevents us from hearing the young artist expected this evening. When about to enter her carriage she slipped and fell on the pavement, and while it is believed she is not fatally hurt, it is feared that she has injured her right hand. It is with deepest emotion that I am forced to the painful duty of announcing this tragic accident—tragic when it is realized what the loss of the artist's magic fingers may mean to her and to all true lovers of music."

The most profound silence reigned over the great concert hall during the disjointed though dramatic speech of the manager. When he bowed himself off the stage, a subdued murmur, like the roar of the surf on a melancholy shore, rose and fell all over the house.

Up in her little room Margot was lying on the bed, her languid eyes closed, her poor little mangled arm lying outside the coverlet. A nurse tiptoed about the room.

All over the boarding house a hubbub of whispering was going on, for those who had not gone to the concert hall had heard of the accident, and some of them had seen the slight form carried in through the door, limp and helpless in the pretty finery in which they had decked her.

In the wide lengths of his rooms on the first floor Manning was striding up and down. Now and then he would sink into a chair, groaning and shuddering, only to spring to his feet again with impatient pain.

He had waited in the chill coldness of the February night for Margot to pass into the carriage. When she came out of the house with two of her artist friends, Manning sprang out of the shadow of the porch on to the stoop and with impetuous haste rushed down the steps toward the carriage, throwing the door open for Margot. When he turned aside for her to pass into the carriage, he saw her trembling and swaying with a strange somnambulistic expression in her eyes. She must have fallen immediately, for when he put forth his hand to assist her, he saw nothing save the dim, sinuous outlines of the white figure fallen like a lily whipped by a brutal wind at his feet. The horses, cold and impatient, tossed their heads and stamped their feet. One of the wheels turned. It touched and crushed a little outstretched white arm.

It was Manning who had carried her indoors, and it was Manning whom her friends were reviling and holding responsible for the accident. In her state of excitement and nervousness, the sudden shock of the appearance of the man emerging from the porch had startled her so that she had fainted.

A few days later Margot was taken back to her mountain home.

* * *

March was gamboling and playing its pranks more boldly than ever in the mountains. The roads were trackless, but a certain traveler who had come as far as possible by stage and then by horseback still plodded on and stubbornly kept going ahead. When he came within sight of Margot's home he gave a slight cheer and urged his horse to a quicker speed.

And it was Margot herself who met him at the door, and stood there in the glistening sunlight reflected from the snow-clad hills.

"Margot!" was all he said, and stood with uncovered head.

"Is it you?"

"Yes, I had to come to you—since you were gone from me."

"Come indoors," she said mechanically, and he followed her into the glowing warmth of the farmhouse kitchen.

He stood by the stove and warmed his hands, watching the girl's dazed face tenderly.

"Come here, Margot," he said suddenly, and he held his two hands out.

She flushed painfully, but she did not obey him. The bewilderment in her eyes was deepening.

"Come, Margot—dear!"

"Why have you come?"

"I love you, Margot!"

"Oh, no, no—"

"And you love me, Margot."

"No, no—"

"Yes, yes," he said, and went to her, and took her in his arms.

"You cannot deny it, Margot. You know it is true. I know your letter by heart."

"And I yours," she said pitifully—"the one you never wrote."

"But I will *say* the words to you. I will live them."

"That is better," said Margot, softly.

He suddenly remembered something.

"Your little hand—" he began, his voice trembling.

She drew her hand from his and held it up before his eyes, tapering and moving the slender fingers.

"See," she said, "they, too, are quite well and happy now."

(Frank Leslie's Popular Monthly, December 1901)

✳

EYES THAT SAW NOT

Graytown had put out its lights and retired for the night, with the well-bred decorum of small-towned respectability, when John Swinnerton came home smitten with blindness. Only the station porter saw the little party that met him almost at the door of the Pullman. John's mother was the first to greet him.

"John," she said, as he stepped off the train—"John, it will be all right. Mrs. Thomas knows a specialist in New York who—" The rest of the sentence was lost in the hubbub of arrival.

His father standing by heard and smiled in pity. "John, old man!" was all he said.

There was some little delay while Jerry clumsily drove his cab up to the board platform, and Elizabeth, who had also come down to the station, found herself alone with John for a moment.

"I'm so sorry, John," she said.

Her chagrin at the trite inadequacy of her words received instant compensation when John replied melodramatically, just as she feared he would:

"It is nothing. Say no more. The light without has gone to feed the flame within."

Then she guided him into the cab, and the others silently clambered after and took their places. Jerry's fumbling at the door-catch and the sharp bang of the door's closing awoke in each the same memory. Certainly there had been happier home-comings than this of John Swinnerton to Graytown.

There was no conversation during the long ride to the Swinnertons' home, the residence of Graytown's leading family. To Elizabeth's relief, John's mother had insisted upon sitting by him, and as John sat idly holding his mother's hand, Elizabeth was shocked to surprise herself smiling at the idea of John's fancying it to be her hand.

Once home, the party broke up immediately. The hour was late, and John, the bereft sense of his affliction fresh upon him, craved the solitude of his old room. He could feel the way even now. His mother attempted, in the overflowing tenderness of her heart, to follow him.

"No, mother, not to-night," he remonstrated, kissing her, and gently pushing her from the room.

He heard her crying in his father's room as he undressed. Then he lay down, and, utterly fatigued and worn out, fell asleep almost instantly.

Graytown, after the manner of most inland towns, followed with close interest the careers of its young men, even after they had fled, as is their wont, to the great cities, which drew them forth into the vortex of human activity and strife. Nor was this interest less tenacious for the fact that they left behind them scores of young unmarried women, who watched their struggles for riches and honor, and while waiting found encouragement in sundry notes and epistles confided to envelopes bearing the postmark of one or another far-away metropolis. So was John's career the cynosure of Graytown in general and of Elizabeth in particular.

Graytown's solicitude for the welfare of the native was none the less genuine because an inquisitive sympathy was its accompaniment. Thus, on the morning following the sad reunion at the railroad station, John's arrival and misfortune were known to the whole town. Early-morning neighbors on their way to office and shop stared cautiously at the red curtains that shut out the light from John's room. The newsboy when he brought the morning paper asked the cook how John was. When John's mother opened the library door on the veranda to receive from the postman the day's mail, his inquiry brought tears to her eyes.

Behind those red curtains, insensible to the thrill of curiosity he was causing his neighbors, John himself lay wide-awake. He had been stirred to consciousness as the machinists, who lived on the street's new extension, hurried past the house with rattling dinner-buckets to the shop before the five-minute whistle blew. He lay quite still for a long time, listening to their heavy, shuffling tread. Then a rooster crowed. John knew him well. He was a descendant of that old black Spaniard he had tried to kill with a Flobert rifle on one of his college vacations. From far below the bluff on which the house stood came the rattle of the morning train, loaded with fishermen going "up the river" for the day. It was all just as he had known it before he left home for the first time three years ago, yet it came to him now with a note of pathos and isolation. These people were going on without him. It was nothing to them that his career, as it seemed, had been suddenly cut short on the very threshold.

Then he drifted into another train of thought. He began to review his three years' work on the New York morning newspaper on which, as he put it, he had served his literary apprenticeship. All the incidents sedulously chronicled in his diary were recalled: the nights spent in the morgue—waiting for the identification of the mysteriously found body, and watching the reporters, who were always turning up with some false clew; the scenes in the Tenderloin, rich in color for the book he meant one day to write; the women's clubs he had attended, with orders from the city editor to "write up a funny story about them." Then there was his sudden resolution to give up the newspaper business for a serious attempt at real literary work, and his subsequent transfer to a copy desk, with the new idea of saving a little money before making the plunge. And then this catastrophe—his total blindness.

Yet, strange to say, this catastrophe failed to daunt John's hopes and ambitions, as it might have done with a young man of less buoyancy and self-confidence. His overweening vanity, the very strand in his character which showed weakest, was the strongest now to save him from utter collapse.

As the scenes of his reporter days recurred to him his imagination grew warm; a woman's face thrusting itself into the tangled mass of color and incident fixed his resolution.

"I'll do it, by all the gods!" he cried aloud.

His mother, waiting outside in the hall, heard him. Emboldened, she brought in the breakfast-tray.

"John dear," she said, "I didn't know you were awake. I've been standing out here with the breakfast things, listening, and I'm afraid the oatmeal's all cold."

John pushed the tray aside impatiently.

"Mother, I'm going to make you very happy," he said, brusquely.

John's mother set the tray on the floor near the bedstead's head. Then she sat down on the bed near him.

"There is really nothing to worry about, John," she began. "Mrs. Thomas said—"

"No, it's not that," John broke in. "I have given up all hope of ever being able to see again. You know I had a long talk with old Doctor Vermile just before I left. The old man's been my friend ever since—well, never mind. You know what he said. Now let's put that aside."

"My brave boy!" John's mother interjected.

"It's just this, mother," John went on. "I have had three years of living where life most abounds. I have studied human nature thoroughly. I have plenty of incident and plenty of color. My inability to see is a physical misfortune. It doesn't impair my ability to write, nor destroy my knowledge of life. Mother, I intend to devote my life to literary work."

"And Elizabeth and I will be your secretaries!" exclaimed John's mother, enthusiastically—"that is," she added, "until you are able to see again."

The early-morning conversation with his mother marked the beginning of a new period in John's life. He devoted himself assiduously to what he called literary work. But he came to it by degrees. First of all he went over the notes he had laid up as treasure for his after-literary life: all the bits of *genre* description; all the quick impressions formed by seeing people, as the reporter alone sees them, at the great climaxes in their lives. His mother, to begin with, read his notes and scrap-books to him, but later it fell to Elizabeth to be his sole co-worker and amanuensis.

As a reporter, John Swinnerton had nursed the ultimate ambition of the literary aspirant. His scrap-books, containing under date and head-line all the printed results of his assignments, all his "stories," were a source of boundless pleasure to him, and of unfailing inspiration to Elizabeth.

She would read him some story of how the excursion steamer *Oligarchy*, coming up the bay in the fog, had met the Havana liner *Orizaba*; how both boats were steaming at each other with such speed that great disaster and loss of life seemed inevitable until, by a quick twist of the *Oligarchy*'s steam steering-gear to port, in spite of the other boat's contradictory whistles, the excursionists had been saved, as the two boats cleared by about six inches.

The story in itself was interesting to Elizabeth, but the story of the story, as told by the reporter, who had fallen into the bay after it, she thought the most wonderful thing she had ever heard. Her eyes sparkled. She caught up a pen.

"John," she cried, "write that just as you have told it to me, under the title, 'The Story of a Story.' Now, then, begin!"

John dictated.

His narrative to Elizabeth had been instinct with the charm of a personal experience told in simple, direct, graphic language, and his assumption of the first person had led her to identify herself with the actor in the scene, as her imagination, warming at his words, had reproduced the experience to the smallest detail. But his dictation lacked every grace; all the strength and picturesque beauty of his narration were wanting. While he had been talking he was himself, natural, spontaneous; now he was somebody else, an author dictating a story. Like the mere ecclesiastic who enters the pulpit in cleric robes, but lacks the message of the living word, so John left out just those elements that were the very soul of his story.

As the time-chipped phrases of the daily newspaper fell from his lips,

Elizabeth wondered that the fortunate possessor of such rich experiences, possessed by one, too, who was capable of forming such vivid impressions, could so miserably fail in their ultimate expression.

The story he dictated spoke of a "heroic young reporter," of a "gruff sea-captain"; told how "the young hero" "boldly plunged into the dark depths" that "funereal-like enveloped him," and so on *ad nauseam*.

With others stories which followed, it was the same or worse. Experiences that would have delighted a literary artist became mere collections of literary mosaics, arranged with little more than a newspaper idea of journalistic effect.

Elizabeth's life now became a series of exhilarations followed by greater depressions. When he told her, in that vivid conversational way of his, how for three days he had searched for the mother of a girl who had brought death to three others and finally to herself, how at last he found her destitute—her daughter having taken the savings of years—and how she had only said, with that queer look of tenement-house pathos, "Well, I suppose the only thing to be done now is for all of us to pitch in and give her a first-class funeral." Elizabeth thought that now perhaps John would rise to his opportunity. But no; as each grotesque experience was related to her she would thrill with the awakened instinct of creative power, but when John's blundering, bald-phrased dictation began she shuddered, and her artistic perceptions underwent crucifixion.

Just three years ago, John, encouraged by Elizabeth's girlish admiration for what they both regarded as his undoubted marks of literary talent, had announced his intention of leaving Graytown and going out into the larger world to win something more than her loving approval and applause. Elizabeth remembered, and how, inwardly, she had been passionately jealous of his work. In the months that followed, her resentment against the ambition which threatened to come between them and push her aside had steadily grown, and in time her bitterness began to open her eyes to the true extent and value of his presumptive ability. She had slowly acquired a contempt and cynicism for it which was pitiful in the extreme. For it must be remembered that Elizabeth had loved John ever since as a young girl of fifteen, recently orphaned, she had come to live with his mother, and John, then a bright-faced college boy home on a vacation, had teasingly asked her whether he was to address her as "Sis" or "Sweetheart."

Now that John, helpless and almost at her mercy, was forced to abandon the very work that had taken him from her, she gradually relapsed into the old habit of encouraging him to pursue a work which she now realized could only reap a harvest of bitter disappointments and failure for him in the end. How different from the days when she and John used to go out into the woods together, and his wild imaginings would conjure up the most vivid and fanciful impressions! Elizabeth now saw, with all the quickened sensitiveness of latent power that was in herself, that John could never realize his literary hopes.

Still, she cheered and comforted him, but as the days drifted into weeks and the weeks into months, despair and hopelessness seized on her heart, and John's all-absorbing vanity grew more formidable.

As the number of completed stories increased, the difficulty of placing them had to be faced. One after another they came back, looking at first as if they had been examined, but by-and-by Elizabeth knew that the leaves of manuscript had not been disturbed. Then she had to summon every resource of her woman's nature to reassure John.

The path of fame was none so easy, she would tell him. He must have patience and keep steadily at work. His reward would come some day.

But she could not sustain him on this philosophical ground much longer. In the beginning she had encouraged him in his pathetic hopes, because her belief in his ability had been actual. Moreover, now, when he was stricken and helpless, the light flame of their boy and girl love had deepened into a lasting and immeasurable tenderness for him.

For some days she had lacked courage to tell him of the return of a certain manuscript in which he had special faith. The long delay in hearing from the magazine to which they had sent it at first depressed and then cheered him.

"Beth," he would say, pathetically, "really, you know, they would not hold the thing so long if they were not uncertain about its value."

Elizabeth could not bear it any longer. She went on a personal mission to the city. She told him she would call at the office of the magazine while there.

When she came back to Graytown she brought news that gave new life to John. His story had been accepted. The first rung on the ladder had been mounted.

After this desperate invention Elizabeth took the story to her room and read it over and over again, hoping against hope that she might be able to discover in it something that would make it sufficiently attractive. And as she read, the plot of the story grew into her consciousness, awakening in her all the power of the literary artist. She could almost hear John's rich voice, with its ringing enthusiasm, as he had glowingly told her the story.

A sudden excitement fired her. With a quick nervous pencil and an old pad of John's, she sat down by her window and began to write feverishly.

A few days later she made her second trip to the city, and just three months after she put the magazine, with the story printed over his name, into John's hands. All that day long there were joy and peace in the Swinnerton household. And if Elizabeth, in her little white room upstairs, smothered her sobs at night in her pillow, she smiled by day.

The effect of the publication of his first story upon John was instantaneous. Plans and ambitions wilder and more futile than ever occupied his mind. And Elizabeth had to bear the brunt of them. Hour after hour she took his dictation. She thought of those prisoners condemned to work forever at machines that merely registered their efforts—a round of endless labor with nothing but a dial face to show what might have been accomplished.

But when she went to work on John's dictation, the passion of the writer possessed her, and she forgot that she had been walking the treadmill of letters. The instant acceptance and publication of most of the stories—were they not John's as much as hers?—whetted confidence in her ability and acted as a spur to her pen. Gradually all the stories bearing the name of John Swinnerton found acceptance wherever sent.

Then the critics found him out. Articles, well written, which could not but appeal to his peculiar vanities, appeared in the press. He became popularly known as "the well-known short-story writer, who unites the observation of the reporter with the grace of the artist."

He was now a full-fledged author, and a successful one.

Meanwhile Elizabeth kept an almost jealous guard over him. No one, not even his mother, must read his precious work to him but her who had shared his labors. And John's fond little mother, with tears in her eyes, kissed the girl's wistful white face and promised.

To John, Elizabeth said:

"John, you are now a very important man. You must live a secluded life. It will not do for you to be disturbed by the vulgar outside world—not yet, at least."

"You are all I want," said John.

Elizabeth's lip quivered.

"Then, too," she continued, her voice shaking, "you must keep very quiet. You must not be excited or disturbed. Your work demands it."

John's mother said to him:

"Dear, you must do all Elizabeth says. She knows best."

"She is a wonder!" said John, softly, and John's mother started at the little sob that involuntarily escaped Elizabeth.

John began upon a novel. The plot he had planned out long ago, and

Elizabeth had thrilled and glowed over it with all the sympathy of the nat-
ural-born writer.

It was done at last. Wooden characters strode through melodramatic situations with the commonplaces of newspaper phraseology upon their lips.

Nevertheless, the day came when Elizabeth put the book into John's hand.

"Your novel, John," she said, hurrying from the room to her own chamber, and locking herself in.

An hour later she found him still alone with the book. He was rubbing it
gently over his cheek, handling it as if it were a thing of life, to be touched
reverently. He opened it, fingering with delicate affection the bold lines of print.

"My book, Beth!" he said, almost in a whisper.

"Your book, John!"

"Beth, you don't know what this day is to me. A little while ago I was
alone in the darkness, vainly groping toward the light. Now I have found
it. Then I was only a blind man, without the right to hope. Now I am an
author whom the world recognizes."

He paused.

"Beth, when I was blind and obscure, I did not dare hope for that which
you must know has been my heart's desire ever since I have known you."

Even in his emotion John's words did not escape a certain affectation of
manner.

"I resolved to struggle to the light for your sake only, Beth. You were the
prize which was to crown my efforts. Dear, you must know that glorious and
intoxicating as is the beckoning hand which leads me on to where the star
of fame is poised, dizzy and alluring, yet the star of love shines above it,
supreme, and without it the star of fame is blurred and dim, a dazzling light
without warmth and life. My struggles you have witnessed—and shared. The
result you see. It is no martyrdom now I ask you to take up with me, but the
love of a strong, successful man, an author blind, but with insight into the
human heart. Beth, will you—can you—"

He stopped. The novel he held out between them. All of a sudden she
struck it to the floor jealously, and put her hand in his in place of the book.

"John," she said, in a voice barely above a whisper, "you love *me*—
better—than—"

"My work?" he laughed, joyously. "Yes, yes," he said. "It is only a record
of my brain. You, you dearest and sweetest of women, you are my heart,
my soul! You will be my wife, Beth?"

With a smile that seemed the most pitiful thing in life, she raised her own
misty eyes to the wondering, groping, sightless ones.

"Yes, John," she said, simply.

* * *

It was spring-time, three years since the night John Swinnerton returned to Graytown. In two months he was to be married.

He sat impatiently by an open window, restlessly turning his eyes toward the little path that led up to the house, just as if they were endowed with sight. Suddenly they dilated with excitement, as he felt, rather than heard, some one enter the little gate.

A few moments later a big burly professional-looking man was closeted alone with him. Outside the door, her hands trembling as though afflicted with ague, her ear straining at the key-hole, knelt, or rather crouched, his mother.

Scarce an hour later John's mother was sobbing in his arms.

"Oh, John, John, John!" she was crying. "I knew it. Mrs. Thomas said . . . and oh, thank God!"

John's face was aglow. "Mother dear," he said, "we must keep this from Beth a little longer. Let us surprise her when she comes back from the city."

* * *

When John Swinnerton first saw the light again, it awoke in him a sudden shock, almost repulsion. His eyes, which had been trembling in the dark so long, pained him excessively after the operation. By a strange revulsion of the delight with which he had looked forward to this event, a feeling of inexplicable depression and melancholia assailed him, a premonition of disaster amounting almost to superstition. It may have been due to the fact that Elizabeth was absent in the city with an aunt, who was in John's confidence, buying her trousseau. However it was, when they told John of the success of the operation, and he saw for the first time in three years a peep of light warming his eyeballs, he marvelled at the depression that weighed down his spirits.

But he was up and about and quite strong and hearty when Elizabeth returned home.

He had watched for her all morning—watched the little path with eyes that behind their darkened glasses saw clearly.

His mother, who met Elizabeth at the door, acted in what seemed to her an extraordinary fashion, laughing and kissing her hysterically, and then pushing her toward John's door.

When she stepped into the room, John, instead of coming to meet her, stood back from her sombrely, pale to the lips with tense emotion, his two hands, quivering and trembling, outstretched to her.

"Here I am, dear—" she began; "and your mother—" She stopped short, for her eyes had travelled upward to his face, and with a sudden shock she saw the glasses, and all in a moment she understood.

She caught at the edge of the table dizzily, trying to gather her scattered senses. And then John, unable to restrain himself longer, strode across to her with an exclamation of the most immeasurable love, and folded her in his arms.

When the first hysterical inrush of her emotion was past, and John was holding her at arm's-length so that his greedy eyes might feed once more on her delightful beauty, a horror of the events of the past three years swept over her and took full possession of her.

What had she done? What would John do when he knew the truth? John, who despised dishonesty in every shape and form; John, who had been given new life from the very success which was not his own; John, who was so greedy and proud of his attainments, whose whole life had been one upward struggle and straining after the unattainable prize, which she by a trick had placed in his hands? She could not go on deceiving him. He knew nothing as yet; otherwise he would not have taken her to his heart. Ah, she knew John so well! And as all the horrible questions came up in her mind one by one, like a long thread of dismal phantoms in a nightmare, she almost lost consciousness as she stood there before him, vainly trying to put them from her mind and feign understanding of what he was saying, to listen to his whispered and broken words of love. Ah, could she do without them now? They had become her life! John meant them. He had said he loved her for herself alone; then she had not won his love by her trick. Oh, no, no; not that! But would he spurn and hate her when he knew the truth? She had long studied his complex character. She had been cynical in her grand disdain of the vanity which was so dominant in him. He had called it "self-confidence." Was it stronger than his love for her? Ah, that was the question!

Gradually she drew away from him.

"You—you—you—" Words failed her, and she began to sob.

"Why, my darling!" He knelt beside her. Out in the hall they could hear his mother weeping also. She had not resisted the tempting pleasure of listening to them at the door. "They are so sweet!" she apologized to herself; and still crying softly, she passed down the hall.

"Let me think—I must think—" cried Elizabeth. "No, John, don't touch me. Let me alone a moment."

"But, dearest one—"

"John, do you remember what I once asked you—whether you loved best me or your work?"

"And I said you, of course," he replied, quickly.

"John, answer me that when—when you—John dear—when you have read over—some—of your stories, John."

Still mystified, but greatly moved by her apparent distress, he replied, "But, dearest, I know them already, almost by heart."

"No, no!" She was losing herself in her passionate distraction. She caught up his book and thrust it into his hands. "Can you see well enough to read? There—do—just a few chapters—" Her breath almost left her.

His eyes strained as he turned the title-pages, and slowly, painfully, he began to read.

The silence in the room was horrible. It would not have been broken but that the book dropped from his nerveless hands. He staggered back, his hand to his head, like one who has suddenly lost reason, memory, understanding; and as she approached him with wide bright eyes full of piteous supplication, he stepped backward away from her.

"John," she said, "for the love of Heaven, speak to me."

Her voice recalled him. "You!" he turned on her with savage fierceness. "What have you done? What horrible deceit is this you have practised on me? My God!"

"John, I—"

"Whose work is this?"

"Yours, dear—all yours!"

"Mine!" He laughed mockingly.

"Yours—and mine, John. You were my inspiration. You gave the life, the spark. I could not have written a line but for you. Your soul, which could not find expression through your medium, dear, entered into mine, and I—"

"Ah-h!" he said, "I understand. It is all clear to me now. You—you stole—you took—my—work. You are guilty of the most despicable, the meanest of thefts."

He sank down in a chair, burying his face in his hands, and groaning in the agony of sudden disillusion.

"John," she cried, her two little hands stretched toward him appealingly. "I can't bear it. John, love, it was for you!"

He looked up at her. "For God's sake leave me," he cried. "Your jest has come to its end."

* * *

She was gone. He rose and stumbled about the room, more helpless than when he was totally blind. He began feverishly gathering the scrap-books in which the printed stories which had been cut from the magazines were pasted. Then he groped his way across the room to a chest of drawers. He drew out the original manuscripts—"the copies," she had called them. These at least were his own. He carried them over to the table, and spread them out side by side in order, opposite to the stories in the scrap-books bearing the same titles.

He was shaking pitifully. His hands trembled violently as he turned page after page, and as he read, a great light, a light that was startling in its poignant clearness, dawned upon him. The crudities of his own work, the set, stupid, inane phraseology, the long, tedious, duologues! And then, opposite, the delicate wit, the intangible art, the philosophy, the pathos!

His shoulders heaved, his heart suffocated him with its tumultuous beating, and his brain was swimming with vertigo. His thoughts would not tarry with him. They wandered inconstantly without any abiding-place in his mind. One great feeling welled up and took full possession of him, a longing that was almost madness for the presence, the touch, the sympathy of her he had spurned.

He sprang to his feet and strode to the door, throwing it open violently.

"*Beth!*" he called, and the startled cry of fear and longing rang up through the deserted halls.

In her room she heard it, and was glad.

(*Harper's Monthly,* with Bertrand W. Babcock, June 1902)

A CONTRACT

Masters sat at his desk. His eyes had wandered past the mass of correspondence, papers and maps before and about him. Half absently he was watching a little rift of white clouds drifting lazily across the turquoise blue of the skies, a great snowflake fallen on a blue sheet of water. Now it drifted slowly toward the west, growing ever smaller and mistier until it melted into the endless glow of the sky and became a part of it.

As it vanished from his sight Masters aroused himself from his reverie. He had been likening the flaky cloud against the blue to a piece of gauze twisted with a magic hand about the waist of a pale blue kimona of the sheerest silk.

"Ah, these skies of Japan!" he sighed with a great indrawing of his breath. He was in a sentimental mood as usual of late, for Masters was in love.

A polite Japanese looked in at him from an adjoining office, with the calm, half wondering, wholly unreadable expression of the better class. Seeing him, Masters sat up in his chair abruptly.

"Ah, Ito, come in."

Bowing profoundly, his secretary approached the desk, where he stood in respectful attention.

"You wanted to see me about some personal matter, I believe? What can I do for you?"

"If your honorship would be so kind to sign this honorable insignificant paper," said Ito, "I shall be thousand thanks to you until before I die."

"What is it?" asked Masters, examining curiously a paper written in Ito's fine Japanese characters, deeply ruled down either side in red ink.

"That, your honorship," said Ito, without change of expression, "is one little bit betrothal contract."

"A—w—what?" exclaimed Masters, dropping the pen he had just dipped in the ink bottle. It was his custom to sign without question the various papers of the company prepared by the secretary and translated into Japanese, a language he was not completely familiar with in written form.

"Insignificant betrothal contract," repeated Ito, still unmoved.

Masters sat back in his chair with a slight frown.

"Why do you bring such things to me in the office here?" he demanded sharply.

"Your honorship forgetting," said Ito, gently, "that I beg for one private consultation with you."

"True," Masters nodded, "but what have I to do with a betrothal contract? I hope, Ito," he added, whimsically, "you are not a nekoda in disguise and are not about to trick me into a marriage."

"No, no," returned the other, hastily. "I beg your honorship's ten millions pardons. This is my own insignificant contract."

"But why should I sign it?"

"Ah, now I will take the pleasure to explain." And Ito permitted a shadowy smile to flit across his face.

"I am about to make proposal of marriage to Japanese maiden."

"Yes," said Masters, with interest.

"Vell," said Ito, "before her father giving that necessary consent unto me, I got get endorsement from you also, Master-sir."

"From me?"

"I explain further. The honorable father of this honorable lady don't quite appreciate me."

Masters smiled.

"Nevertheless," continued Ito, "he have greatest respect for your excellency." He bowed very deeply here. "Now, if you making request for me for this marriage he agoing to consent right away at once. Will your excellency honorably condescend to sign this insignificant contract?"

"Oh, very well," said Masters, picking up his pen, "glad to do anything I can to assist you, 'm sure."

As he wrote his crisp, bold signature across the bottom of the sheet he asked with mild interest: "And who is the happy bride?"

Ito did not reply. He had taken the contract from his master and was examining his signature very carefully. He blotted it thoroughly and then slowly folded the contract.

"You say her father knows me?" asked Masters, striking a match and lighting a cigar.

"Yes, your honorship."

"What's his name?"

"Ten million pardons, but his honorable name so augustly insignificant your excellency could not remember it. Five thousand such name in Japan."

Masters smiled good humoredly.

"Keep your secret, my boy," he said.

Arising he pushed his chair against the desk. His face had a strangely sympathetic expression on it as he looked down from his height on Ito.

"As I said, Ito," he remarked kindly, "call upon me for any assistance you want. I am sure you—er—deserve this young woman, and don't blame you at all for wanting to beat down the old man's objections."

Ito began a series of intensely low bows.

"And," continued Masters, cheerfully, "I've no doubt she is charming—one of those delightful little Yum-Yum creatures, who walk on their heels and trip on their toes—cherry-lipped, peepy-eyed little witches."

Ito had ceased his low bowing. He had flushed a dark, angry red.

"She is not like that," he said, "she is one honorably insignificant grand lady."

"Anyhow," said Masters, "I wish you all kinds of luck and happiness."

He held out his hand and heartily shook the small cold one of his secretary. Then picking up his hat he passed with his long, swinging stride out of the office into the glow of the sunlight.

Once in the street an odd fancy struck him. Why should not he have a long, formal contract also? Well, he would try his luck. He swung up the street, disdaining the whines and calls of the jinriki men who followed him with their vehicles. As he reached the great terminal station at Shimbashi a new idea occurred to him.

"To make the illusion more complete," he said, "I shall celebrate my betrothal in advance."

He turned out of the station, hailed a jinrikisha and gave an order to be taken to a gay tea-house in the city.

Meanwhile Ito, who had left the office a few moments after his master, arrived at the station, bought a ticket for a neighboring suburb and in half an hour had kicked his shoes into the hands of a kneeling servant in the household of Omizutani, and with low and graceful obeisances had greeted the master of the house and formally presented the contract.

Ito had deceived Masters. The document he had shown him was something more than a mere contract. It was in fact a demand couched in superlatively polite language upon his debtor, Mizutani, requiring his consent to the marriage of his daughter, O-Kiku-san, to Ito, the secretary of Masters.

Mizutani was not slow to act upon the demand. With the most extravagant expressions of good will toward Ito and his employer he sent immediately for his daughter.

The maid had put the last touch to the little shining head of O-Kiku-san. She brought a little mirror to show her mistress the effect of the elaborate butterfly coiffure. The bewitching young face smiled back at the girl from the small beveled mirror.

"I am happy," she murmured softly, "as all the gods of sunlight."

As she bowed herself before the little shrine in her room she murmured appealingly: "Oh, Kwannonsan, let not my joy pass from me but abide with me forever."

Word had just been brought to her that below in the guest room her lover awaited her. She had commanded her maid to dress her in blue, shimmering blue like the water, and to tie about her waist an obi of the finest white silk. She had one huge poppy for her hair and another for her bosom. It was thus, he had told her repeatedly, he loved to see her best.

The little, happy smile that had glistened in her eyes as though the sun had melted into their velvet depths slipped out of them dismally as she entered the guest room and paused between the parted shoji. One dazzled glance of confusion and disappointment, then she subsided to the mats and made her prostration before her suitor.

Her father addressed her in his stately accent of command:—

"Ito Adachi," said he, "desires thy unworthy hand in marriage. It is my command that it be given to him."

O-Kiku-san's clasped hands fell apart. She raised a pair of startled eyes to Ito, bowing profoundly before her. Then bewilderingly they sought her father's. Before the deepening frown of displeasure she fancied she saw in his face her little head bowed like a flower nipped by a winter wind. She brought words of submission. Then her voice, frightening her with its shrill edge of pain, she suddenly, piteously besought her father that he would pray excuse her for one little hour that she might meditate alone. She was not feeling well; the sun had been hot upon her head in the fields that day, and she was faint and weak. When she had left them the older man turned to Ito.

"I beseech you," he said, "to pardon my daughter's honorable rudeness."

"I beseech you to feel assured that I appreciate her honorable indisposition," returned Ito.

"She is honorably grateful to you for your condescension in desiring her for a wife," said Mizutani.

"I am deeply touched," said Ito, "by the honor she does me in accepting me."

"I beg you to permit me show her this honorably magnificent letter from his excellency, the Eijinsan."

Ito with extravagant words of politeness relinquished the contract, and then with more elaborate apologies the master of the house withdrew.

Mizutani found his daughter prone before the shrine in her chamber. She was bathing the feet of the goddess with tears. He raised her gently to her feet.

"My daughter," he said, tenderly, "it was not my desire to marry you to this youth. I have consented to it only because he comes to me with a command from one who holds me in his debt. Nevertheless, I will turn him even now from my door like an honorable dog if it is thy desire."

"Who is the honorable creditor by whose command he comes?" she asked.

"His master, the honorable Eijinsan."

She whitened. Her hands crept out quiveringly from their long sleeves. She seized the contract and read it through. Only one tear; it fell upon the bold superscription at the end. She drew her finger across it and almost blurred it out. Then she ceased to tremble. The face she raised to her father was smiling, the eyes glassy, lips apart, revealing the straight little teeth within.

"Dear, my father," she said, "how good are the gods. They bring to me a husband, to you the favor of your creditor."

"And will you accept this young man?" inquired her father, surprised by her sudden smiles.

"Assuredly," she returned "let us hasten down to him at once and beg him to accept our most humble thanks for his condescension."

The night was sad. But who can see tears in the darkness? A cold bath in the early morning and a clever maid may bring the roses back to pale cheeks and brush away the shadows from the eyes. So the following day old Mizutani, after a piercing glance at his daughter, sighed with relief. He had no wish to lead her into a marriage that might bring her unhappiness. Whilst of ancient and noble lineage Mizutani was one of the men of new Japan, imbued with the ideas of the West. And while his daughter had been brought up with great care the old man's pet ambition was to marry her to a man of her choice as well as his own.

Sewing in the sunlight of her little garden she started suddenly at the sound of quick, firm steps coming up the graveled path. The color faded from her face and the sewing dropped from her nerveless hands. Masters approached just in time to restore to her the little spool of silk that had rolled to his feet. His smile was like the sunlight and he looked so masterful and big that all the resentment and anger of the night passed from the girl's mind like a cloud dissolving in the mist.

"Last night," he said, "I indulged myself in a strange—ah—celebration."

He went a little closer to her and endeavored to look under the drooped lids.

"Can you guess," said he, "what I was doing?"

"I am honorably stupid," she apologized simply.

"I celebrated my betrothal," he said smiling joyously. "Unique idea, wasn't it?"

She nodded as though she understood, though she was only vaguely conscious of what he was saying.

"Wasn't it though?" he added as though she had assented. "Fancy a fellow celebrating his betrothal all alone; that is, except of course for—er—incidental entertainers and—er—servants to wait on one."

"And—and—your betrothed, was she not present?" she essayed timidly.

"Well, you see, she isn't my betrothed yet. I intended asking her last night. Then I got a fancy that it would be a good idea to draw up some sort of contract first, like my secretary did. Had a little dinner all alone first of all to put me in tune, and then—behold—see."

He suddenly put into her hands a most extraordinary document. He had fashioned it somehow after the manner of Ito's, with deep red lines running down either side.

"Beautiful, isn't it?" he asked boyishly.

She looked at it almost fearfully.

"Now," continued Masters with his winning smile, "that I've drawn up the contract, I believe I ought to propose to the girl's—ancestors."

"Her honorable parents, you mean," corrected O-Kiku-san, and she pricked her finger with her needle till the blood fell.

"Oh, we call them ancestors; same thing, isn't it?"

She shook her head.

"Too old-fashioned," she said and smiled faintly. "Anyhow," she added, "you are English gentlemans—why, pray, do you keer mek Japanese contract?"

"There you're mistaken," said Masters, "if you please—born in Japan."

She sighed. "You Japanese citizen sure thing," she admitted grudgingly, and then without waiting for him to speak, she added quickly, "all the same you jus' foreigner, all the same."

"Well, I like that," said Masters, indignantly.

"You honorable ancestors western barbarians," said O-Kiku-san.

"True," agreed Masters, "but you see in the progress of our ascent it is only natural that I, the latest descendant, should be born in Japan. The next of our line possibly may be partly Japanese, and the next."

"You makin' ridigulous nonzenze ad me," she said reproachfully.

"No I am not," protested Masters, "but you are very unkind. You are trying to rob me of my birthright. Am I or am I not Japanese?"

"Japanese citizen, yes," she admitted. "Japanese man? No, naever."

"Why not!" he inquired angrily. "Isn't this blessed spot my home?"

"Yes," she admitted, "bud you bin edicated away." She waved her hand vaguely seaward.

"What's half a dozen or even a dozen years, to be more exact, compared with all the years of my life here?"

She shook her head, smiling sadly at his persistence.

"Why am I not Japanese, then?" demanded Masters.

"Because you live mos' you honorable life wiz thad English colony ad Japan."

"Nonsense. Haven't I known you ever since you were a little pickaninny with a flower ornament in your little hair and a parasol of all the colors of the rainbow?"

"My honorable fadder was a member thad English colony," she said slowly. "He worg wiz you honorable fadder."

"Then, see here, if you've lived most of your life among the English in Japan, and I—Well, you must see how it is. You can't get around it, you know. I certainly am a Jap," and his blue eyes snapped merrily.

"You certainly is," agreed Kiku, pressing her lips tightly together.

Masters promptly possessed himself of her hands, needle, thread and all.

"Now," said he, "that we've come to the conclusion that I myself am a Jap, do you see any reason why I shouldn't marry a Japanese maiden?"

Kiku shook her head mutely. She let her hands remain passively in his. She had long ago recognized the futility of gainsaying him in even the smallest way.

"Very good then," said Masters. "Why, then, shouldn't we—you and I—get married?"

She lifted her head with a startled movement.

"Pray, why," she inquired piteously, "do you mek such silly nonzenze ad me?"

"Nonsense?" repeated Masters, "I never was more earnest in my life."

An expression of horror crept into her eyes. Her head drooped forward lower and lower until it fell upon her hands.

"Answer me," commanded Masters, with the first note of alarm in his voice. Her strange attitude mystified him. "Will you marry me, Kiku?"

"I already betroth," she said in the smallest voice.

Masters dropped her hands as if they were those of one dead.

"You mean," he said, "that you—I can't believe it. It was always an understood thing between us that we—Do you mean to tell me that you have been deceiving me and that you have been betrothed all the time?"

"I only gitting betrothed yistidy," said Kiku.

"Who the devil is he?" demanded Masters, savagely.

"That not perlite, call my betrothed debbil, excellency—"

"I'm not an excellency, and I'll call your b—, and you haven't got any betrothed. I'll go and see your father now, and I'll wring his little neck if he's sold you to any one except me."

He burst in upon his father's old partner like a thunderbolt. His voice shook the fragile house with its thunder. The old man was dumbfounded. So surprised and shocked was he in fact that it took him several minutes before he could explain to Masters that he had betrothed his daughter to Ito at Master's own solicitation, he having graciously condescended to sign the contract.

"It's a—trick," said the young man, beside himself with rage at his secretary, "and I'll fire that fellow to-morrow."

"But my honorable daughter?" squealed Mizutani, "what before all the gods she goin' to do?"

"She? She'll marry me."

"But, my lord, pray have little pity."

"Pity?"

"I think my daughter giving her honorable heart unto her lubber."

"What?"

"She tell me so."

"She told you so?"

Mizutani bowed his head.

"She told you she cared for—that little mannikin—for—"

"Yes, excellency."

Masters was silent for the first time.

"That alters everything," he said, suddenly. "Good day!"

Mizutani sent at once for his daughter. He wrung his hands in the utmost distress. He almost fell on his knees before her.

"Eijinsan will ruin us, oh, my daughter," he shrieked.

"What can we do?" said Kiku.

Her father tried to appear commanding.

"You must fly," he said, waving his hands, "to the Eijinsan. Hasten with the speed of wings to his honorable residence. There you must beat your head at his feet and implore his honorable pardon. Then if he is still unrelenting you must make the grand sacrifice."

"Yes?"

"You must break your betrothal with Ito Adachi and marry his master."

O-Kiku-san bowed her head with meek joy.

They were soon seated in their jinrikisha and speeding toward the city. Kiku was silent and thoughtful, one moment intensely sad, the next trembling with joy. The old man was so completely agitated by his fear of Masters and his pity for his daughter, who he thought must loathe the prospect of marriage with a barbarian, that he was shivering.

On arriving at his office Masters had rung his bell for his secretary.

"Ito," he said, "I don't like the way in which you tricked me into signing that so-called contract yesterday."

He waited for the other to reply, but his secretary merely bowed politely.

"However," continued Masters, fumbling with the pencil in his hand, "all being fair in love and war, I suppose I'd have done the same in your place. As she admits she cares for you, of course you had a right to override her father's objections."

Again Ito bowed deeply. Masters flung around in his chair.

"I congratulate you and—If you'll stop doubling yourself up you'll be able to listen to me. I'm going on a trip—er—across the ocean, and—what are you salaaming about now?"

Another clerk thrust in a pert head.

"Mister Mizutani and lady," he announced.

In his excitement Masters knocked over his chair as he leaped to his feet. Mizutani walked behind his daughter, but he almost jumped forward at Masters' sharp, "Well, what is it now?"

"We come to beg one little interview with you," said the old man.

Masters nodded curtly. He kept his eyes off Kiku, who was the only one in the room smiling.

"Will you kindly make honorable excuse to Mr. Ito," said Mizutani.

"No," said Masters, "he has a right to hear anything you have to say."

"As your excellency desires," said Mizutani.

He fidgeted a moment, then tremblingly laid his hand on his daughter's sleeve.

"Excellency," he said, "my daughter begs ten million pardons of you; also she rady mek marriage wiz you."

For the first time the impassive Ito started.

"She is betrothed to me," he said quickly.

"A million pardons," said Mizutani, "my daughter no longer betroth to you."

"This is a pretty business," said Masters, "I'd like to know just what it means."

"My daughter like to make marriage wiz you," said Mizutani with diffidence.

"She wants to marry you for your money," said Ito boldly. "She loves me."

The short silence that ensued was broken by Kiku.

"Excellency, don't believe him," she said.

"But you told your own father so," said Masters slowly. And the old man hung his head.

"I doan keer mek him tears," said Kiku bravely.

"What do you mean?"

"Thad honorable lubber," she indicated Ito, "mek proposal unto my fadder. Thad fadder 'fraid offend you and he betroth me. Therefore I kin nod disobey, o' coorse nod. Also I desire that he nod know I brekin' my heart, so I laugh like big bebby. Say I glad, I de-lighted. Ver good hasten that honorable marriage of love."

Masters burst out laughing.

"Well, I ought to have known Kiku; and as for you—" he turned to Ito, who bowed as politely as ever, "you see how it is. What are you going to do about it?"

"Commit suicide!" said Ito promptly.

"Nonsense," said Masters.

(*Frank Leslie's Popular Monthly,* August 1902)

THE LOVES OF SAKURA JIRO AND
THE THREE HEADED MAID

Sakura Jiro had not been in the country long, nor, indeed, had he attained to that exalted position that he afterward occupied in the regard of fad-seeking society women, fascinated by the serpent of mysticism, when he found himself walking through East Fourteenth street. Nowadays Jiro rarely goes beyond the environs of a certain pretentious hyphenated hostelry, but in those days he had no social position to cherish on the better streets. On the day when ambition was suddenly presented to him through the medium of a glaring poster, Jiro had eaten no breakfast. His resources would not permit that extravagance. Jiro had been expecting a remittance from home that thus far had obstinately refused to come out of the East.

Jiro's people were not always to be depended upon. Their respect for him had not been increased by his latter courses. When the time had arrived for Jiro to go into the army, he had demurred.

"What I mek myself fighter for, which-even?" he asked his American friend in Yedo. "Me? Why, I a poet, a dreamer, no swallower of blood."

His friend agreed. "Why not go to America?" he had suggested.

"I go ad your honorable country," Jiro decided.

That had been some eight months before. Up to this time Jiro's relatives had furnished him with the means to pursue his study of the "barbarians" who fascinated him. Now, seemingly, they had deserted him. The conviction had been steadily forced upon Jiro that he must find employment. So he had gone to certain Japanese business men in New York. Some of them had liked him and some of them had not. One of the former told him that he had a very promising opening that would just suit Jiro.

"You will have to attend to my Japanese correspondence, be down here in the morning to open up the place, do the type-writing, wait on customers, and solicit orders from the mail department in the evenings. It's a very fine opening. You will start on seven dollars a week, and win rapid promotion as ability is shown," was the attractive proposition made to him.

Jiro had just come from this man's place as he wandered depressed through Fourteenth street. He had paused to look at the red-brick building which housed "those strange barbarian gents who come from liddle bit isle to run New York," when a gaudy poster caught his eye. The main figure was that of a man picturesquely attired. But it was not the dress or the frankly Irish face that held the attention of Sakura Jiro; out of the mouth of the poster man rolled a mass of flame as red as flaring ink could make it. Underneath was a legend that Jiro made out to be something about "Ostero, the Spanish juggler."

The thing amused him. Familiar as he was with the marvelous feats of his countrymen, it seemed ridiculous, and sad too, that a mere fire-eater should be billed as a feature.

"Any babby in all Nippon do thad," he muttered.

Yet, yet if people wanted to see such a poor antic as that, why couldn't he—? Yes, he could; he would. Jiro, with the quickened movement of a man who thinks he sees a way out of despair, moved farther through the street. At last he stood before the entrance of the place where "the wonders of every clime, assembled from millions of miles into one colossal aggregation, were offered to public gaze for the nominal sum of one dime." Up to the box office he went. The ticket-seller eyed him stolidly.

"Say, you god one manager ad this place?" queried Jiro.

"Yes, we've got one manager," testily answered the other.

"Say, I wan' go in unto this place to see thad same manager, augustness," continued Jiro. "I belong unto thad—thad—thad—profesh."

It was an inspiration, the source of which was a chorus-girl who lived in Jiro's boarding-house.

"Got any credentials?"

"Creden'ls! Whad may those honorable things be?"

"Oh, can you prove you belong to the profesh?"

"Say, augustness, you look ad me liddle bit while."

Jiro was busy fumbling in an inner pocket. Then he drew forth what seemed to be a long, slender Japanese dagger, which he handed to the man behind the window.

"It's jus' a liddle knife, you see," observed Jiro, carelessly.

"Seems to be nothing more. Well?"

Jiro laid his hand palm upward upon the ledge in front of the window. Then, with a sharp, quick movement, he seemingly drove the blade completely through his hand, so that the point protruded on the other side. Smiling, he held aloft the pierced hand.

The ticket-seller looked startled. Jiro held out the hand to him.

"Pull out thad honorable knife," he said.

The ticket-man hesitated.

"Pull it out. See, ther' 's nod blood."

With a nervous movement the man removed the knife from the wound of Jiro. The Japanese passed his other hand lightly over both sides of the wounded member. Offering it again to the gaze of the other, he smiled.

"Say, it's good as new. It naever hurt."

The ticket-man's eyes bulged.

"Say, young fellow," he gasped, "you're all right. Men like you ought to have carpets put down for you. The earth ain't good enough for your feet. Pass in."

Jiro went in. The crowd about the entrance, having seen a part of his feat, sent up a cheer. Before Jiro could reach the interior hall, where were assembled the "illustrious galaxy," an attendant sent by the box-office man rushed the manager to the side of the Japanese. There was some business parley, and then the manager conducted Jiro through the place. Jiro, however, thinking to appear familiar with American ways, held back from any bargain.

"We'll have to have another platform in here if you join us," the manager explained to Jiro, as they traversed the main hall.

While they were talking Jiro regarded with tolerating cynicism the performance of "Ostero, the Spanish juggler." All of the attractions were ranged about the room, each upon its own platform. Next to Ostero was Yido, the snake-charmer. Just across the hall was a figure inclosed in a cabinet that pleased Jiro. It was Marva, the three-headed lady. In his own country Jiro never had heard of any such wonder; but these Americans were capable of producing anything, and why not a three-headed lady? So Jiro had no doubt that it was genuine, and must be a mark of the extreme favor of the gods.

"Thad a beautiful thought of the gods," he told the manager; "she mek good wife."

"Yes, she would," said the manager; "but think what a talkin' to she could give a fellow."

"No, nod thad; but there's three mouths to kiss." For Jiro had learned American ways.

The manager pointed across the hall to Ostero.

"He's rather stuck on her himself," he said—"Ostero there—though Kelly's his real name."

Jiro now saw that all of the Irish Spaniard's feats were directed at the three-headed lady. His mind was now decided.

"Gentle lady of the three heads," he murmured, "I'll join myself unto this honorable company."

"I'm wiz you," he told the manager.

"Good!" exclaimed the purveyor of amusement. "We'll put you up a stand there by Ostero. It will be the East and the West, side by side, exploiting the best of their characteristic civilizations."

Then he sent for the press-agent, and the fact was duly chronicled. Thus it was that Sakura Jiro, descended from the samurai, came to earning his living in Fourteenth street through illusionary feats.

For a time Jiro prospered. His tricks and demonstrations, though of a subtle, weird, delicate character, excited the wonder of Third Avenue and the approbation of the snake-charmer, his neighbor.

"You are a real addition to us with talent," she told him on an off day when the crowd was small because of the storm.

Although the manager and his patrons were pleased with the new acquisition, there was one who could not be won to more than a passing interest in anything Jiro did. The three-headed lady, although possessed, in popular belief at least, with three times the eyesight of ordinary folk, remained indifferent to the subtle courtship established by Jiro. In vain he threw three balls into the air, to have them descend a shower that filled a bushel basket; in vain he grew a multitude of arms out of his body; and all in vain he borrowed lace handkerchiefs, to turn them into white rabbits that ran about upon the heads of the favored spectators.

"Them are all very fine," the three mouths said, "just like any lady that happened to be born a Hindu could do; but there's nothin' manly and bold-like 'bout them."

Ostero had only to put a quid of tobacco into his mouth, with his Gaelic grin, and shoot out balls of flame, to move the triple-necked lady to admiration.

"That Kelly's a monstrous fine man, bold and brave-like," would float across the hall.

Then the inspired Kelly would stand upon his head, while flames belched forth from his toes.

Jiro was not despondent at first. Every time Kelly, basking in the lady's favor, invented a new trick, he would follow suit. In this way were born many of those illusions that in later days made the name of Sakura Jiro renowned among polite people. Alas! it was to no purpose.

One dull, rainy day Jiro gave signs of breaking down under the strain of the competition that led nowhere. He had just borrowed a baby from the throng and grown from its hair a beautiful flowering plant that, springing upward inch by inch, was applauded by the outsiders, without winning more than a pitying smile from the lady with whom Jiro now openly admitted he was madly in love.

"What's the use?" he sighed.

Yido, the snake-charmer, lounging easily upon a corner seat composed of the intertwining bodies of two boa-constrictors, leaned across to him.

"You're not doin' the right thing to win her over, old man," she whispered.

It didn't occur to Jiro to ask how the snake-charmer knew. He was concerned only with her hint.

"My tricks—they are good," he hazarded.

Yido answered:

"Good! Of course they are. They're 'way above the heads of our people, and'll make your fortune some day; but they'll never give you her."

"Why nod?"

"The way to get her is to do something more in Kelly's line, but something better than he can ever do."

Jiro looked across the hall at the radiant blond three heads of his mistress. All the intense longing of his soul throbbed through his being. He could not live without those three heads. How dear they all were to him! He must win the right to kiss them. He would! For, despite his months of residence in America and his Oriental familiarity with illusions, Jiro still had faith in the reality of his three-headed lady-love. Perhaps Yido was right. He would adopt her suggestion.

"Not only do that, but make her jealous. Get me on your platform to aid you in some new feat you think up," went on Yido. "Besides, the manager is thinking of getting rid of one juggler and paying the other more money."

Here were incentives enough. Jiro, earning an increased salary, could easily afford to marry, even if he added to himself all three of the heads requiring separate hats and individual meals.

* * *

Four days later, the manager, in leading the crowds from platform to platform in his adjective-distributing trip, paused dramatically before the platform of Jiro. He waited a moment for complete attention.

"Ladies and gentlemen," he said, "each of you has some ambition in life dearer than all else. Each of you has some wish to whose fulfillment every step of your life thus far has been directed. To some of you it is a great fortune, to some a limit to your fortune with which you will be content; to others simpler, more elementary things, such as the possession of a little home of your own. The people here on our platforms are no different from you in this. They, too, have ambitions. Sakura Jiro, known throughout the world as the 'Japanese wonder,' has an ambition, great as have been the things he has already accomplished. He has striven during his whole life to perfect a feat he is now about to perform. Now success seems within his reach.

"You, ladies and gentlemen, may know the joy—the holy joy, I might say—that comes with the accomplishment of your greatest, your dearest ambition. You are now about to witness the accomplishment of the ambition of Sakura Jiro, known through the world as the 'Japanese wonder,' and to share with him the joy—the holy joy—of accomplishment."

It was a good speech, the manager felt. It had been written by the new press-agent. Women throughout the crowd were in tears, and men felt a quickened pulsation. Some held up their children that all might see clearly what the manager told them in an addition to his speech made without the advice of the press-agent. About the hall the other attractions leaned far out across their platforms, lost in an absorbing interest. The lady of the three heads was watching the scene with all six of her organs of sight. The intense gaze of all was concentrated upon Jiro.

Upon the platform with the Japanese wonder was Yido, the snake-charmer, in rather unusual attire. She wore a dainty red dress cut as a kimono. Upon her head was a white cap, and a housewife's apron was about her waist.

"She looks quite domestic," one woman told another.

With a low obeisance, first to the snake-charmer and then to the throng, Jiro walked steadily to the back of the stage, where a long rubber tube led down from a gas-jet. With another bow he turned the cock and placed the tube to his lips.

"Heavens! He wants to kill himself!" cried a woman.

"His dearest wish is to die," added a man who appeared to be a country clergyman.

The manager waved a silencing hand.

"Hush! Stuff!" he said sternly.

Jiro filled his lungs with gas without seeming to be affected beyond a slight bulging of his eyes. Then he picked up from a little table a long iron tube, the end of which, resting on the table, terminated in a gas-burner that looked as though it had just been taken from some gas-cooking range. The other end Jiro applied to his mouth. Slowly he blew through it with distended cheeks.

The domesticated snake-charmer applied a match to the burner on the table. The gas ignited. There was a burst of applause from the crowd, in which the ossified man joined. Quickly the snake-charmer set a frying-pan over the flame, the source of which was in Jiro's chest. From a little pail at her side she poured a batter into the pan. It sizzled and smoked. Four cakes were cooking in the pan. When they seemed done, she turned them with a little shovel. The other attractions were dumfounded. Marva was pale, and Ostero looked completely crestfallen.

"Breakfast is ready," called the snake-charmer.

Jiro lowered the pipe from his mouth. Pale and trembling, he approached Yido. She offered him the cakes. One he ate, amid thunderous applause. The second he passed to the audience, where it fell from the frightened fingers of an old woman into the eager hands of a newsboy.

The third cake Jiro hurled defiantly into the face of Ostero. He was now staggering, and had just strength enough to toss the last feebly at the feet of Marva, his triple love. Then, with a half-sigh, he toppled over on the floor.

Upon the instant there was wild confusion. The spectators were seized with a panic. Unmindful of the dignity of her position, and forgetful of the presence of spectators, Marva, slipping off her two false heads, vaulted over the rail to the floor. Her two abandoned heads flapped forlornly behind in their place in her cabinet. In a moment she had two heads on her body, but one was that of Sakura Jiro, the Japanese wonder.

"He did it for me, he did it all for me!" she sobbed.

The snake-charmer bent pityingly over both.

"If he had only known," said the snake-charmer.

"I love him," fiercely retorted the one-headed lady.

* * *

When Jiro regained consciousness in the hospital, four hours later, he found one of the three heads dear to him bowed above his bed.

"I feelin' so queer, an' you look lek you only had one head," he moaned, gazing up at her.

"You did it all for me, dear," she said amid her tears.

"I am mad," he said. "Where are those udder heads?"

"Why, dear, I have only one, like you," she said. "It was all a trick. But this one head is yours. I love you."

"Dear leddy, I so happy I shall love you enough for three," he said.

(*Century Magazine*, March 1903)

MISS LILY AND MISS CHRYSANTHEMUM:
THE LOVE STORY OF TWO JAPANESE GIRLS
IN CHICAGO

Yuri (which is "Lily" in English) and Kiku (which is "Chrysanthemum") met in one of the noisy and crowded railway stations in Chicago. They were sisters, half Japanese and half English; but neither could understand one word the other spoke, for Yuri had been taken by her English father, who had been long since dead, from Japan when a little bit of a girl, and had lived most of her life in England and afterward in America, so that she had forgotten her mother tongue; while Kiku had stayed with the little mother in Japan, whose recent death had left her so lonely that she had come all the way to America to join her sister, of whom she had only the dimmest memory. For in this double orphanage, thousands and thousands of miles apart, the two had felt strangely drawn to each other.

They were very much alike in appearance, only Yuri looked older and perhaps sadder than Kiku, who really was the younger by two years, and who was fairly beaming with excitement. She chatted away in Japanese to Yuri, forgetting that Yuri would not understand her, and turning half apologetically to be interpreted by the kind English lady who had known her very well in Japan and had brought her to her sister.

"Your sister is pleased to be with you," she said to Yuri.

The girl flushed with pleasure and put her arm affectionately about Kiku. "And I am glad to have her with me." Then she added, "But I would rather have gone home to her."

* * *

Six months passed rapidly, and Kiku had learned to speak English brokenly. The two little strangers boarded together on the South Side. They had an east room which overlooked Lake Michigan. Each morning as Yuri rose softly from the bed, so as not to awaken Kiku, she would throw open the green shutters, and resting her elbows on the sill, look dreamily out across the lake, letting the cool breeze fan her, and watching with eager eyes the sun rise. In those early hours, before Kiku had awakened, Yuri would make great plans for their future. She thought of how much she could save out of her salary (for she was employed as a teacher in one of the public schools in Chicago), so that she and Kiku might return together to Japan. She knew it would take some years before she would have sufficient to take them both back, for Kiku's pretended cheeriness had not deceived her, and the pitiful quivering of the girl's lips told of her homesickness.

Yuri had looked forward for years to the time when she should have enough to take her to Japan. Perhaps she loved even more dearly than Kiku the home that she could not remember. She had almost lived on the hope of going there; but now a new difficulty stood in her way—Kiku had had only enough money wherewith to bring her to America, and was entirely dependent now on her sister, whose salary had only recently been sufficient to lay any aside. Moreover, Kiku was pining for her home, and Yuri knew that when the little fund in the bank should have grown large enough to permit of the trip, it must be Kiku, and not she, who would go. Kiku was nineteen years old; Yuri, though only two years older, felt as a mother to her little foreign sister. A love wonderful in its strength, devotion and unselfishness had sprung up between these two. Kiku loved Yuri with a pride in her that was pathetic in its confidence, but Yuri's love partook of the supreme and tender love of a good mother.

"Oh, Kiku," she would say, before starting out in the morning, "you must be careful when you go out not to go far, for I don't want my little Yap to lose herself," and Kiku would say with her pretty English lisp, "Ess, liddle mozzer."

* * *

Walter Palmer was a young lawyer who boarded in the same house as Yuri and Kiku. He had been in love with Yuri-San for many days, but the girl had known nothing of this. Her life had been a hard one, and the struggle she had had in order to put herself through college and support herself at the same time had occupied all her thought, so that she had paid but little attention to the amusements and distractions that occupy the minds of most girls of that age. She was an extremely pretty girl, with dark, shy eyes, shiny black hair, and sweet, tender mouth. She had never mixed with companions of her age, on account of the strange antipathy the English had shown to her in her childhood, because of her nationality; which prejudice, however, they had long outgrown. Yet it had had a rude effect on her life, making her supersensitive. It was not that she distrusted and doubted the sincerity of all whom she met, but she sought to save herself the little cuts and pains which had seemed but her birthright. From the time when the little schoolmates at the public school had called her "nigger," "Chinee," and other names, which to the Western mind at that time meant the essence of opprobrium, Yuri had distrusted, not them, but herself. That she was inferior to them she never for one moment thought, but that she was different from them, and one whom it would be impossible for them to understand, she firmly believed; hence her strange love for the home she had never known. Holding herself aloof from all whom she met, she had lived a lonely, isolated life ever since her father's death.

So Walter Palmer found little opportunity to speak to her, and it was only in the mornings or evenings as she went to and from work and passed him in the hall, on the stairway or on the doorstep, that the young man had the chance to see her and get a shy glance of recognition, and the girl little knew that he would loiter sometimes around the halls and places where he knew she must pass, for half an hour at a time, simply for the sake of seeing her. He was much in love, and often as he sat in the dreary law office, with his work piled high around him, there would rise before him a picture of a young girl, with a strange, half-foreign proud face, and he would forget the musty law-books, and the confessions or accusations of his numerous clients.

Although scarcely past his thirtieth year he had already made quite a name for himself, so that his practice was extensive, and he had become recognized as one of the first young lawyers of Chicago. He had known Yuri for six months, and during all that time had been unable to speak to her because of the girl's reticence and reserve.

* * *

Then Kiku had arrived. She was a wonder to all the other lodgers in the house. She was more Oriental-looking than her sister, but perhaps her chief beauty lay in her animation and bright spirits. She would dress in a style peculiarly her own, half Japanese and half American, and there was something fascinating in the manner in which she would twist a sash about her waist and tie it in a large fantastic bow at the back, as though in imitation of the Japanese obi. And because she was lonely all day while Yuri was at the school Kiku roved about the house and soon made the acquaintance of all the other lodgers, none of whom Yuri had known during all her stay at the house. So it happened one day when Yuri returned home that she found the little room deserted and Kiku nowhere in sight.

Yuri was uneasy, as it was after four o'clock, and Kiku had promised her not to venture out alone after that hour. While she sat wondering in distress what had become of Kiku, the sound of laughing voices floated up from the lower hall, mingled with which were the familiar, half-halting lisps of her sister's. She opened the door, and walking to the head of the stairs looked down at the gay group below. A pitiful tremor flickered across her face as she realized that these people had suddenly come between her and her sister, and that Kiku should not find her sufficient; for Yuri had all the subdued half-jealous passion of a Japanese girl, even if subdued by enforced unselfishness. As Kiku saw her at the top of the stairs she only jerked her little chin saucily and motioned her to descend. At the same time, a young man who had laughingly placed his hand on Kiku's shoulder raised his head, and saw Yuri with the pained embarrassment and surprise on her face. In a flash his hand had dropped and he was seconding her sister's invitation to her to join them, and with half-unwilling, half-hesitating step Yuri descended.

The next morning when Yuri went to the school Walter Palmer walked with her, and the next morning, and each morning after that, he waited for the girl. Mostly they talked of Kiku, and of her future, because it was on this subject that Yuri was most intensely interested, and Palmer would have praised her sister if but for the sake of seeing Yuri's eyes shine with pleasure.

"It would do her a world of good," he said one day, "to take her out on the lake. Can we not go some evening?"

The girl looked at him half hesitatingly. Then she said impetuously: "Yes; I believe I can trust her with you;" adding deprecatingly, "she is such a little thing, and a stranger to your ways; please be careful with her."

"But you will come, too," said the young man eagerly.

"Oh, no," she answered, smiling; "I cannot spare the time. There is so much to do when I return in the evening; and besides, I am studying the Japanese language, and I shall make no headway if I do not persevere."

Palmer swallowed a huge lump of disappointment.

* * *

It was a beautiful moonlight night when he took Kiku on the lake, and perhaps its stillness and beauty set the girl thinking; for as they pushed out from the shore she raised her little brown face to him and said in her strangely frank and confiding manner: "What is this 'lofe' of which they speak in America?"

Palmer started sharply, and looked at the girl's innocent, questioning face without replying for some time. Then he said: "That is a leading question, Kiku-San. There are many of us here in America who ask the same question. 'What is this—love?'" He smiled half tenderly at the girl's wondering eyes.

"Ess?" she answered, her voice raised questioningly, "but we do not 'lofe' like that in Japan," speaking as though he had explained to her the meaning of the word. It seemed to please her, and she repeated softly, "Lofe— lofe—it is very queer, but we have no meaning for the liddle word in my home. Tell me the meaning," she persisted.

Palmer turned his eyes reluctantly from hers, which were fastened on his face. He stopped rowing and leaned on his oars.

"I must be stupid, Kiku-San, but I cannot analyze the word any more than you can, though—I—I think I know what it is."

Kiku stirred restlessly. He could not fathom what was going on in her little head, or what had caused her to put the question to him. He had been thrown a great deal in her company of late, and often in the evenings Yuri had left them together while she prosecuted her studies, and Palmer knew that Kiku had more than a common liking for him.

They were both silent for a time; then Kiku said softly: "If you do not know what this lofe means, how then can you be 'in lofe' with me?"

Palmer was mute, and his face had grown an ashy gray in the moonlight.

"I," he said, "I love you?" And then, "How can you know—how can you think that?"

"They tell me," said the girl calmly; and she added shyly, "They tell me— that you—that you—lofe me," and her voice lingered softly on the last words.

"Who told you that?" asked the man harshly, his voice sounding strange even to his own ears.

"The pritty American ladies at the house," she said. "Is it true?" There was a certain stubbornness in her voice, mingled with wonder and half-pleased vanity.

* * *

"You must not ask such questions," he said evasively.

The girl's persistency fascinated him, and there was something tender and winning in her innocence. He could see her face distinctly in the pale light, and the moon's soft rays touched it gently, and seemed to spread a halo around the shiny, dark little head. Her eyes were luminous, and in spite of her innocence there was a hesitancy and pitiful faltering in them and about the soft little mouth. Her face in its mixed beauty intoxicated the man. He could not remove his eyes from it. He forgot Yuri. He thought only of the girl sitting opposite to him, with the sweet face softened with the questioning that her innocent soul could not solve. With a sudden fierceness he reached over and caught her little soft hands in his, whispering huskily:

"What makes you look like that, Kiku-San?" (San is the equivalent in Japanese for Miss, and is sometimes used as an endearing expression.)

Kiku did not attempt to withdraw her hands from his, but let them rest there in silent contentment. And thus they sat hand in hand, the boat drifting with the tide, and the moonbeams deepening, and enwrapping them with a silence and mystery that was replete with delight.

Then her soft little voice broke the silence that had fallen between them, and her eyes fell on their clasped hands. "And is *this* lofe?" she asked softly.

Palmer looked at her with eyes that took note of every outline of her face and form, and he was silent. Suddenly the girl raised her head and pointed toward the city.

"See," she said, "how far are we—so far! This must be lofe. We have no fear, though so far away from all life." Then she seemed to recall herself.

"My sister, Yuri-San, she will expect us. Surely had we better return."

As she spoke her sister's name the man suddenly shivered, and a cloud of agony flickered across his face. He seemed as one who had been asleep and but rudely awakened. His hands dropped hastily from hers, and he seized the oars in silence.

* * *

It was past one when they reached the house. Yuri was sitting up waiting for Kiku. The room was in darkness, and she sat at the window looking out across the lake with her head on her arms.

"Is it you, Kiku?"

"Ess, liddle mozzer," said the other, and put her arms softly about her sister, sinking on the window-sill beside her.

"You are tired," said Yuri with concern; "we must not sit up any longer, little sis." She began helping her undress, but Kiku stayed the busy hands, and, holding them tightly in her own, clung with a sudden tenderness and almost with terror to her sister.

"Is *this* lofe?" she said wistfully.

"Love, love?" asked Yuri, shivering a trifle. "Why, little sis, what a great big question that is! Of course it is love, and such love as never was perhaps between two sisters."

Her voice was quite hushed as she kissed the upturned, questioning face. Kiku's restlessness puzzled her.

"I fear you have been out too long," she said gravely; "come, sister will undress you."

Kiku shook her head. "No!" she said almost fretfully, "Kiku does not wish to go to bed yet. Kiku wants to hear about this—lofe."

Yuri laughed, the easy, good-natured laugh of an American-bred girl.

"Why, you absurd little goosie; what can I tell you, save that this is 'lofe,' as you call it?" And she bent down and kissed Kiku on the lips.

Kiku shook her head impatiently.

"But *he* did not do that," she said with puzzled eyes.

"*He!* What do you mean?" said Yuri with a sudden fear at her heart. "Who did not do that?—and what—what—oh, Kiku—what is it, little sis?"

Her quick questioning excited Kiku.

"*He*," she said with a sudden scorn at Yuri for not knowing who "He" should mean. "Why, the pritty American gentleman. See, he *lofe* me, and he do *only* this"—and once more she caught Yuri's hands in hers and pressed them with a strange passion.

"He—he—did—that?" Yuri said with slow indignation. And then both were silent.

* * *

When Yuri started out the next morning she was alone. It was the first time since she had known Palmer that he had failed to accompany her. The girl's face was troubled, and there were shadows under her eyes which bespoke the sleepless night she had passed.

She was thinking of Kiku. She realized with a sad tenderness that Kiku, being such a stranger to Western ways, must ever be misunderstood by those about her. Her great love for her sister made her sensitive on her account, and it was with apprehension and a good deal of bitterness that she thought of Palmer.

She had never admitted, even to herself, that she loved him; yet, as she felt the sudden wave of helpless agony that swept over her whenever she thought of him, and of how stunned she had been at Kiku's half confession, its truth came home to her with a brutal pain. All her life she had been forced to battle for herself; was she strong enough now, she asked herself, to take up her sister's burdens also? That Kiku was as dear as, if not dearer than, the other to her she told herself repeatedly, calling up a pitiful resentment against the man.

She left the school early that day. Although ignorant of her mother tongue, yet she had many friends among the Japanese. She could not have told what impelled her to go to them, but feeling helpless in this new pain that had come to her she sought them out, and tried in their unfamiliar companionship to forget her own unhappy associates. When she returned home that evening a young chemist of great wealth, named Nishimura, accompanied her.

As they came to the front of the house two figures sitting together on the front steps rose. One ran down to meet them. It was Kiku-San, with shy, shiny eyes, and the one who stood back and looked at Yuri, with a sudden blinding agony before his eyes, was Walter Palmer.

Yuri was smiling bravely. She introduced Nishimura to Palmer, and then turning to Kiku made some gay remarks about her ruffled hair. Though she spoke to Palmer she did not once look him in the face. With arms entwined about each other the two girls mounted the stairs to their room.

Then Kiku began to speak breathlessly: "And I know what this lofe is," she said triumphantly. Yuri turned her face away, and Kiku continued. "I—lofe—him," she said slowly. "I lofe the pritty American gentleman. I dream of him in the night, I think of him all day, and I am very sad. Then he comes home very early, and he speaks to me about this lofe. He say it is nothing. That it is foolish to talk about it—that it is not good. Then I laugh at him, and I say: 'No, then I not believe, for I know this lofe—for I lofe you—and you lofe me, and because of this we would be contradict.'" She laughed happily as she ended.

"What did he say then, Kiku?" said Yuri quietly.

"He laughed and he frowned, but he say nothing."

"And what else did you tell him, Kiku?"

"Oh! I talk much," said Kiku saucily. "For this lofe is so strange. I talk, talk, talk, and he keep still and listen. I tell him I want to be with him largely."

* * *

Two months later Palmer joined Yuri as she walked to her work. It was the first time in many, many days. There was a large vacant field that Yuri would cross to make a shorter cut to the school, and it was generally here that they would separate, he taking the cars for the downtown part of the city. But this morning he started to cross the field with her, though a silence, eloquent in its sadness, had been between them from the start.

Palmer's eyes had been on the girl's face almost from the beginning, but she turned from him, and her abruptness amounted to rudeness, and was meant to be noticed.

Palmer stopped in the middle of the field and broke the strained silence.

"I cannot stand it," he said brokenly.

Yuri turned on him with a wild swiftness.

"*You* cannot stand it," she said witheringly. "*You*—you. What have you to say about it? Can't you see, don't you know—it will *kill* her if—if you are not kinder to her. And then—you tell *me* you cannot stand it. What is it you cannot stand? What has she done to you?" She stopped, her indignation choking her.

This was the first time the subject had been broached between them.

The young man's shoulders drooped.

"Don't look like that, Yuri," he said, thinking more of the girl herself than what she had said. "Don't hate me. I tell you I don't deserve it. What can I do? What have I done? I could not help it."

* * *

Her anger had died out. Her eyes softened a trifle.

"Then you will make it all right, won't you?" she said wistfully. "You will tell her—you will tell her—poor little Kiku, that you are not offended with her, and you *won't* try to keep away from her. She is such a little thing, and she does not understand people like we are. It is cruel not to be kind to her."

"What can I do?" he asked, his teeth grating against each other with pain. "Surely *you* ought to understand? You know how it all came about, and you cannot blame me altogether. She was such a child, and I tried to discourage her, but I couldn't bear to hurt her."

"You—couldn't—bear—to hurt her," said Yuri slowly. "Am I to understand from that that you never really loved, never really cared for my little sister?"

The man was mute.

"And you let her believe it!"—her voice rose in its pain—"you let her believe that, and then you come to me—you come to me, and pretend you are sorry—that you cannot understand—that ——— Oh! I hate you—you are contemptible—a brute—a—a coward."

She turned to leave him, but he stood in front of her and burst out passionately: "You *shall* not leave me like this, Yuri. Yuri, turn your face to me. Let me look into your eyes. They accuse me so—and I—I have no words for myself. I do not know what to say—but, Yuri—I would not lose—your—your—regard for anything in the world. You will understand and perhaps you will forgive when I tell you, Yuri, dear little Yuri—it is *you* I love—I love *you!* How then could I care for any one else in the world? Can you understand now why I have had to evade even your little sister, whom I—I—cared for only because she was *your* little sister?"

The girl's face was white and drawn.

With a sudden agony she turned and ran blindly from him, scarcely knowing where she went, but wishing to get farther and farther away from him:
to forget everything—the hideous pain of living, and the feeling almost of
exultation that the knowledge of his love gave her.

Kiku was in a high fever when Yuri returned. She called constantly for
her sister, and pitifully begged to be taken home to Japan. Yuri could not
understand her well, for in her illness she spoke always in the soft accents
of her mother tongue. But she knew what the girl was crying for and would
whisper back softly, "Yes, I know; yes, I know, little sis, you want to go
home, and you shall go home."

* * *

Two more months, and Kiku, clad in a soft, clinging kimono, was on her
way home. The girl's face was sadder and more subdued than when, hardly a year before, she had come to America. Her heart bounded with gladness as she thought of Nippon, and because she was scarcely more than a
child her thoughts were more with her destination than with the man who
had taught her the meaning of the Western "lofe."

And alone in the little room Yuri was crying over the little Japanese relics and remembrances that her sister had left behind, and almost wondering whether the one year so full of laughter and tears in which Kiku-San
had been with her were not all a strange dream. Of Palmer she would not
think. His white face haunted her constantly, and she hated herself because
the bitterness she had conjured up against him was slowly passing away, to
be replaced with a feeling of pain and yearning and longing that the girl could
not comprehend. She tried to assure herself that she would have all her heart
could desire when, after her marriage to Nishimura, she was once more in
the sunny land which she had dreamed of since her childhood's days, and
on which all her hopes for the future had been built. She knew Palmer had
been sick. When she met him she dared not look at him for fear of finding
him changed.

Once as the winter months advanced, and Yuri's little cold hand tried in
vain to turn the latchkey in the door, a firm hand closed over hers, and taking the key from her, deftly turned the lock. Then as they stood in the little
porch alone together, he said with such piercing tenderness in his voice that
the girl's defiant eyes filled with tears:

"Yuri, dear, cruel little Yuri."

She did not answer him for a moment; then she raised her head and looked
at him. He was smiling, and it angered her. "You must not laugh at me,"

she said as childishly as Kiku might have done. Suddenly she thought of Nishimura, and she tried to steady her voice.

"See," she said, "I am to be married next month to—Mr. Nishimura."

The man's face suddenly changed, and its ashy misery appealed to her. With a sudden passion she pulled the little ring from her finger and forced it into his hand.

"No, no!" she said frantically as he turned from her, "I won't! I can't— I—I ———" But Palmer's hand had closed tightly over hers and the little ring, and he was drawing her into his arms with a glory over his face that only "lofe" could have reflected.

(*Ladies' Home Journal*, August 1903)

THE WRENCH OF CHANCE

Part 1

Japan had treated Michael Lenahan well from the first. A fugitive from English justice, he had found a refuge in the sheltering arms of Nagasaki. As a matter of fact, his opponent survived the beating he had received, and so the only crime of which the Irishman was actually guilty was that of desertion from the navy, though a charge of murderous assault hung over his head for a time.

For two days a search was made in Nagasaki for the fugitive. During those two days the Japanese chose to befriend him, blocking all efforts to capture him. While the shivering young Irishman remained in hiding—in a cell in a Japanese police-station—no English-Irish-Japanese vocabulary was eloquent enough to express his gratitude toward his protectors, two little impassive-faced policemen, who came of Samurai stock, but who, in these degenerate days for Japan, served in the menial capacity of law officers for the glory of still being permitted to wear a sword.

When one day, however, one of the aforesaid policemen opened the door of Michael's cell, brought him out into the light of day, and, pointing to the harbor, showed him the departing vessel which had lately been his home, he broke into oaths of such power and picturesqueness that his listener needed not a translator.

Michael tore his fiery red hair, shook his big knotted fists, kicked the ground with his great ungainly feet. Robinson Crusoe was no less desolate than Michael Lenahan, aged nineteen, deserter and deserted, alone with a race of people he termed "oogly haythens."

His wrath and despair subsiding, he accepted the bitter consolation of a dozen thimblefuls of sake offered him by the now grinning little policeman, and which barely wet the greedy and already experienced throat of Michael.

For several years Michael led the miserable existence of the expatriate. The open port of Nagasaki held a nameless fascination for him. Hither came all manner of foreign peoples of the same skin, and often tongue, as himself. They made Nagasaki bearable to the homesick Michael—they and the foreign liquors which flowed freely there. Michael would have pitched his permanent tent in Nagasaki, but beneath all his loud-mouthed bravado he was a coward at heart. He might brawl around the little Japanese seaport with all manner of foreign sailor-men, breathing defiance and contempt of Great Britain, but the advent of an English boat was the signal for the swift and terrified departure of Michael. While the ship remained in port, Nagasaki saw him not.

As time passed, Japan held out a less-grudging hand to the invading commercial nations. The English ships came very often to Nagasaki, forcing Michael to play a constant game of hide-and-seek. Drink-besotted, cowardly, penniless, his nerves began to trouble him. When one day in a summer month he came face to face on the street with a former shipmate, Michael's last bit of courage deserted him. He turned and fled wildly countryward. Always he had despised the mere country, and had clung feverishly to gay little Nagasaki and its environs. Now in terror the inland country seemed to beckon to him with comforting fingers.

Twenty years after he had come to Japan found him settled in a small inland town, holding the unique position of "Professor of Irish" in the town's high school. As Professor of English he had been engaged, but with characteristic effrontery he had changed the title conferred upon him. Japan's first selection of foreign teachers had not been of the most choice. She took them from among the foreigners who drifted upon her shores—men often of the lowest type.

The small town to which Michael had come hailed his advent with pride and delight. It was an ambitious little hamlet, bursting with eagerness to share in the new progress sweeping like a fever all over the Empire. The opportunity of securing a foreigner to teach in their chief school was not to be lost. Fate put Michael Lenahan, a disreputable, illiterate, drunken sailor into their hands, and they seized him with avidity. The whole town gave him of their best. In time they found him out, but looked upon his faults with tolerance and leniency. That he was a "foreign devil" and "beast" was, of course, palpable, but he was to be endured for what he would give them—knowledge! They even indulgently gratified his demand for liquor, and imported to the town for his sole use great quantities of brandy and other alcoholic spirits.

Time slipped sleepily by. Michael's great fear had almost left him. When he was not upon one of his periodical sprees his mind felt at ease and at peace with the world. He was almost happy. He had even grown used to the complexion of those about him. They were still "oogly haythens," but he is willing to leave the punishment for their worship of idols to the saints presiding over purgatory.

One day Michael appeared at the house of the chief man of the town, announced that he desired to become a Japanese citizen, and asked that he be given a Japanese wife. Neither of these requests being considered extraordinary, they were complied with promptly. With considerable ceremony Michael Lenahan's name was changed to Taganouchi Taro, and he became a Japanese citizen. With even more ceremony a wedding was arranged for him; the girl upon whom he had fixed his fancy—one of his pupils—became his wife.

Henceforth the pugnacious little government of Japan was prepared to protect her citizen, Taganouchi Taro; for the rest of her life Yugiri-san must be his slave. Michael believed that Japanese wives were little more than slaves. Oddly enough, though damning the race for its subjection of the charming sex, he experienced a strange sense of pleasant power at the thought that now he, too, could do as he pleased with this pretty, helpless creature who had become his own.

During the short seventeen years of her life Yugiri had made a protest against parental control only once—the day her father announced to her her betrothal to the "Professor of Irish."

What! Marry the beast of the town! No, no, she could not—would not do it! she had declared in this her one little outburst of passion. But her protest was termed "unmaidenly" by her mother; by her taciturn father, who, since the Restoration, like many another Samurai, had become impoverished, she was heavily reprimanded.

Smothering back further words of appeal until the day of the wedding she wept only when alone. But when the big barbarian came to take her, as his wife, to his home, Yugiri made a desperate effort to drown herself in the poor little stream that ran through the woods back of her home. Frustrated in even this effort, and fearing that the gods were punishing her for some crime committed in a former state, she bent to their will, to go a tearful, but subjected, victim to the house of the Irishman.

Taganouchi Taro (late Michael Lenahan) was in the large room which constituted the entire upper story of his house. The blotched condition of his face, his bloodshot eyes, and unkempt red hair revealed the fact that this citizen of Japan was just recovering from the effects of a prolonged alcoholic debauch.

Open though it was on all sides, in the Japanese fashion, to the free air of heaven, the entire floor was permeated by a rank and foul odor, the sour stench of bad tobacco and whiskey. The matting—so immaculate and sweet-smelling in the houses of the Japanese—was fit only for such a creature as the ex-sailor. Broken glasses, bottles, corks, matches, ashes, papers, shoes, and the habiliments of Michael strewed the entire apartment. Because they have no furniture, the Japanese have a beautifully clean space to move about and walk upon in their dwellings. There was no furniture in the apartment of Michael, but neither was there a spot where a foot might step with ease.

The Irishman sat up on his couch-bed and looked about him. Several times he cleared his husky throat. He drank continually from a huge crock of cold water that some one had placed beside him while he slumbered. Over the dull face of the professor there gradually stole a look which signified that memory had returned to him. Anon chuckling, and then cursing softly, he recalled the events of the previous month.

Tiring of the drowsy dullness of the little town, he had gone on a trip to Nagasaki. There he had fallen in with some kindred spirits. While celebrating in a gala tea-house of the town, who should rise up from an adjoining table and confront him but the man he thought he had killed. In a moment he knew the truth—knew that his fears had been unfounded, and that for twenty years he had been an exile without real reason.

His first sensation was one of mingled rage and resentment against Japan—as if the land where he had spent his exile were responsible for the mistake he had made. His next was one of hilarious elation at the thought of his new freedom. He would celebrate the occasion as it deserved, and then he would return to the little town, pack what things he possessed, obtain what money he could, and shake the dust of the almond-eyed isles forever from his feet, sailing for greener isles of which he knew. To his wife he gave not a thought. She was part of the country.

Now as he sat in his bed for the first time in weeks, in his own home again, he suddenly thought of Yugiri. Of course he could not take her with him. She did not belong to the new scheme of things Michael had planned for himself. But he felt sorry for her. That she would feel the parting he felt sure. Though he had never restrained his heavy hand from her, yet in his new and happy state, nourished upon the exhilarating spirits he had imbibed, Michael felt loath to hurt her feelings by acquainting her with his intention of deserting her. He sighed and frowned, then brought his heavy hands together in a loud clap.

Noiselessly the screens of the apartment were opened. A woman came through the opening, stood silently a moment looking at the man on the couch, and then, like a puppet, made a mechanical obeisance to him. Her face was devoid entirely of color, save the scarlet line of her lips. Her eyes, long and very dark, were shadowed by some mystery of expression, enhanced by the long lashes and the curved line of eyebrow above them. They were the features of the Japanese woman of patrician blood—small mouth, thin nose, high brow, pointed chin, and inscrutable eyes. Small and exquisite as a child's were her hands. Obedient to her husband's commands she went toward him. He reached out, seized her sleeve, and drew her down beside him. She was now upon her knees. He kissed her. She made no resistance.

"Hoom!" said Michael; "so you're after sulking, huh? Well, well, well! Aren't you glad to see me back, my girl?"

"Velly glad," she said in English; but beyond the parting of her lips to enunciate the words the stony expression of her face did not alter.

"You don't look it," said he, and pushed her back from him. "Fine wife you are! Not even a smile for me, huh?" His large mouth curled up in an ugly sneer, and the drooped head of the girl moved upward. The smile she brought to her lips was that of a mechanical doll.

"Call that a smile!" snarled her lord, indignantly. "Now, see here, Giri. I've been a good husband to you, haven't I?" He was now working himself up to a mood of righteous indignation which would make it easier for him to say what he wished. He waved his hand about the room, blind, no doubt, to its aspect.

"Look at the grand house you're after living in. Sure it's silk itself you're dressed in, and your poor sisters contented with cotton and crape for their Sunday best. Do you know how much I paid your father for the fine pleasure of your company? It's no lie I'm telling you, my girl. One hundred yen was the sum the old divil got out of me pockets. In Ireland I'd have had a bride as a gift, and a bit of a dower—a pig or two—thrown in with the bargain. Now you've been my happy wife for five unhappy years. It's a grand time I've given you, but like all grand things in the world, my girl, it had to come to an end."

Here he got out of bed, fumbled about, searching for his clothes, and began to swear savagely. Silently she brought him his garments (he still wore Western clothes), put on and laced for him his heavy, dirty boots. Then she brought a basin of water, and herself washed his hands and face. Finally she got a box of blacking, and, kneeling, began to polish his shoes.

He had been seeking for certain words with which to inform her of his intentions, when something in her attitude as she knelt there cleaning his boots touched a softer spot in him. After all, Yugiri had been a good wife. She had from the first waited upon him hand and foot, almost as if he had been a helpless baby. She had meekly obeyed his every command, had endured vile tongue and heavy fist. She had been faithful and true to him. Of these qualities Michael was mindful. It was too bad she was a heathen, and he could not take her back with him.

As the girl painstakingly polished his boots, Michael frowningly thought over the problem presented—not whether he should take her with him, but how he was to break the sad news to her.

Suddenly, in the silence that had fallen between them, outside in the street the sweet shrill call of a bugle sounded. As the two in the littered room of the Irishman heard it, their eyes unconsciously met. A flush had swept like the dawn over the face of the kneeling woman. Her eyes grew large and humid. They seemed to look beyond, not at, her husband. Though she had finished her task she still remained upon her knees, her hands now crossed upon her bosom.

To Michael a brilliant idea came. That even this little town was sending of its best and bravest to the war with Russia, that the whole country was palpitating with the war delirium, he knew. Even Yugiri's heart had leaped at the mere blowing of the bugle.

A devilish twinkle came into Michael's eye, and a cunning expression was on his face as he sat down heavily on the floor by his wife.

"Giri," said he, "it's a bit of sad news I've to tell you. Now you're after thinking me a bad and cruel husband to you, because of my little taste for the divil. But never mind that. There's a good spot in the baddest of us, my girl, and sure there's one in Michael too."

He seized her hands gayly, and still in jubilant mood continued: "Now what sort of a soldier do you think I'd be after making?"

Again the flush rose to her face, slowly and painfully now. She sought to avoid his eyes and turned her head droopingly away. As insistently he pressed her hands, she suddenly withdrew them passionately from his. There was a smothered sound in her voice, almost as if she spoke with difficulty. Somewhere behind it were the tragic welling tears.

"I pray you—do—nod—mek—liddle joke about soach—soach madder," she said.

"Joke!" shouted Michael, now thoroughly enamoured of his plan. "Shure it's the first time I've been in airnest for days. The fact is, I'm aff to the bloody war with Roosia!"

His wife raised her head and looked at him, closely, searchingly, as if she sought with all her soul to pierce his bleared, besotted mask.

"Well," said her husband, engagingly, "and what have you got to say to that, my dear?"

Her hands were still crossed upon her bosom. They slipped down mechanically to her side. Her voice had a most pitiful note.

"What I gotter say? I—I—dun'no' whatter say. I guess—mebbe—you like mek liddle joke ad me—mebbe?"

"No joke about it," said Michael grandly. "It's a heathen Jap am I—a heathen citizen of this glorious heathen land. For its heathen sake I give my worthless life."

Yugiri moved slowly nearer to him. A strange light had come into her eyes now. Her lips were parted, but she did not speak. Suddenly she put her head down at the feet of Michael Lenahan. It was the unconscious movement—the attitude of a dog or slave.

"Oh, my lord," said she, "I am forever now a miserable worm at your feet, fit only for your augustness to tread upon."

A bland happy smile overspread the countenance of Michael. Stooping with good-humored condescension he lifted the humble one into his arms. But even in her abasement now she seemed to shrink from his caresses, and in her eyes were both loathing and terror.

The following day, when, after the fashion of a Japanese soldier, Michael took leave of his wife upon the doorstep of their house, Yugiri's words were heartfelt, albeit they were by the fatalistic ones spoken by all true Japanese women, sacrificing their dearest for the Mikado.

"I give you to Tenshi-sama. We will not meet again. Come not back to me. Sayonara!"

She remained at the door watching him until he could no longer be seen. Then she entered the house quietly. To a servant-boy she gave an order. Immediately he ran joyously to obey her. Shortly after, a small sun flag was flying from the roof of the house, signifying to the world that this was the home of a Japanese soldier.

Now Yugiri was alone in the great apartment that had been her husband's. For a long time she stood in silence, her eyes travelling over the disorder of the room. Overnight, as it had become colder, Michael had slipped the sliding walls into place, and now the apartment was close and stuffy. The golden light of the morning percolated through the paper shoji, but so tightly had the Irishman closed the screens that none of the fresh air of the beautiful day entered the room.

A young girl came noiselessly into the room. She gave one quick look at her sister's rapt face, then clapping her hands over her mouth and nostrils hastened across the room, with the evident intention of opening the shoji. She was stopped by the gentle voice of Yugiri.

"Haru-no, I desire the shoji closed."

The young girl turned, with surprise in her eyes.

"But the place smells sickly, Yugiri-san. Do let me purify it. Mother bade me assist you with the work to-day. This room—" She looked about them, then turned candid eloquent face to her sister.

"Oh, Yugiri-san, how happy you must be to-day!"

"Yes," said the other, dreamily, "I am very happy now."

"To think of what you have endured. The beast was worse than any mother-in-law! But now, you will be happy once again."

Smiling gently, Yugiri put her arm about her sister's waist.

"Listen, little sister," said she, "I will tell you what it is that makes me happy now. Not because the barbarian has gone away! Because the gods are good, O-Haru-no! I am the wife of one both brave and noble, who will give his honorable life for Dai Nippon! That is why I will not have his august room touched, nor his honorably beautiful dirt swept away. That is why I will keep his—his augustly beautiful odor in the house so long as it will condescend to stay. Sister, I had misjudged my husband. The gods made him a hero—not a beast!"

*   *   *

Two Japanese officers were sitting at a small table in a tea-house of Nagasaki. One was a tall vigorous young man of about twenty-five. His flushed face and sparkling eyes bespoke an impetuous and ardent temperament, and his entire personality at this time evinced some deep-seated joy.

There was something of the fanatic in the face of his companion as if for a certain principle he would have sacrificed his very soul; but in the brooding melancholy which rested like a shadow about his lips and eyes it was clear that he was suffering from some deep disappointment. His eyes dwelt almost enviously upon the face of Lieutenant Sato, and as he spoke his nervous hands moved the small teacup round and round on the table.

"It is not," said he, "that I criticise my superiors. I would not be a true son of my fathers were I to question those in authority over me. I realize that it is for the good of Dai Nippon that these rules should be thus stringent. It's fate I curse—fate which has made me physically what I am. To think that while my whole soul is fairly bursting with longing to do something for my beloved Emperor and country, a paltry physical defect should prevent me—and at such a time! It is maddening—maddening!" His hands clenched spasmodically, and so bitter was his feeling that smarting tears sprang into his eyes.

"My dear Tahaki," said the other, pityingly, "your case is truly a sad one. I hardly know what to say to give you consolation. I can only devoutly express the hope that the condition of your eyes will improve to such an extent that—"

The other broke in impatiently:

"My eyes have been the same all my life. They will never change. Yet they forbid me service at the front. God! To be forced to stay behind here like a woman—ah! I had far better follow the example of my illustrious ancestors. Seppuku is more honorable than idleness at this time."

"No, no—you talk rashly. No one is so foolish nowadays as to commit suicide. That is, happily, a thing of the past. After all, you may get the Saseho appointment. Your service there in the hospital will be as great as that we—the fighting ones—can render to our country."

Tahaki smiled bitterly.

"It is hardly likely that I will even get the hospital appointment," said he, drearily.

A silence fell between them. Then, almost mechanically, their attention was attracted to the noisy talk of the red-headed foreigner at the next table. He was a great ungainly fellow, possibly forty years of age. With some sailor companions he was gulping down great quantities of liquor, stopping ever and anon to toss some jest to the attending waitresses.

The tea-house at this hour was filled with Japanese soldiers, seated at the various tables, and in the quiet, sake-sipping, celebrating their last night in Japan. The loud-voiced talk of the foreigners had drawn only casual glances from the engrossed soldiers thus far, but a sudden burst of ribald laughter attracted the attention of the two officers at the next table to them. The Irishman had arisen to his feet and was holding his glass tipsily aloft:

"In case some of you lads may not have heard me name, I'm proud to say it's Michael Lenahan. That is my true and only name: Michael Lenahan! Michael Lenahan! For twenty years, me lads, I've borne another—a haythen name. A citizen they made me of this haythen man, and a haythen wife they gave me. But the blissed saints be praised, to-day it's free man I stand before you. Me name is Michael Lenahan. Glory be, for to-morrow it's out on the bounding ocean I will be, sailing for the old country."

He took a long and deep draught of the beverage he held, then with a chuckle which caused him to lurch forward against the seat he had vacated, he continued:

"Shall I tell you lads where I told the Missis I was after going? 'I'm off,' ses I, 'to the bloody war with Roosia.' Ses she, with the watery tears arunning down her pretty little face, 'It's a worm I am. Tread upon me, Michael Lenahan.'"

Amid the wild and cheering applause and laughter of his friends Michael unfolded to them the history of his life.

An angry red had settled on the face of Tahaki. He leaned forward, frowning darkly. Tahaki understood and spoke the English language well, and as Michael told his companions of the trick he had played upon his "little haythen wife," the Japanese swore fiercely under his breath. The next moment he was repeating the story to his friend. Its effect on the latter was electrical. Younger and more headstrong than Tahaki, he was scarcely restrained from springing upon the Irishman. That such terms of contempt should be expressed against his country and a woman of his country at such a time aroused in him a frenzy of resentment.

Later, another officer came into the tea-house and joined the two in pledging the health of the Emperor and the nation. Then Tahaki, moody and heartsick, made his excuses and bade his friends good-night.

The two remaining officers listened for a while to the raised voice of the now maudlin Michael. He was in tears now, and had lapsed into Japanese.

"It's remorse that's consuming my vitals," he groaned. "So back to-night I'm going for my girl. It's a grand treat I'll give her. Two, not one, will sail the ocean, and one will be the little haythen girl I'm after telling you about."

"Talk about fate!" growled one of the officers. "Tahaki was bewailing the fate which keeps him here in Nippon. Think of the wife of yonder brute. Why, the very gods are laughing—jesting at her. Probably to-day she has been rendering them thanksgiving for her freedom. To-morrow his foot will be upon her head again. A generous Providence truly!"

Lieutenant Sato brought an impetuous young fist down upon the table.

"'Providence!' I intend to be that woman's Providence to-night. What better service could I do the unfortunate one than rid her of such a—"

"What!" gasped his companion, "you would—"

"Kill him? Bah, no! He isn't worth that honor at my hand. I would simply—Listen. You have heard of the practice known as 'shanghaiing'? Now that foreign beast there has lied to his wife, her relatives, and the people of the town that befriended him. They believe that he has gone as a soldier for Japan, and they accordingly exalt him. Well, he *shall* go!"

"You mean—! My dear fellow, the British government may make trouble. The thing may leak out. You—"

"This fellow is a Japanese citizen. Leak out? Let it. I myself sail to-morrow night for Manchuria. I never expect to come back. Before I go, however, I desire to perform one act of kindness for a countrywoman of mine. No, you cannot dissuade me!"

He arose to his feet and, clapping his hands sharply, attracted the attention of a number of soldiers across the garden. He signalled to one of them, who came quickly across the room.

Sato spoke in a low voice to the stockily built young Japanese soldier, who threw one quick glance at the Irishman, and then, with the grin of a bulldog, nodded his head. A few moments later he crossed to the main exit of the tea-garden and took his stand outside in the street.

"That," said Lieutenant Sato, quietly resuming his seat, "is Santo Gonji, a jiujitsu expert. One touch of his hand will disarm yonder braggart, and to-morrow night will see him on board a Japanese transport bound for Manchuria. Ho, there, Miss Snowball!" he called to a passing waitress; "bring us some more sake." Then, to the speechless officer, "My friend, we will now drink the health of this brave new soldier of Japan."

Part 2

Love at first sight is a usual and indeed cultivated thing in Japan. The youth and maiden ordained by fate in the persons of their respective parents to become life-partners cherish, even before they meet each other, romantic hopes, and it is more often the case than not that the electric spark of love is struck at sight.

So it was with Tahaki. Of a naturally melancholy disposition, there were latent in him all the wells of concentrated love and passion, needing only sight of the possible one to flame into life. He could not at once analyze the new emotion which possessed him. Hitherto his mind had been filled with one absorbing thought—his country! Although he had passionately longed to serve at the front, his had been the fate to see his former friends and comrades depart without him. Even the Saseho appointment failed to soften his disappointment, though the heavy work it entailed at least took his mind from the morbid thought of self-destruction.

Now into his dark-seeming life had come a new force. The world in a moment had turned rose-colored. He was conscious of a glorious upleaping of his heart, of thrilling pulses beating ecstatically within him, of vague delicious longings, of yearnings and desires to be better, worthier. This was love which had transformed him. Yet he had seen Yugiri but once.

A week passed before he saw her a second time. During that period he could have learned something of her history, for she was one of the nurses in the hospital, but he was of a disposition too proud and reserved to make inquiry about a woman.

Taking a brief restful stroll one evening in the twilight he encountered two of the nurses from the hospital engaged in the same recreation.

One was in uniform and wore the nurse's cap; the other likewise was in conventional uniform, but her head was bare.

It was at her Tahaki looked. He had recognized her at once, and half unconsciously had stopped. She looked up at him in some surprise, smiled, blushed, and bowed. But Tahaki had not returned her salutation. His eyes had become riveted upon an ornament in her hair. It showed quite clearly there—the marumage! Suddenly he was conscious sharply of the truth. She was a married woman!

As she moved away he remained standing in the street motionless. He felt like one stricken with a sudden paralysis of mind. Then it came over him in a flood—he loved her!

*   *   *

In the early dawn of a day seven soldiers of Japan slipped out of life and started on the terrible journey to the Meido. She who had eased for them their last moments of life, and whispered words of coming comfort for their souls, knelt now by the cot of an eighth, a very young Christian who, perhaps, was to join his comrades soon. For him Yugiri was repeating a new kind of prayer—one the soldier had himself taught her. Now as the words dropped like very pearls of speech from her lips, a strange smile stole into the eyes of the dying boy. He made an effort to lift his head from the pillow, sighed, whispered, and again smiling, lay quiet—rigid.

Yugiri's dark eyes lifted from the face of the boy soldier and met those of the young surgeon on the opposite side of the bed. She spoke lowly, almost wearily:

"Do you think the gods will cruelly refuse to receive his soul, sir doctor?"

"I do not know," he answered; "but I am sure of one thing, madame. If you will condescend to pray for him, the gods will hear."

Following the doctor into the operating-room, she swayed slightly on the threshold. She caught at the arm of a passing nurse for support. Dr. Tahaki pushed out quickly an invalid-chair, and made her lie down at once.

"How long have you been on duty?" he asked, sharply.

"Thirty-three hours," said Yugiri, and her tired eyes did not open. It seemed as if she now heard the voices of the doctor and the nurse in a dream. Some one had said she should not be disturbed. There was a patient to be moved into another room, so that she might sleep in peace. Sleep! Why, there was work to do—work—work! Service for Dai Nippon! Soldiers of Tenshi-sama were suffering, crying, calling for her succor. There was a dearth of good nurses. She, above all, was needed—needed always. But even as she fought against the encompassing sleep it wrapped her closely to its soothing arms, and soon came blessed oblivion.

The light of sunset had replaced the dawn when she awoke. An orderly turning on the electric lights in the room aroused her. She sprang to her feet and began examining her chart. Then, looking up at the young man:

"Omi—the young Adachi—do not tell me he is—dead?" The chart in her hand fluttered as she held it.

"Yes, madame. Adachi died at five this morning, his honorable hand happily in yours, madame. Do you not remember?"

She put her hand to her head, and stood silently a moment. Then:

"Oh, how sad—how very sad!" she said, and turned to hide her tears.

That same evening she seized an opportunity of speaking to Dr. Tahaki, with whom she was on terms of a friendship so perilously dear that she dared not analyze it at all.

"Dr. Tahaki, do you believe in dreams?"

"Sometimes, madame. Why do you ask?"

"I had a very strange dream when I slept to-day. May I tell it?"

"Please do so, madame."

"I dreamed the young Adachi and my husband were together. Their souls were homeless and wandered out into space, side by side, seeking Nirvana. This they could not find without my insignificant help. I tried to go to them, but something seemed to hold me fast to earth. I could not even move, and always they stretched their hands to me and besought my help. What is the meaning of such a dream? Why should my husband and Adachi be together?"

He regarded her sombrely a moment. Then, averting his eyes from her face:

"It is reasonable enough. Adachi recently filled your mind. His death affected you painfully. Naturally you dreamed of him. So your—the other one, madame, doubtless occupies your mind."

She shook her head.

"This must be the reason," she said; "my husband, like Adachi, has made the supreme sacrifice. He, too, is—dead."

She had turned very pale. Knowing not what to say, he did not speak. After a moment she continued, quietly:

"That must be the meaning, doctor. Adachi and my husband are together. Adachi was a Christian. My husband, too, was—a Christian."

Tahaki made a slight exclamation; but before he could say anything she added, in a tone almost of defiance and hauteur:

"Yes—a Christian. Also a foreigner—honorably Irish. I am very proud of it."

"A foreigner!"

She bowed; then with a swift, proud uplift of her chin:

"All the greater his heroism, sir doctor, for he gives his honorable life for an adopted land."

"Was not his name honorably Taganouchi?"

"That unworthily was his adopted name, sir doctor. He became a citizen of our Japan. In his own most honorable country he bore another name—augustly Michael Lenahan—Dr. Tahaki, why do you look at me so strangely?"

"Madame, condescend to repeat the name you spoke just now."

She did so twice; then, still with her eyes upon his face, she spoke tremulously:

"You have heard the name before, sir doctor?"

He bowed in silence.

"You are honorably acquainted with my husband?"

"No, madame."

"You have met him?"

"I have seen him."

"Where?"

"In Nagasaki."

"Ah, it was when he so honorably marched with the soldiers of beloved Tenshi-sama," bowing deeply as she spoke the Mikado's name.

"No—not—Madame, pardon me."

"You speak—you look strangely. You are aware my husband is a soldier?"

"I had heard so, madame."

"It is so. I tell you so. Why, you look—as if—do you not believe me?"

Tahaki spoke slowly and carefully, as if choosing words wherein he might speak the truth to her and still spare the laceration of her heart:

"Sooner would I tear my miserable tongue out than give you pain. Yet truth, though harsh, is better for you to hear, dear madame, than a lie. The man whose name you mention is not a soldier of Japan."

For a moment she seemed about to swoon, then the proud blood flew to her cheeks and brow. She drew herself proudly erect.

"You make mistake, sir doctor. I, his wife, know."

Tahaki bowed in silence; then, as he moved coldly away, she went quickly after him, caught his sleeve and held it with trembling hands. For a moment he stood looking down at her in silence; then, as if he could not help himself, her name escaped his lips passionately:

"Yugiri-san!"

She dropped his sleeve as if it were something unclean.

"Now I know," she said, "that you—that you—lied to me, and also the unworthy reason why."

He smiled bitterly.

"Listen to me, madame. I am a gentleman—a soldier. It is not possible for me to lie. I claim the right to speak your name, and you are free to hear me. The law gives you just freedom. The beast deserted you. You are divorced."

"Who calls enlistment in Mikado's army desertion?" was her passionate rejoinder.

"Madame, knowing who was your husband, I will not believe you deigned to care for him. Therefore I will not hesitate to speak the truth. The day you thought your husband enlisted in the army, that day he took ship for his home. I with two of my comrades heard him boast of his intentions in a Nagasaki tea-house."

She looked him fully in the face.

"It is not true," she said. "I do not believe you, Dr. Tahaki."

But within an hour she had come into the little office of the doctors. About her whole personality there was a subtle change. Shame, pride, joy—all were reflected in her face as she went slowly toward him. He was alone in the office, and rose as she entered. He took the hand she proffered, and enclosed it with both his own.

"Dr. Tahaki, I should have known that *he* could do no worthy thing. And you—why, how could I misjudge you, knowing you?"

Their hands clung, tingled and thrilled in the clasp of each other, then fell grudgingly apart. But each understood the heart of the other.

Part 3

In a little Chinese farmhouse at the base of a hill there was an outpost of forty-two men, sleeping on the floor in their clothes. The lieutenant in charge of them was the only one of the company awake. He had made an effort to sleep, but had found it impossible, owing to the noisy snoring of one of his men. This fellow was sleeping on his back. His mouth was wide open.

Lieutenant Sato marvelled that his companions could sleep near him. Smiling half irritably, he walked over to the fellow, struck a match, and bent to examine him. The light revealed what at first looked like a mass of tangled wool of a ruddy color—the curious red hair of the soldier. Instantly Sato drew back, frowning slightly. He did not attempt to sleep after this, but began to pace the floor back and forth, his hands behind him, his head bent, as though he were plunged in some reverie.

About two in the morning he was startled by an unmistakable sound—the challenging of his picket. He rushed across the room, thrust his head out of the window, and saw the Russian column.

If the Japanese soldiers had slept soundly, undisturbed by the snores of their comrade, they knew at least, even in sleep, that other sound. They were all upon their feet, with their rifles and ammunition. Almost in a flash they had sprung out and had gone to meet the head of the column. They had no notion of the size of the enemy; they knew only that they must overcome him, and unhesitatingly they went, all—save one.

That one, unlike his comrades, had neither heard nor answered the call to arms. Mouth agape, he still slept loudly on. Not even the noise of the going of his comrades had awakened him, nor the frenzied kicking at his shins administered by the departing ones.

A Chinaman rushed down from an upper floor to give the alarm. He saw the place was apparently deserted, and hearing the unearthly music of the sleeping one, stood for a moment petrified with superstitious fright. Then emitting a loud squeal of terror, he scuttled across the room, and fled up the little rickety steps down which he had come.

The shriek of the Chinaman awoke the sleeper. He stirred, turned over on his side, sat up. For a moment he remained stupidly blinking, then suddenly bounded clumsily to his feet. His head struck the ceiling, revealing the fact that he was a giant in stature. For a moment he stood listening, his big hand at his ear. Then clumsily he secured his rifle, stuck out his foot to make sure he was treading on no one, found by instinct the door, kicked it open with his foot, and sprang out into the night.

The little handful of men who had gone forth in the darkness to meet the enemy were now engaged in hand-to-hand fighting. That is, they had literally fastened themselves upon the Russians, and were using their bayonets, fighting unknown numbers of a column coming up the hill. The Russians for the moment were stopped by the sudden onslaught of the outpost.

Now as they fought—the Japanese in silence, the Russians with grunts and mutterings—a strange and almost eerie sound reached their ears. At first it seemed the harsh calling of some bird of prey, but as it drew nearer, the little band of Japanese engaged recognized it.

Nearer and nearer came the sound, and now the Russians, too, must have recognized it—the wild singing of a soldier gone mad with the fighting fever. Soon he had sprung into their midst, a great gaunt giant, whose tawny hair glistened redly in the moonlight. As he lunged and thrust right and left he kept on singing—singing as though he were a boy playing some joyous game:

> "Oh, Paddy dear, an' did you hear
> The news that's going round?
> The Irish are forbid by law
> To walk on British ground."

The companies on the hill and in the grove near at hand had heard the few shots that had been fired. They now charged down toward the fighting-zone. When they reached it, fifteen of the outpost of forty-two were still standing their ground, but the voice that had strengthened their arms by a thread of Irish melody was heard no more.

Presently it was done. The Russians had been repulsed.

A streak of gold crept up the eastern sky, hung glimmering over the hills, and spread in the glow of morning over the land. It was almost silent on the field of battle now—a small engagement it had been, but the sight the rising sun looked down upon was awful. Here and there in every direction forms were lying, some of them face downward to the earth, others with their stark faces upturned to the sky. And in the very heart of the field a mountain of forms lay massed together.

Lieutenant Sato had abandoned the heroic fifteen left of his little band. From one soldier to another he went, turning them over and examining their faces. His sword hung by his side—the blade was nicked and broken; a streak of blood ran down his face; his cap was gone. But forgetful of everything save his one object, he sought among the dead and wounded.

As he came to that human mountain, he stopped. He set to work, pulling the forms apart. Two soldiers close at hand fell to helping him. It was slow and terrible work, for some of them were still alive. One by one they were moved. At the very bottom of them all was Michael Lenahan.

Sato threw himself upon the ground and burst into tears. One of the men who had assisted him made a pillow of twigs and put it under Michael's head. The other went to fetch a litter.

Of a little Chinese temple on the hill they had made a Red Cross hospital, and now rude litters, some of them made of four sticks, were bearing the wounded, victor and vanquished alike. One knew who was Japanese on this litter, who Russian on that; for the wounded Japanese were silent as the dead, while the groans of the Russian made the sound of mourning loud in the air. But from the stretcher of Michael Lenahan there arose a new kind of sound—one not often heard on a battle-field. Snatches of song floated upward from beneath the Russian coat thrown over him. Sometimes there would be a short silence, followed by muttering—an oath. Again a bit of song would ring out. Then, after a longer silence, a voice softened to the tenderness in tone of a woman: "Giri!" said Michael, softly, "Giri, my girl! I'm coming back for you. Giri—my girl—my wife!"

Michael had crouched in the corner of a little "heathen" cell, cowering with the terror of the pursued. He had fled with the fear of a wild beast at the mere sight of an English ship in a Japanese harbor. For twenty years he had hidden himself in a little inland hamlet of Japan; always in his heart had lurked the dread and fear of the fugitive from justice. Most of us believe that he is a coward who will strike a woman. Michael differentiated not between the sexes, save in this: Woman was the weaker, therefore she might be beaten with impunity. He had, in fact, oddly enough, somewhat the same regard for the sex as the people among whom he had lived for twenty years, but his foot was bigger, his fist heavier, and hence the lot of his woman the harder.

Yet this shivering refugee, this wife-beater and drunkard, in the face of an actual torrent of battle plunged into the heart of it, with never a thought of fear in his heart, and on his lips a song.

Part 4

"Your eyes look tired, beloved," said Tahaki. They were alone for a moment. All the night they had worked side by side. Outside in the hall the white-frocked nurses rustled back and forth. They who had been on duty with Tahaki and Yugiri through the night had now retired. Yugiri had expressed her determination of staying on through the day. She smiled now at her lover, and shook her head without speaking. He was not ready to cease work, and she would drop by his side with weariness sooner than abandon him.

"Do take a little rest," he urged. "The day nurses will be here in a moment. There is no need for you to remain."

"But you," she said, "have had no rest at all. My place is by your side."

"There is one more case," he replied. "After that, perhaps—"

"Well, then, I will wait also."

Nurses and a surgeon pushed a wheel-stretcher into the room and ranged it beside the operating-table. Dr. Tahaki turned, looked casually a moment at the form upon it, then scrutinized it sharply. Covered with a sheet, it was still and silent as a corpse; so still, indeed, that the trained eye of the surgeon guessed the truth before they had drawn aside the linen. Uneasily the nurses looked from one to another. Dr. Tahaki, frowning slightly, was drawing over his hands a pair of rubber gloves.

"Are there two patients here?" asked Yugiri, in surprise. "How long the honorable body is!"

"A giant," whispered another nurse; then, shivering, "How still he is—perhaps unconscious."

"But a moment since," said another, "I had to cover my ears from his sounds. A loud crying! I could not bear to hear it!"

"Crying!" said Yugiri. "A Japanese soldier cry! Surely you make mistake, Miss Sono."

Tahaki and the other surgeon were now ready.

With the assistance of the nurses the body was rolled from the stretcher to the table. The sheet fell backward from the lower part of the body, revealing the great ungainly feet and limbs.

As if forced, Yugiri's eyes from the feet moved slowly toward the head. Like one in a trance she stood, unable to speak or move. One of the nurses pushed her lightly aside, then drew the sheet carefully from the body. The great red head was now uncovered.

Yugiri-san had moved slowly toward the head, and now, with her fingers trembling, she touched it—turned its face toward her; and there she stood, her eyes riveted upon the face of her husband.

A hush had fallen upon the operating-room. The two nurses who had brought the patient looked blankly at each other. Tahaki, at the foot of the table, was staring at the face with distended eyes. The younger surgeon spoke lowly:

"He has come too late to us, Tahaki. Dead—as you see." Then in a very gentle voice: "A sei-yo-gin! Yet—a soldier of Japan! The gods reward him!"

He looked up to give an order to the nurse, but stopped, startled by her attitude. Her hands rested flatly over the face of the dead; she was leaning over, but her face was uplifted, and her eyes, full of a terrible reproach, were fixed upon Tahaki.

(*Harper's Weekly*, October 20 and 27, 1906)

THE MANŒUVRES OF O-YASU-SAN:
THE LITTLE JOKE ON
MRS. TOM AND MR. MIDDLETON

O-Yasu-san's arrival at her aunt's hotel caused a sensation. She came, as her new guardian expressed it, in bits. First, her father's servants brought her baggage, diminutive boxes and trunks, thirty-five in all, for she was modern and very fashionable; then, two austere-looking ladies, who described themselves as chaperons; a governess, bearing the young lady's books and school mat and stool; a tittering maid, Yasu herself, flanked by her fiancé's father, her fiancé's mother, her fiancé's paternal and maternal grandparents, her fiancé's several sisters, and a quite uncountable number of kotowing relatives, of both sexes and all ages.

When, however, the last farewell had been bobbed and bowed, and the little train had at last dispersed, Mrs. Bailey found O-Yasu-san and the aforesaid tittering maid alone on her shapely hands. The maid had retired behind the skirts of her mistress, and the latter small individual, very much composed, and almost condescending in her manner, made known her identity. She was very attractive and entirely Japanese, in spite of her blood, save for two things at once observable. Her hair curled, and, where the charming obi of her race usually encircled the waist, there was a very tightly-laced French pink corset. She said:

"How dodo? I come. You velly nize aunty-san for me. Yaes."

Whereupon Mrs. Bailey laughed and kissed her, for she was Nina's child.

Many years before Nina Bailey had made one of those unusual marriages which occur in an ordinary English family only once, perhaps, in generations. She had married a Japanese while at school in Paris. He was an attaché of the legation there. The marriage was a happy one, in spite of predictions, though it lasted only a year. The Marquis Hakodate, grown old in a day, took his little girl back to Japan with him the day after her mother was laid to rest, and, in Japan, O-Yasu-san had passed all her days. Her education had been that of the ordinary Japanese girl, save that she had been taught the

English language. A fiancé had been chosen for her. She indulged in dreams of young love in consequence, though she had never seen her fiancé at all. He was at college, somewhere.

Then one day her maid brought her the astonishing intelligence that a "foreign Mrs." was in the *ozashiski*. O-Yasu-san descended at once, precipitately. A hole made by a moist, plump finger in the *fusuma*, a bright eye and keen little ear alternately applied thereto, and O-Yasu-san had learned the history of her blood. She was not gloriously and honorably Japanese, after all, it seemed, but half barbarian. That accounted for—and excused— her uncertain temperament. The foreign Mrs. within was her aunt-in-law, wife of her mother's brother, and she had come to Japan, armed with a letter from O-Yasu's English grandmother, begging the Marquis Hakodate to permit her granddaughter to become acquainted with some of her mother's people, and to that end that she live with her aunt during the period of that lady's stay in Japan—a few months only. The Marquis Hakodate not only was willing to lend his daughter, so he courteously declared, but all his household and ancestors also. They were all at the service of the honorable Mrs. Mrs. Bailey, at first, had felt genuine alarm when the army of relatives and servitors presented themselves to her. Finally, however, O-Yasu, her maid, pets—a monkey, a chin and a pussy-cat—and her baggage, of course, settled down, and all seemed just as the lady had desired. Then, one night, plunged in sad and troubled thought, a solution suddenly presented itself to her for certain difficulties of the heart that at this time were afflicting her. She sent for Mr. Middleton the following day. She was a most resourceful lady, was this beautiful "Mrs. Tom," as she was called by her friends.

* * *

O-Yasu-san blew into the pink and white "boudoir" of her aunt. She was arrayed for conquest. Mrs. Tom was to receive friends this afternoon, and Yasu was to have the honor of pouring tea. The lady had given some pleasant thought to the graceful picture of little Yasu-san in silken kimono, sitting on her heels, pouring and serving tea for the gay galaxy of magpie callers. But now, as the girl came into the room, all smiles and twitters, Mrs. Tom threw up her white hands in horror.

"Whas matter?" demanded O-Yasu, in alarm, her bright eyes round in innocent astonishment.

"I told you to wear your kimono," said Mrs. Tom impatiently.

"Yaes," assented Yasu smilingly, "I got one on. See! Behold that *kee-mono!*" And she lifted up the accordion-pleated black voile skirt which an accommodating jinrikiman in her confidence had bought for her at a European store. Underneath the skirt in question the scanty folds of a ruby-colored kimono were visible, while a tiny white-shod foot peeped out, guiltless of shoes.

"My dear," said Mrs. Tom, almost tearfully, "you look a perfect little fright, and I wanted you to look your best—all Japanese."

"I am not *all* Japanese," Miss Yasu asseverated stiffly.

"But you look so sweet in your national dress. There, run along and get into it quickly."

"I am *nod* sweed," Yasu denied with fervor. "You gotter find out 'bout me. I nod sweed. Besides, I like wear this kind dress. So you do also."

Mrs. Tom was not fond of argument, nor was she used to being disobeyed. She shrugged her pretty shoulders a bit contemptuously.

"Oh, well," said she unpleasantly, "if you must wear European clothes, do so altogether. I *have* seen Japanese women appear half-way decent in a Paris frock; but you, my dear, are half-and-half. You look just ridiculous."

"Me?" said O-Yasu, with a queer little gleam in her eyes. "I *am* half-and-half? I like be that—ridiguluss." And all further parley, promises of sugary rewards, which had previously been quite enough to win her over to any desire of her aunt, were vainly tendered. Miss Yasu Bailey Hakodate, as she now was known, refused to be moved. And so, thus arrayed, she served the "exalted guests" of her aunty.

* * *

"How old are you, O-Yasu-san?"

The speaker, a very large and languid-looking Englishman, was seated on a stool, hard by the little table at which O-Yasu-san knelt. He was regarding the girl with a degree of interest mixed with humor, and occasionally his eye wandered craftily in the direction of his hostess, and always hers met his in a curious look of meaning.

O-Yasu paused a moment before answering the query addressed her. Then she looked directly at Mr. Middleton, and he forgot his question in unexpected internal speculation on the color of her eyes. They were golden, fringed with silken lashes of black. He thought of yellow-petaled daisies. Then her small, staccato voice, with its queer little ring of sarcasm, reached him:

"Thas not perlite question you mek," she said, "and my honorable aunt say in England nize gintleman not call maiden by her Clistian name."

He laughed, and gave her more attention now.

"Well, but we are in Japan," said he, "and it is polite here to inquire a person's age—is it not? Don't you Japanese consider that a compliment?"

"I am not Japanese," said O-Yasu-san, and put four lumps of sugar viciously into the Englishman's cup—a thimble in size—adding as she handed him the sickly-sweet beverage:

"In Japan thas perlite you dring *all* thas given unto you."

He tasted, then regarded her in mock reproach.

"You are *not* Japanese, I quote," said he, "and I refuse, therefore, to suffer."

Whereupon he set his cup down, and O-Yasu quite unaccountably fell to tittering and giggling to herself in a curiously suppressed, yet wholly youthful, fashion. Mr. Middleton watched her, his hand curled up near the side of his upper lip, where once a military mustache had flourished. "I am curious to know if you are laughing at me," said he.

"I god liddle joke all in my own haed," said Yasu, smiling vividly. "Some day I tell you. You want hear?"

"I am perishing to," he said.

"Very well," said she. "To-mollow, perhaps, I telling you."

"Oh, I am to see you, then, to-morrow?"

"Yaes—you want see me?"

"I intended to ask you if I might."

"Aevery day," said Miss Yasu, lowering her voice confidentially, "I take liddle walk out to Shiba Park. You know that white lotus pool? Thas where I like go—er—mebbe, to-mollow."

"Good!" exclaimed the Englishman, and, under the watchful eye of his hostess, he reached across and took O-Yasu's little limp hand in his and shook it cordially. Then he smiled—but it was at Mrs. Tom his smile was directed.

A little later, shaking hands with his hostess, in that affected uplifted mode then prevailing in society, she said, smiling teasingly—there were a dozen friends at hand:

"Aha! my friend, another conquest for our little maid, eh?"

He responded more warmly than they had agreed upon:

"Quite adorable—altogether ———" The rest was lost in the hubbub of chatter about them, but what he actually conveyed to Mrs. Tom's ear was this:

"Easy as fishing. Little lady herself arranged it all. Didn't have to suggest seeing her again. She even mentioned Shiba Park—the place of rendezvous agreed upon. Everything is falling in, apparently, with our plans. The gods wish us well, it seems."

Mrs. Tom's voice was raised, her face seemed grave, in spite of its seeming graciousness. Her friends heard her say:

"How sweet of Yasu-san. We shall be delighted, of course. I'm sure every one will envy me my little task of chaperon. Yasu is only a little girl—a mere child, you know. To-morrow, then. *Good*-night!"

Now, O-Yasu-san said nothing to her aunt of her engagement with Mr. Middleton, but, the following day, she appeared at the pool in question, a perfect little flower in appearance, gorgeous in purple kimono, flowered obi, gay parasol and glossy hair, bright with gilded ornaments. She found her swain in the company of Mrs. Tom, who surveyed her very benignly.

"*Ohayo gozaramazu,*" said Yasu, bowing extravagantly to the Englishman, and then very coldly to her aunt:

"Goo-by. I got nize ingagement make a talk with this English mister. Please mek excusing yourself."

"Dear," said Mrs. Tom, in her most syrup-like tones, "young English girls must always be chaperoned, you know. I couldn't think of letting you be alone with Mr. Middleton, my dear."

O-Yasu snapped her parasol closed, and said crossly:

"*I* am not English-jin."

She sat for some time thereafter on the curved stone wall of the pool, apparently oblivious of the two a short distance removed from her, and certainly themselves oblivious now of her presence. O-Yasu contemplated the sparkling-bodied goldfish and dropped pebbles, one by one, into the water. But, in the midst of some very ardent declaration, Mr. Middleton's eyes encountered the side-long contemptuous smile of O-Yasu-san. He colored to the ears and said in a rough whisper to Mrs. Tom, "Careful!"

She glanced about with the stealthy look of the guilty, and he crossed to O-Yasu at the pool. She leaned over the water, and he, watching her, saw that she was laughing in that elfin way of the previous evening.

"Oh, Miss Yasu, you were going to tell me, last night, some secret. Don't you remember?"

"Anudder day I tell my liddle—no, grade *big* joke on you."

"On me?"

"Yaes." Her eyes big and innocent. "I telling on you."

"Tell me, too." chimed in, sweetly, her aunt.

She shook her head vigorously now.

"I naever tell unto *you*," she said.

"Why?"

"Be-cause you gotta big mouth. You speag all things loud—mek big noises. I nod telling you."

And having oracularly delivered this astonishing snub—a truth, more-over—to her speechless aunt, she deliberately turned upon that lady a small, disdainful back, decked with an obi butterfly bow of huge dimensions.

Mrs. Tom looked up at her friend. Then she turned a trifle pale. *He* was laughing.

The meetings at the pool occurred daily now—even on rainy days when, arrayed in preposterous rubber coats, they sought the shelter of some flow-ering arbor. And every day O-Yasu laughed to herself, and said she had a "joke," and sometimes she would make believe to tell her "joke." Once it was a bunch of hair, which she withdrew from the bosom of her kimono. It belonged to her aunt. Yasu had playfully hidden it to show the foreign mis-ter. Another time she appeared with her aunt's shoes upon her own dimin-utive feet, and, in the midst of her innocent mirth, showed the gentleman the size of the same. And again she appeared "writing on her eyebrows," aunty's pencil being useful for that purpose. And so on, until, bit by bit, she had playfully stripped the lady of all her clever feminine devices to stop the march of time upon her beauty. And always the Englishman laughed.

O-Yasu had become a vital factor in this curious triple courtship. It was said among the foreign colony that the Englishman was a suitor for the hand of O-Yasu-san.

Mrs. Tom's plans had been more than successful, and she had reached a stage now where she found herself attempting to unravel the net in which she had unconsciously enmeshed herself. She had acquired an almost ab-normal hatred for her niece; for, though the girl had made possible her dai-ly meetings with her lover, yet Mrs. Tom had awakened to the electrical fact that O-Yasu-san was acutely aware of her manœuvres. She tried to convey this discovery to her lover, but O-Yasu, always obtrusively close at hand, overheard the words and stood before them a picture of obtuse innocence.

"Make no mistake about Yasu," had said Mrs. Tom bitterly, "*she* knows exactly why we come here." The Englishman had whispered feeling words of the apparent innocence and sweetness of the "child."

"Yaes, yaes, *me* knows—me knows allee 'bout it," asserted Yasu sweep-ingly. "Mister Middleton—he—he—lub me. Thas vaery nize. Thangs. Much 'bliged. All lide. Me mek marry wiz you ride 'way. Put you nize head mos' respectfully unto my august father's most honorable feet. Say like this: 'Guv me your most beautiful daughter.' My fadder say: 'She is nudding but a worm, but tek her. Help youself. When you like marry?' Then I am ad lid-dle hole on *fusuma*. I rush in quick like thees," and she illustrated with a rush toward the Englishman, seizing his hands impetuously in her own. "I say: 'Ride away, ride away mek that marriage. Hoarry. I got liddle joke telling him.' Then my fadder say: 'What is thad joke?' And I answer at once, like filial daughter, 'I *lub* him—and he also lubbing me. *Thas* my joke,'" and she brought out the word "love" with such fervid violence that the Englishman tingled; and a good part of that night he spent smoking under the stars, repeating to himself over and over again:

"And to think *that* was my poor little devil's joke. What a ——— I am."

Mrs. Tom took to writing letters to him:

"*My dear Jim:*

"Wake up. Beware of that little Japanese fraud. Believe me, she is absolutely alive to ———"

And, just then, O-Yasu-san looked over her shoulder.

"Why," said she, "you writing unto my lubber! 'Jim'! Thas hes beautiful name of heem. What you writing?" For Mrs. Tom had crushed up the letter and now sat with it clenched in her delicate fist. She stood up suddenly, her eyes narrowed menacingly. From her queenly height she looked down at little dwarfed O-Yasu. For a moment they surveyed each other in silence. Then O-Yasu said, in that guileless, naïve way which never deceived her aunt for a moment:

"Never mind, I see thad letter some udder day. All hosbands read those letters to their wives. Mr. Meedleton going show me thad letter some day."

Mrs. Tom spoke succinctly:

"You and I understand each other perfectly, O-Yasu. I will tell you one thing, however. You will never marry Jim Middleton, and, in a few days, I will see that you are returned to your own people—the people to whom you really belong."

The following morning the Marquis Hakodate called solemnly upon Mrs. Thomas J. Bailey, and most of the morning was shut up in her room with her. Alas! the hotel walls were not paper *shoji* and O-Yasu was unable either to see or hear; and a prying maid in her confidence, who had crawled along a perilous rain pipe to gain egress in some way to the room, was observed by a stupid, open-mouthed bell-boy, who, a lover of the aforesaid maid, gallantly ascended another drain pipe to rescue her. Whereupon, a wordy war ensuing, the argument came to a violent end, maid and boy crashing down to the court below and picking themselves up ruffled and bruised from head to foot.

Presently O-Yasu-san was called into the room. Her father's face was very grave; her aunt smiled upon her. "O-Yasu, dear," said she, "your papa deems it expedient that your marriage to the Marquis Momoso should take place immediately. I congratulate you upon your good fortune."

"Thangs," said little Yasu dryly, but she turned her eyes inquiringly upon her father. Still grave, he said briefly: "Have your insignificant belongings packed at once, my daughter, as I wish you to return with me to your home this evening."

After a deep bow signifying obedience to her father, O-Yasu turned a beaming face upon her aunty.

"Thangs ag'in," said she; "you mos' kind aunty in all the whole worl', b-but *please* permit me stay wiz you liddle bit longer," she pleaded.

"My dear little girl," said Mrs. Tom, smiling graciously, "I only wish you could stay with me longer, but, of course, it must be as your father says."

Whereupon, O-Yasu turned to her father quickly. His eyes regarded her tenderly and lovingly, for it had been many days since he had seen her. She said:

"Dear my father, it is the wish of my honorable aunty that I should stay with her much longer, and she begs that you permit it."

This was said in Japanese, while Mrs. Tom drew her brows petulantly together, and clasped her finger in nervous exasperation. Bowing deeply, the Marquis Hakodate said in English, a language he spoke perfectly:

"I thank you, madame. It is very kind of you to wish the longer stay of my daughter, but ———"

"Oh, please, *pl-ease,* father," coaxed little O-Yasu, seizing his hands, and holding them tightly, and entreating his glance. He coughed uneasily, for he had been made aware of the danger from the designing Englishman pursuing his daughter. "Please, permit me to remain," begged O-Yasu, tears in her voice now.

"Till to-morrow, then," said he gruffly; "to-morrow morning—at eight o'clock, you must leave."

O-Yasu looked piteously at her aunt, who was looking above the child's head into space. Then she said meekly, "Thangs. Vaery well. I will go home to-morrow—at eight."

The following morning, some time before sunrise, she shook into wakefulness her grumbling but finally excited and curious maid, and for some time thereafter the two fell back and forth into each other's arms, thus smothering back the ebullient mirth which possessed them. In the gray of the morning the gaping-mouthed bell-boy spied them stealing forth, but he told no one. He was in the secret—via the maid. Also his services were required.

When Mrs. Tom, at seven A.M., discovered that O-Yasu was gone, and with her her maid and all her petty belongings, a thrill of fear shot through her. Some women would have reasoned that O-Yasu had returned to her home. Not so Mrs. Tom, who at this time was palpitating with all the intuitions of a woman guiltily in love. Her mind could jump to startlingly true conclusions. That is why the address she gave to the runner who brought the jinrikisha to her was the same as that given earlier in the morning by O-Yasu to a public jinrikiman of Tokyo.

Mrs. Tom's boy, however, flew swiftly to the southward, while O-Yasu's man had gone east. And Mrs. Tom's boy stumbled as they passed through one of those strange waste places of the city which seem almost like deserted country—stumbled, fell, and broke the shaft of his vehicle. So there was Mrs. Tom, doomed to wait—and wait—and wait, until the gaping bell-boy should return from his quest for another carriage.

Meanwhile: Rap! rap! rap! on the woodwork of the English mister's room. A murmured grumble inside. Rap! Rap!

"What is it?"

"Veesitors, Excellency," shrilled the English mister's "boy," a weazened, wise old fellow of sixty.

"Visitors," exploded the voice within. "What the —————— You, Tomagawa, what do you mean by waking me at this hour?"

"Veesitors!" patiently repeated Tomagawa, a note of reproach in his voice.

A noise heard inside—the tramp of a heavy man, barefooted, across the floor. Then the door opened a crack. As it did so a little figure darted forward, thrust itself through the aforesaid crack, and, a moment later, Mr. Middleton found himself encircled in the convulsive arms of Miss O-Yasu Bailey Hakodate. Her maid had also entered the room, quite as a matter of course, and she now stood off at a respectful, admiring distance, examining the bare legs of the foreign mister from several oblique angles.

"Oh, my lubber, my lubber!" sobbed little O-Yasu-san, clinging frantically to his waist—she had tried vainly to reach his neck. "Soach a trubble—soach a trubble."

The speechless Englishman with one desperate pull freed himself from the embracing arms, threw one agonized look about the apartment and, with a dash, plunged into his bed—the only modest place of hiding for a decent gentleman. Curious the moral sense of Mr. Middleton, who thought nothing of making love to another man's wife, yet panically hid his naked limbs from the innocent gaze of little O-Yasu-san. However, she followed him swiftly across the room to his place of refuge, and now, upon her knees, she wailed aloud her "trubbles."

It seemed she had a cruel, ugly old aunt, who hated O-Yasu very much. She had sent for O-Yasu's father and had told him many wicked lies about her dear lubber (and she put her face fondly and warmly against the hand which she clutched tightly with her own). She, the ugly, very old aunt—she was very near forty, perhaps more—asserted O-Yasu, had told the Marquis Hakodate that he, Mr. Middleton, was in pursuit of his daughter. Her honorable father—a descendant of a thousand samurai, she asseverated, was greatly enraged, and was now looking all over Tokyo for the despoiler of his house. He had with him the two sharp swords of his ancestors, and he intended certainly to run them through the heart of her dear, dear lubber. Therefore, she, weak and helpless as she was—and here she let fall a sob, which induced the Englishman to put his free hand over the little one clinging to his other one—had come thus early to save his life. *She* knew that his intentions were of the most honorable, for had not he always courted her in the presence of a chaperon—the very aunt herself? But how could they make the Marquis Hakodate believe this also? Why—simply by an immediate marriage. (Here the Englishman let fall her hand and regarded her with his eyes bulging out, and his mouth gaped open.)

It could be easily arranged, urged O-Yasu. Why, there was a clergyman—a "Clistian" she called him—just around the corner, and she had brought a jinrikisha right to his very door for the purpose. She stopped, sat back on her heels and regarded her "lubber" in a most engaging manner.

"Miss O-Yasu," said he, when he had found his voice, "please go outside for a moment. I won't be an instant getting into my things."

"You going to do it?" she questioned joyfully, astounded at her own success.

"You mean, marry you?"

"Yaes."

"If you will have me," said he, quite simply.

She had arisen now, and stood looking at him a bit uncertainly. Then:

"Sa-ay, I got you sk-skeered mebbe?"

"No."

"Sa-ay," she was retreating now toward the door, "I—I just meking liddle joke ad you. I gotter make nudder kind marriage. Me? I just want disgusting you at my honorable aunt, account her hosband, my honorable uncle. Aexcuse me—I going now."

She had reached the door now.

"O-Yasu!"

She stood still, looking at him somewhat fearfully now.

"You *will* wait for me, won't you?"

"My fadder *nod* goin' kill you," said she. "Thas lie. I jus' want mek liddle marriage wiz you for liddle bit while, *till* my honorable aunt go away.

Then I, gittin divorce, ride away. Git marry agin wiz my honorable Marquis Momoso."

"Very well," said he cautiously. "Then wait outside; there must be a marriage, however."

"Ye-es," she hesitated, and then cried out:

"No, no—I got a changing of mind now. I not going mek you do that. Good-by!"

"Tomagawa!" shouted the Englishman at the top of his voice, and then, as the weazened face of his "boy" appeared at his door, he added peremptorily:

"Hold this young lady till I can join you."

"Sertinly, Excellency," smiled Tomagawa, and seized little O-Yasu by the sleeve, holding her a prisoner.

By and by, fully dressed, Mr. Middleton opened the sliding doors of his chamber. For a while he stood in silence, his arms folded, looking at O-Yasu. Then quietly:

"You may go, Tomagawa. I will take your place."

Released, O-Yasu remained still, her shamed eyes avoiding the Englishman's, but, when he put his arm about her, she laid her face against his coat and began to cry.

After a time:

"You goin' *mek* me marriage wiz you, mister?"

"Yes, Yasu-san."

"Why?"

"Because—I'm—I'm quite mad about you," said he.

"But my honorable aunty?"

"There was no 'aunty' for me, Yasu, after the second time I saw you."

"Oh," said she. "Then, if thas so—then—then my honorable uncle not going lose her ride away."

"I suppose not. We won't talk about it. Come. Are *you* willing?"

"Yaes," she nodded.

"Why?"

"Same reason you got," said she. And they went out together.

Mrs. Tom Bailey lay in her shaded room. She still shook and trembled from her late seizure. Ever since her return from the house of the Englishman she had gone from one fit of hysterics into another. One moment her mind was flooded with the imagined scenes of the past few months; she saw herself the central figure in a quiet, perfectly-refined little every-day divorce—later an accidental meeting with her friend, and still later a marriage. And then, jumping in, like an elf, upon these mind pictures, fluttered the gaudy, mocking little form of O-Yasu-san, and she clenched her delicate fists at the thought. About her wisps of rice-paper were scattered like snow, the pieces of O-Yasu-san's letter which she had torn to pieces in a frenzy:

"*Darling Aunty Tommy:*

"I got marriage with Mr. Middleton," wrote the jade. "Listen, honorable aunt-in-law, I did not intend making this beautiful elopement with that loavely man. I just want making revenge on you, because I listening at the *shoji* on that day you making plan with him—for just little bit while, so you can see him much. I say that I going unto that Englishman making a big raddle and noise. Mebbe, he gitting skeered, and run away from Japan. But he not want doing thus. Say he got mad with love for me, and so we make that marriage, sure enough. That's very nice. Thanks you for making me aquinted with my honorable hosband. Good-by. Mebbe my honorable uncle thank *me* also. Yes?" and she signed her name in dashing letters—Japanese—at the end.

Marie held the ice-bag over her mistress' temple. She spoke thoughtfully:

"Madame was always better at zese times when m'sieu' was wiz her. Perhaps, madame ———"

Mrs. Tom buried her face deeply in her pillow. From there her muffled voice came:

"Cable, Marie—cable—cable. Say—we are—going—home."

(*Saturday Evening Post,* January 25, 1908)

A NEIGHBOR'S GARDEN,
MY OWN AND A DREAM ONE

I have always loved flowers. The wild ones tossing up their bright heads in the fields and woods I have gathered at will and filled my house with. But toward the exquisite darlings which bloom in gardens I have felt as I do to precious jewels which I see set out in a shop window or ablaze on the person of some fortunate lady: they are things I love to look at, but do not own. At least, I have only a few bits of fine jewelry, just as I have only a few flowers I can call my very own.

Though I have never desired to possess jewels, I have positively hungered for a garden of flowers. I have spent sleepless nights in which I planned to have one all my own, and have gone to sleep to dream of it. Since I came to America, however, I have been a dweller, until recently, in the big, grimy cities where the ugly buildings and the noises made of life to me a veritable inferno. It is not always the ones who live among the flowers that love them most. The city child—child of the slums, sometimes—with its one pot of geraniums, will often expend upon it more care and thought than some women give to the flowers which seem literally to garland their home, inside and out. I often think of my mother, and her pathetic attempts to recall the bloom of the flowering land of Japan which had been her home. The first time she made the long journey to this country, she carried with her a dozen or more boxes in which seeds and slips were planted, and even at sea she had her little green growth always with her.

Here in America she was never without her own bit of a garden, her "flowering spot," as she named it, and often it consisted only of an ugly hotel window ledge, or the roof of some city house. But she never lost her passionate love for flowers, and she passed this trait along to me. I consider flowers the loveliest things in creation, and yet, as I have said, I have never owned any, hardly.

About four years ago I bade the city a sincere and cordial farewell. For a time we lived in the suburbs, where, on a tiny lawn, I cherished a few pansies and geraniums, but I could not have a garden, for with my work as a writer I found that the most I could do in life was to produce a book and a baby a year. Besides, I wanted the real country for my garden. By and by fortune made this possible. I dwell now in the heart of Westchester, near the metropolis. I have a little acre of land all my own. Around me are sumptuous homes, mansions set amid grounds kept as perfect and smooth as a well-swept parlor. My little frowsy acre, with its unshorn lawns and overgrown carriage drives, seems a reproach to an otherwise immaculate community. I'm sure my neighbors regard me with suspicion, convinced I am an eccentric individual who prefers my place unclipped. But, in truth, I love the smooth, sweet, rolling green expanse of well-cut lawns, and I should like to own the flowers and flowering shrubs which grow within the gardens of my neighbors. But I keep no man, and have neither the strength nor ambition to push a lawn-mower over an acre of lawn.

When the babies have ceased to come, and when the ones that are here have ceased to need me all the time, then I expect to have flowers of my own. Meanwhile I content myself with wandering into the gardens of my neighbors.

I am not interested in the work of the mere professional landscape gardener; so after a brief look at a few of these places, I turn away. In nearly all the places hereabouts I perceive only the work of the conventional hired gardener. I like a garden which shows individuality, which not only is a bit of earth in which to grow flowers, but in which, like a room in which one lives, one's actual personality appears. My neighbors seem impressed, however, with the necessity of formal gardens on their places. Italian, Dutch, even Japanese, gardens are out of place in America, and look incongruous in the shadow of an American country house. So I was disappointed in my neighborhood, and after a few weeks of searching after gardens I stayed at home, contented with my frowsy acre, flowerless though it was.

I wish I lived, as I hope to soon, in a simpler community, where there are greater woods, and perhaps a river, or at least a little stream or brook twisting in and out. The gleam of the Sound is, I suppose, beautiful enough, but it does not run inland. A big body of water tires me; but a river or even a little brook, never does.

In the spring, Norah, the Irish girl who cares for my three fat babies, came to me with a great bunch of lilies-of-the-valley in her hand, and a mass of buttercups in her apron. The lilies, she said, were for me, the buttercups for the nursery. She had found the lilies, she said, in the little fenced-in yard we used for drying clothes.

I greedily took the buttercups as well from her, and in my pretty shallow fern dish arranged the lilies—the leaves discarded—with the buttercups amongst them, with an exquisite result. Against Norah's protests that buttercups were not fit for a parlor, the lovely posey found the place of honor in what my little boy calls "mamma's best room." Then at once I demanded to be taken to the spot where grew the lilies. I had thought my acre yielded only two large lilac trees, one wistaria vine, some Virginia creeper and two peony bushes. Such a bare acre, with nothing at all set out, save the great trees! Yet the fair actress from whom I purchased the place had smilingly informed me she spent five hundred dollars each summer on flowers. Whereupon she showed me an enormous round bed, wherein each year a florist raised certain ornate annuals. Also there are no less than nine garden boxes on the great verandas; besides, set out at various points along the carriage drive, are huge red tubs. The bed, boxes and tubs, so far, had been empty since my advent. I cannot afford five hundred dollars to fill them with the desired annuals, and at this time I cannot make up my mind whether to plant a maple tree in the huge round bed or to turn it into a great sand pile for fat babies and doggies to roll in.

But I digress. Following Norah, I went into the little yard in question. No lilies. Norah kneeled down and put her hand under the fence. Lilies! I turned pale, kneeled also and looked. A neighbor's garden—and right next to me, where I had never thought to look at all.

With Norah's aid I climbed up the fence and after a cautious look at the rather frowning looking, and seemingly deserted house a short distance away, I surveyed the place. It was only a very little garden, filled with old-fashioned and odorous flowers. At this time of year only a few of them, comparatively speaking, were in bloom, but the lilies-of-the-valley underneath a great oak tree, which crowded against my fence, were all a-bloom, sending up a wonderful fragrance in the dewy morning. Also the honeysuckle was in bloom, and hyacinths.

"I wish," said I to Norah, "that we owned that place instead of this. Now, the woman who lives there has planted flowers for her fortunate successor to come into, but my actress planted only for herself, five hundred dollars' worth a summer, and scarcely a flower left for me. I'm going to get acquainted in the neighborhood. There must be gardens somewhere. If the people don't call on me, I'll call on them, or rather on their gardens, and if they snub me, Norah, I'll send you over to *steal* their flowers. You do get your hand so beautifully under fences." Whereat the scandalized Norah left me in what she would have termed "doodgeon," and I was left alone ruminating on the fence, and enviously regarding my neighbor's garden.

I was awakened from my reverie by the melodious accents of the now much excited Norah. She had discarded her erstwhile grimy apron and now appeared before me in a beautiful white starched one, which she tied on her excitedly as she spoke thus elegantly:

"For the love of God, ma'am, get down from that fince and put some clothes on yer back!"

I sprang down as airily as a mother of three may, and demanded of my servant what was the matter with the clothes I had on—a decent skirt and waist, the latter with sleeves rolled comfortably to the elbows.

"There's three grand ladies in yer parlor!" said Norah in a loud whisper, "Hurry!"

I forgot my progeny of three and flew houseward as though I was not married at all. Up the back steps I sped, and a few minutes later I was descending the front stairs, dressed as I should be—according to Norah, anyhow.

The three "grand ladies" consisted of a mother and two rather pretty daughters. They were acquainted with city friends of mine, were delighted to have me as a neighbor, so they said, and finally the older lady said smilingly:

"And I want you to come over as soon as possible and see my garden— I am sure you must love flowers, too."

I gave a little jump in my seat. "Have you a garden?" said I.

"Yes, and one I planted all myself! There is not a flower in my garden that I did not plant or raise myself, sometimes from my own seeds, and I've—"

Here the younger girl interrupted, apologetically I thought. "It's mamma's fad," said she. "She thinks more of her flowers than of her children."

"I don't wonder!" I exclaimed shamelessly in the face of the two pretty daughters. "Why, I'll confess to you the truth. Ten minutes ago I was sitting on my back fence, looking at and coveting my neighbor's flowers, some of which, you see Norah had already stolen for me," and I indicated my posy.

This brought out a burst of mirth, explained presently by the mother:

"My dear, that little old garden was my first attempt. Four years ago we lived in that place, but after my father's death we moved into the big place we now occupy. If you think well of that little garden, I wonder what you will say of my present place. Now, you must come, just as soon as possible;" and I said I would.

* * *

I will call my neighbor Mrs C. Her place is on the top of a hill. She has about seventeen acres of rolling lands and lawns. I felt a bit disappointed as I climbed up the winding path which led to the house. From the front the place has the usual aspect of the conventional rich man's country place. How smoothly are the lawns cut! Here and there shrubs laden with spring blossoms are set as formally as pieces of furniture in a parlor. But the lady herself came halfway down the path to meet me, both hands held out. She drew me around the side of the house, saying:

"My dear, *my* garden is at the back. My men care for the front of the place. I disport myself back here."

Then I found myself in her garden. Even thus early—it was the middle of May, I believe—it was a mass of bloom, bloom of that fresh lovely kind which the first flowers show. The exotic radiance which comes in midsummer, or even the dreamy deep purple red-browns and golden colors of the fall, have not that same appeal of the spring colors the first of the year.

Some people set out their gardens as they do a room. They hang twin pictures side by side, or a large one in the center. They fill their room with furniture, so that it looks and feels like an overcrowded shop, with the goods on exhibition. Everything just so, almost as if tagged. But I like flower beds, as I do pictures, set out haphazard, with charming inconsequence and irregularity. Indeed, much art could be expended on the irregular disposition of flower beds in a garden. That's why I fell in love with the garden of Mrs C.

She had planted her flowers willy-nilly, anywhere and everywhere, and yet there was a studied design in the placing of her beds. No gigantic middle beds. Irregular rows of long beds running two and three parallel with one another. Corners massed high with tall growing varieties, climbing roses smothering the stump of an old dead tree. A bed all in bridal white—what it was I cannot now quite remember, whether sweet alyssum or candytuft— and then a bed to hold one's eyes enthralled. The colors of the flowers seemed those of sweet peas, but they had not the disadvantage of the ungainly vines. They grew in a shady spot, where few other flowers were, and hence their loveliness was enhanced by the cool greenness about them. *Aquilegia,* she called them; columbine. She wanted to pick some for me, but I would not let her. They are of the sort of flowers that look better growing.

There was one great bed of a white blooming flower for the center, while, banked up against it, were the old-fashioned bleeding heart, the bushes fairly laden with red pink blossoms. Her hedgerows were of lilac, the Persian variety, a deeper purple than the English, and while not so fragrant, far more lovely, in my opinion. She showed me where she had planted banks of hollyhocks, and told how when in bloom they literally glorified the whole otherwise homely and out-of-the-way spot she had given them. With these she had mixed sunflowers and other tall bright flowers. Her lilacs, at this time, were all in bloom, a lovely line of purple my eye returned to constantly.

In spring, it seems to me, purple is the predominating color; purple, white and pink. The flowering trees and shrubs are mostly pink and white. I know no lovelier sight than a single tree of magnolia on a green lawn in full, pink bloom—no lovelier sight save the blowing cherry and plum blossoms of far Japan.

Mrs C has built her garden on a rocky hilltop. The huge rocks themselves have added to its natural beauty, and over these she has thrown haphazard the cheerful nasturtium seed, and farther down some odd and tropic-looking plants, which were sent to her from California.

While going with her from bed to bed, a neighbor's voice called across the dividing lilac hedge, and I perceived the face of a smooth-shaven scholarly looking gentleman, at the lilac hedge.

"Ah, Mr B!" exclaimed my hostess, and she led me over to him, on the way explaining: "Now, you must meet my teacher and master in the art of gardening. He it was who first interested me in the work, who taught me, in fact, all I know. Many of my flowers have grown up from his slips and seeds. I call them his grandchildren. I'm afraid when you look over the fence into *my* neighbor's garden you will not want to look back again."

But I could not see much of the Englishman's garden from my position at the hedge, and at that moment I was filled with such a deep admiration for the garden of Mrs C that I did not want to see any other. I felt very ignorant and awed listening to the Englishman talking of flowers, and when he handed me a basket full of rudbeckia roots, I would not have confessed my ignorance of what those flowers were for anything on earth.

I went back home with some odd sensations. Here was I with the beginnings—some roots—of a garden; I had spent an entire afternoon in one of the prettiest gardens I had ever seen. I had made the acquaintance of a character as fragrant as the flowers themselves. She told me how she had come to turn to gardening. The two pretty daughters I had met were both married women, one of them, like myself, the mother of two or three babies. The loneliness of the great place had come upon the mother after they had left home, and about this time also the father fell sick with a malady of the heart. She saw him daily passing away before her eyes, unable to do a thing to hold him, or to prevent the inevitable. She said the thought of her coming agony was more than she could bear.

And then, suddenly, for the first time in her life, she had begun to raise flowers herself. What a surcease for an aching mind! What a balm for a bleeding heart! The flowers, like children, needed constant care and food.

Parental pride in their beauty meant one must never forget them, but always strive to add to the cultivation of their grace. And so my lady of the flower garden had found that which we all seek in time of trouble—comfort.

When I reached home, and went, with my basket of roots, to my lower veranda, the boxes of the actress never seemed so ugly before. Yet there was something appealing to me about them. They were so empty! I had intended to plant my roots in a conspicuous place on my lawn, but I hesitated as I went past the row of empty boxes.

"You wouldn't look so bad," said I, "if there was only something in you. Now, if she hadn't spoken that figure—$500—I might have interested myself in you. Even as it is—"

I dug a bit into the earth that was still in them, and then, after a moment, went to work in earnest. I planted my rudbeckia roots in the actress's flower boxes. Then I went indoors, washed my hands, and dreamed a bit of what my boxes (not garden this time) would look like when full of bloom.

My Own Garden

I decided upon a garden—and ceased to dream. If a woman of the age of my neighbor (she was about fifty-five) could with her own hands set out and plant a garden, why could not I, young, healthy and ambitious, do likewise? Katy could mind the babies for a time entirely, and the brown-faced girl who did my housework was only too anxious to take full charge of the rest of the work. Fanny was a born housekeeper, and I know she always saw through my various brave devices to make her think I was one also. For I'm not.

I sent at once for a catalog to a well-known firm, and in due time arrived a most gorgeous and fascinating pamphlet, giving pictures, descriptions and directions regarding more flowers than I had hitherto dreamed existed. About this time also a publisher friend sent me a book on Hardy Gardening—a delightful, alluring book. There followed a few days of excited preparation, and nights when, propped up in bed, I read and re-read the book and the catalog. Also I telephoned to Mrs C that I was about to start a garden and I had "such ideas" that I didn't want her or anyone to see it till it was quite started. Then!

About this time there came to my door a peddling florist. I bought from him three dozen pansies and a like number of geraniums. Also a few forget-me-nots—all in bloom. I had hardly set these out in a prominent place on my front lawn, when my precious seeds arrived and a few hydrangea bushes. I coaxed my husband into planting the latter for me in the big round bed, formerly the actress's pride and the florist's profit. Then I went to work digging. How I dug! And dug!

It was hard, hard work, but I kept at it till my back ached and I was as grimy as a hired man. I had to pick out the endless number of stones which seemed to be in the earth, and I never realized before how very hard it is to make one's earth crumble up. Mine looked so lumpy, even after I was through, and where I had dug up the sod to make a bed the earth looked sunken; in some places almost like a little hole. However, I patiently carried two or three loads of earth in a wheelbarrow from the aforementioned big bed, and gradually my beds assumed a respectable appearance.

I began to plant the seeds, following the printed instructions on the little envelopes. Suddenly I remembered that I had forgotten to put down the manure and the fertilizer that had come with the seeds. So I had to scatter these *over* where the seeds were planted, supposing it would have the same effect. I refused to refer either to the book or catalog upon the subject, in case I was mistaken.

In the beginning I had intended to have a real garden; but the seed firm sent me only enough for a few beds in those bare spaces about the house which looked as if they were just waiting to be planted with flowers. So I ruefully decided against a "garden" this year. Then I went over to break this news to Mrs C. "It's too late," said I "for a garden this year, but I have set out some beautiful beds all around the house."

After talking with the lady awhile, I was mortified to discover that I had made a foolish mistake. In my zeal to get the planting done and over with, I'd forgotten that the seeds all had different months for planting. I had set them out all on the same day, having spent the previous week entirely in digging. However, I hoped for the best, and I did not tell Mrs C. It was still May—the end of it—and most of the flowers I had planted were perennials. Even if they did not bloom this year they surely would next. Anyhow, I was not going to borrow trouble. Besides, I intended to give so much care to those seeds I had planted that they were bound to do better than the ones just planted in the ordinary way.

I rested for a time from my labors, though three or four times daily I most sedulously watered the earth where I had put down the seeds. The first thing in the morning I was outdoors, down on my knees, trying to find the "first showing." My pansies and geraniums meanwhile continued to thrive, and as they had spread considerably, I moved some of them to the tubs still vacant.

The boxes with the rudbeckia in them looked very promising indeed, and I was proud of them. No bloom yet, but how that rudbeckia did spread!

My mother had given me a few sprays of English ivy she had brought from the home of Dickens when last abroad. These I had previously cherished indoors. I now brought them out and added them to my veranda boxes. They made only a thin little showing, but the foliage of the rudbeckia itself was so thick and green I felt well satisfied.

Then came the wife of the Englishman to call upon me, and proudly I took her out to show her the progress of her husband's gift—the basket of rudbeckia roots. The lady at first seemed quite taken aback. She sat down, almost breathlessly, and she surveyed me with a look of mingled compassion and amusement. Then she said:

"Don't you know rudbeckia?"

"Why—er—of course," said I. "It's a very pretty flower," I added cordially. After a moment's silence, she said:

"It's nothing but the common golden glow. You probably know it by that name."

I did. I had an instantaneous mental picture of my boxes with the six-foot tall golden glow looming up from them and shutting out the blessed light.

The lady at once sought to put me at my ease. She told me stories of the early gardening of Mrs C, and another story concerning a neighbor.

"My husband," said she, "gave her a basket full of common sunflower roots, jokingly remarking, 'Here's a pretty border for one of your beds.' She took him in earnest, and in not so long a time the whole neighborhood enjoyed the unique spectacle of a round flower bed, the border of which was the common sunflower. No one ever knew, save the lady herself, what was planted in the center of that bed, as it always remained unseen, and to this day she has not forgiven Mr B."

The following day found me furiously at work transplanting the rudbeckia to a sunny corner of my house.

Next week I went to the woods, as they do in all flower books, and I dug up a lot of ferns. They seemed a lot to me, anyhow. I carried them home alone. I had been unable to induce my husband or Katy to share these labors. We possessed an evil-smelling automobile, the darling of my husband's heart, and whereas he complained that in these days I was "always muddy," I retorted that he was "always greasy," and when he said that he never saw me save doubled over some patch of earth, I inquired whether he went to sleep under his machine, for I'm sure he spent most of his time at home underneath the automobile. Anyhow, I dug and brought home my ferns without help of any sort.

I began anxiously to look for results from my seeds. A green growth had indeed cropped up. It looked, however, suspiciously like weeds or grass but

for a few distinctly shaped leaves that appeared among it. After a few days
of serious inspection I decided these were my flowers. So I weeded out the
green grassy-looking growth, and left in the distinctly shaped leaves. They
appeared in nearly all my beds, and I was a bit puzzled at their similarity.

I made another call on Mrs C, intending to ask her advice about the matter.
When, however, I saw her "blooming spot" and recalled my own melancholy, shriveled, little "non-blooming spots," my courage failed me. I did
not want anyone to see my beds.

She had heard the story of my rudbeckia fiasco. How tales travel! She
laughed a bit, and then:

"Don't worry about it," said she, "I just know that you are a natural
gardener, anyhow. All of your countrywomen are. I'm ever so anxious to
see your little garden. I know very well it will reflect the color and taste of
your far native land."

Alas for Japan!

I went home in something of a panic. I called up on the telephone the florist
to whom the actress had recommended me.

How much would he charge for setting out for me, at once, a flower
garden—lots of beds, and, if possible, the flowers must all be in bloom. After
a few questions on his part, and explanations, he named a price. I dropped
the telephone receiver. I will not tell you the price he named for fear a certain actress might read these lines and—grin.

A mere townsperson, one who lives in a New York flat the year around,
came out to visit me, poked among my grubby looking little beds and had
the audacity to say:

"You say you weeded these? Are you cultivating dandelions?" (The distinctly shaped leaf plants I had carefully left.)

And the next day Mrs C "dropped over at last" to see "that garden." I
almost wept as I showed her around. Not a single flower, save those I had
purchased from the man who had come to my door! In all my beds I seemed
to have left the weeds instead of flowers. And how those weeds did grow!
What tremendous sizes they achieved in all my most hopeful beds. Some of
them required all my strength to pull out, and usually the horrid roots still
remained firmly in the ground.

I wonder what my garden friend thought as the summer progressed. For
a time I kept away from her, actually depriving myself of the pleasure of visiting her garden, which I loved. A telephone call, however, sent me over there.
It was midsummer now, and her garden was a thing of glory—all reds and
yellows. I surveyed it with speechless admiration, then I turned to her:

"And you planted it all yourself? What an utter little failure I must appear to you!"

It was then she made to me a queer confession. She had indeed planted the garden all herself, as she had said. The garden was her own personal handiwork, she could truthfully say. But she had hired men (strong-armed men, who are good for so much in this world) to do the digging—*and* the weeding!

The digging! Why, that was what had discouraged me from the first. At the outset to be fronted with the heavy labor of a man.

And the weeding! How could *I* tell a weed from a flower in its infancy? But the practiced eye of a regular gardener could at the outset have discerned the difference.

"Next year," say I, "I, too, will have a man. I can do without a spring hat— or rather, babies thrive just as well in rompers as in expensive, starched frocks. The little dears shall contribute to my garden, and the needful article—a man!"

A Dream Garden

We must move away to a new place entirely. It must be close to some densely wooded lands, as without a background of woods, it would seem to me like a picture without an adequate frame, and I want my garden to be a romantic spot, a perfumed, lovely Eden. From this wooded forest, jumping down over rocks and mossy places, must pour a little stream or rivulet. It must wind in curves and dips, and when it reaches about the center of my garden it must become a little lake or pool, wherein I may grow sweet water lilies and lotus, or where, instead, the shining-bodied gold fish may play and swim.

I want no hedge. Rather, my garden will be open on all sides, so I may always see it. There must be a small summerhouse, pagoda shaped, and built of old gray stone. A trellis work of some kind shall be built out slightly over my pond, and over this shall be trained the wonderful wistaria of Japan. This flower is never so lovely as when it clambers over some dipping bough or eave to peer at its own drooping reflection in water underneath. That is how they love to grow it in China and Japan. But the wistaria bloom is short-lived, and when it has died with the spring, what can I do to replace its beauty? Mingle the white-faced moonflower vine among the wistaria, or even some morning glories.

Roses I love, but not as others do. I do not name the rose queen of flowers. To me they are chiefly attractive after they are cut. The climbing ramblers are, of course, very lovely while growing, but the formal, stiff-necked, larger varieties never appealed to me, save as decorative house creatures. They are domestic flowers, house pets, trained, civilized. But, ah, to me they have not the charm of other flowers of which I know!

I know a long, narrow bed of yellow coreopsis. When the wind blows ever so faintly these small gorgeous flowers look like an Oriental army marching with flying colors. Beside them, more brilliantly, more triumphantly, move an army of brazen poppies of enormous size and beauty. But the coreopsis sway with the wind, and every toss of their little heads makes me feel they are a stronger, cleaner race, and more beautiful even than the opium-freighted poppies.

There shall be no pebbled paths cut into my garden. My walks shall be entirely of grass; and that the tread of our clumsy feet, or the high-heeled shoes of some I know may not wear out my sod, I shall have flat, white stones and slabs as stepping stones, as the Japanese do.

Though all flowers are lovely, yet many of their stalks and bushes are unsightly, and spoil the artistic effect of a garden. Therefore I banish sweet peas to a few steps lower than my garden. I wish only to see their heads.

I must have a single cherry tree, set on a bit of greensward by itself. Under its shade I shall break up the earth as a bed, and there I will plant purple and white pansies. They love the shade as few other flowers do. Under my magnolia tree—or shall I have it a plum tree?—I'll have a great bed of lilies-of-the-valley, and these, too, I will mass all about my pagoda, and close to my little pond.

There will be no distinct form or style to my garden. I am not an orderly person, and if I choose to scatter my flowers in madcap fashion anywhere they will grow, I will not spoil the landscape effect. I scorn a bed whose middle piece springs up stiff and tall, with red-piked flowers, while, encircling it, lower and lower, appear other flowering pieces, till the final border, dear to the heart of the conventional gardener. A star-shaped bed, or any fancy shape, makes me positively shudder. Flowers should have a chance for picturesque growing.

I know an old and dried-up fountain in the garden of a little old-fashioned French woman who delights to grow phlox, bachelor's buttons and asters. This fountain is of some fanciful iron. Its central piece is a slim statue figure of a man holding aloft a slender pipe to his lips, from which, I presume, originally dripped the water which filled the little fountain below. The old woman makes of this old dried-up fountain each summer a thing of such ravishing beauty that I yearn to steal it for my own.

In the fountain bed she has great yellow and red flowers. I do not know what they are from where I look in at her gate. There is English ivy and some bright red flowers mingled with it, about the statue itself, and a vine whose flowers appear to be deep purple—a star-eyed, exquisite flower. Then I think there are nasturtiums and geraniums growing in the curved arm of the figure, whose face alone is uncovered by vine or flower.

Whenever I see ferns growing in the woods, I always think: "How easy to transplant! Why, half a day's work and I shall have all I could want." But try it. Large ferns have large roots. One needs great quantities of little ferns to make any showing at all. It is amazing how easily the stalks break; and often, thinking I had a large quantity of ferns, I have returned home to find myself with a mere handful after I had discarded the bruised and broken ones.

Yet, I shall have a part of my garden entirely for ferns. It shall be at the edge of my garden, nearest to the woodland, and I shall look to these neighboring woods as a sort of wild protection for the transplanted creatures from their heart.

When I have planted my beds just as I desire them: the old-fashioned, hardy flowers here; purple-colored varieties there; scarlet beauties here; yellow, golden ones there; delicate-faced ones all by themselves, or with the lilies, and Oriental exotics apart also, I shall plant among my ferns numberless wood violets and maybe a few of the more delicate wild flowers.

Then I'll begin to realize the necessity for a fence or hedge. I do not want one, and I am quite sure it would spoil for me the beauty of my garden. Yet creatures of prey exist who even come into a cherished garden; and whether they come to steal or for vandalism, and whether they be dog, man, chickens or small boy, their work is as devastating. So I've bethought me. I shall have a *snake* as the guardian of my garden. Who does not fear a snake? It shall be a great, beauteous creature whose fame shall be known to all the neighborhood, and I also shall share in its fame, perhaps as a supposed "charmer," or "witch," for *I'll* not be afraid of my flowers' protector, nor will it be afraid of me. Who knows we may walk together, looped in each other's arms; at least it may loop itself on my arm.

"Ugh!" I hear some people say, "Who'll want to go near you then—or your garden?" Keep away, then. Gardens thrive best when only those who love them step upon their paths. I'll twine my green-bodied, yellow-eyed protector at my gate—I'll have a gate even if no hedge or fence—and only those shall enter who fear it not—or know the secret.

(*Good Housekeeping*, April and May 1908)

DELIA DISSENTS: HER DIARY RECORDS
THE END OF A GREAT ENDEAVOR

We dressed in our best. Miss Claire was after linding me her illygunt camio broach, for ses she shmiling:

"If yer're afther rooning for pressydint you must dress betther than ye're aponunt. Think of the broach undher ye're chin, Delia," ses she, "and ye'll hold ye're head hy and horty."

The fuchure mimbers of the yunion began to arrive in boonches.

Some of thim came in carruges owned by the family they warked far and who had innersintly lint thim for the occashun, little dhreaming that insted of a grand parrty the Wolley servants (consisting of mesilf) aloan was afther giving in honor of the Poynt imployees, as Minnie ses tis now the fashun to call oursilves—little dhreaming, as I sed, that we were about to meet for the rightchous purpose of forming a yunion.

The last to arrive was the widder's maid, the little cullud lass I'm afther tilling ye about befure—the wan named Lilly.

The meeting taking place in me kitchen. I natchurally took the place of chareman, and wid me pertater masher thoomping on the table, I called the meeting to ordher. Mr. Larry Mulvaney arose to rayspictably suggist, as he's perlitely saying, that we precede to ilict a prisydint at wance and call the roll.

"Prisydint? is it?" ses I, "and who did ye think ye were afther being invited to meet. Sure it's the Prissydint hersilf whose intertaining the boonch of ye."

A noomber of those marselled oopstares girls started in to titter and at that me blood biled oop widin me. Raymimbering me camio pin I lifted me chin hortily aloft and sed swately:

"We'll now preceed to talk of the roll. Minnie, darlint, will ye kindly show the ladies and gintlemin that we are able to call more than wan roll, but that refreshments are intinded to be sarved afther the meeting is over."

Whereupon Minnie aroze and pulling back the illygunt American flag which Miss Claire is afther linding us as a screen in front of me stachunarry wash tubs, reveeled set enticingly upon thim the rolls and dilicussies in quischun.

"We are here," ses I, raysing me voyse so it cud be hurd all over the naybyhood, "for the purpose of forming a sarvints yunion and to dishcuss the hard sircumstunses under which we puir loan hard-warking crachures labor wid the shweat of our brows and uther parts of us besides. We have been crooly composed upon for sinchuries, but the time has arrived at last" ses I, obsarving the effect of me oratry in the moyst eyes of minny of me lisseners, "when the worm is about to toorn around and walk home. Lit us, ladies and gintleman," ses I wid passhun, "dishcuss the ways and meens of impooving our crool and unforchnut position. Will somewan sphake some wards upon the booted subject, as Mr. James wud be afther calling it."

"I move," ses Mr. Tooth, he being the gardenir at the Doodleys, "that we shtart properly. Lit us ilect a Prissydint."

A fat little schnipe aroze in the rear. She's afther being the nurse over at the Regal's house. She and the frorleen are seeted thegither thick as theeves.

"I take this opporchunity," ses she, "to say that I am an American. I cum" ses she "froom the South, from which as perhaps ye all know hale all the refined rich, grate and reel ladies and gintlemin in these Yunited States of America. I am opposed at the outset" ses she "to sitting in a meeting or joining a yunion where cullured peeple are admitted."

Wid that she toorned a horty glance of disdane and scorn upon puir little Lilly Pearl Jackson, she wid the face the cullur of ye're auld black cat.

I rose in rarth.

"I draw the line at the cullured quischun," ses I. "Miss Lilly Pearl Jackson will be good enuff to kape her seet."

"I sickond the moshun," ses Mr. Mulvaney.

"Passed," ses Museer, feercely pulling at his mustash on aich side of it.

"And now," ses I swately, "we'll preseed to business."

The Rooshun Jew in charge of the ingineering privit illictrical plant of the Oil magnut, hoose afther owning half of the Poynt itsilf, aroze.

He's a silint shpaking gintleman, niver known to open his mouth befure. "For sinchuries" ses he, rolling his black eyes about, "we've been composed upon. You spoke rightly, Miss Pressydint," ses he (I bowed grazefully) "the proverbyull worm is indade about to toorn. I congrachulate you upon this first shtep forward upward—onward. I belave, Miss Pressydint, the idear originated in your fertill brane—the idear germinated there, while you wint about your toil the brillyunt, heaven sint idear came to you, that you would, you could help yere equilly unforchnut bruthers and sisters. And my deer yung lady, while the idear was germinating in your brane, so did the seed in my brane bare fruit of a differunt sort. Behold, deer lady!"

He took from his pocket sumthing rapped about in a peece of oil skin.

"Bruthers and sisters of toil," ses he, "I show you here the object which will wance and for all settle all quischuns of this sort in the fuchure. Poot this" ses he, "in frunt of the roast. Let your masters think it a—stone—for sharpening the carving knife upon."

Wid that he paused, then hissed out the follering terryfying ixplunashun: "*It's an unfirnal masheen!*" ses he.

"Grashus!" ses I, joomping on the table, follared by ivery female in the room, all haulding up there shkirts as though the kitchen were alive wid mice, while the men—the crachures made a onited move tord the winders and doors.

"Poot it in the fire!" yelled Minnie Carnavan at the top of her voyse.

"Throw it out of the window!" yells I.

But Larry Mulvaney had dropped it in the dishpan.

"Let it soke," ses he. "Mr. Moriarty will ye oblige me by pooting out the loonytick."

Ordher being raystored wid the ecksit of the Rooshun the minits of the meeting preseeded.

"Let us," ses I, "dishcuss our sad sichuwashun as ladies and gintleman. Mr. Momose," ses I, "let us here a ward from you, being a furriner, upon the subject."

The little Jap aroze promply, and tooched his hed to the flure itsilf. Whin hes throo bowing and hissing in his breth he shpoke at last:

"In Japan ———" ses he.

"Shpake to the quischun darlint," ses I. "We're in America."

"Wimmen," ses the Jap, "have been given but these wan opporchoonity to show what they can do in the warld—namely" ses he—"the wark of rooling the home. Does it not," ses he, "prove the sex infeerior—incompetent—weak? Man handles his biziness problems well and wiz biziness dispach," ses he; "but wimmen, given this wan only biziness to attind to fale—fale—badly. The soloshun is, let men ———"

The American girl aroze hastily.

"Are you making an attack upon our sex?" asks she wid indignashun.

"No, madame," ses the Jap, bowing for tin minits again. "Only upon ye're misthresses."

"Talking of misthresses," ses Mr. Moriarty, butting in. "Some are grand

and uthers are not. Nuthing makes me madder on airth than to have the ladies of the house interfeering in the shtable, pinning bo-nots onto the harnesses and ribbons about me own auld legs. I'm in favor," ses he, "of doing away wid all ladies in the shtable."

"Be careful" ses I, "of the subjick matter of discurse. Sertin subjecks are dangerous. Rolls, teeching, cullur, unfirnal masheens, and, finnly, sex. Drop the paneful subjick. Talk of misthresses as if they was sexliss."

"My madum," ses a spunky little Irish girl, "requires me to get up at seven A.M. in the morning. Whin are we to be alloud to have a moment for our beauty sleep?"

The quischun aroused instunt intrest among the fare sex—aven the men being intrested.

"Look at us all," ses the frorleen exsitedly. "Sum of us are—homely. Som few are not. Is it fare—is it rite," ses she, "that we be not given a chance all—to be beeyutiful?"

"Frorleen," ses I, "do you think a bit of shlape the morning will take the cracks out of yere face or make Minnie Carnavan's mouth shmaller?"

At that Minnie aroze in doodgin.

"Is it me ye're shpaking about?" ses she shcrewing up her mouth, so it looks like a cracked bad egg.

Up spoke the American girl.

"What of the ladies?" asks she shrilly. "Are they not given the chance to have cumplickshuns ———"

"—of strorberries and creem?" finishes the frorleen, whose own skin is the cullur of pie paste.

A neet little crachure stood up.

"I have a secret to tell," ses the girl, and I seen at wance that she was Frinch, lady's maid to Miss Una Robins.

"Behold zese hands!" ses she. "Do zay look pretty to you?"

"Very," ses Larry, and then shrunk back in his place at the look of contimp I'm afther giving him.

"It ees only looks zen," ses she. "But feel zem—feel zem—annybody—you, Meester Moolvaney!"

But I throost mesilf betune her and Larry.

"Miss—what's yere name?"

"Marie Montybilly," ses she.

"Well, then, Miss Monty for short," ses I, "allow me to infarm you that this is nayther a Coney Island car nor a box at the opera, as Miss Claire would be saying. There'll be no shly haulding of hands in the shadows."

"I mearly," ses she appolygiticully, "vished to show the crool cundishun of me hands. I ern my living," ses she, "viz zeses hands. See! I do so—ladies—so!" And she passed her hands over her face and pinched it.

"Ah," ses the Swedish sewing girl who calls hersilf a seamstriss also, "You are massuse."

"A beauty massoor," corrects Miss Monty hortily. "My hands were vonce loavely and soft," ses she. "But now look—feel ———"

And again I was obliged to poot a shtop to her ackshuns. The teers cum into her eyes. "Ah," ses she, "how my loavely hands are hard—rooined—rooined!"

"And why?" asks I, coming to the point.

"Because," ses she, "all my life is spint in rubbing the face and body of my mishtress wiz alcohol."

"What?" asks Mr. Moriarty. "Did you say whishkey."

"Well," ses I, "and isn't it yere biziness? Wud you rather *cook* the alcohol, thin?"

"No, no," ses she, "I meerly vished to illistrate the sacryvices made by us for ze ladies booty. See! all morning zay sleep—the sleep of beauty. Zen zay wake the wake of beauty. Zen the chocolate—ze barth—ze rub—ze ———"

"That will do," ses I, interrupting. "We'll not go into detales. What is the vote?"

"Later rising hours," ses the American girl bluntly.

"Somewan suggest an hour," ses I shmiling.

"Nine A.M." ses the frorleen firmly.

"My!" I joomped out of me seet. "Mr. John," sez I, "must have brekfust by ate sharp, and the babby is afther wanting his sereal at seven A.M. in the marning."

Minnie aroze.

"Allow me to shpake," ses she defyintly. "It's not so much the hours," ses she, "but the duties!"

A roar wint up at this.

"Yes, yes. That's it."

"That's it! That's it!" shouts the intire yunion at wance. As the noyse grajoolly subsides, I seen the frorleen stand up firmly. She's as historical and ixsitid as Mrs. Wolley whin somethings gone rong.

"First of all," shreeks the frorleen, "set down on paper in order what we desire—demand," ses she. "Our hours must be the same as those of any other warking wimmen—8 to 5—or 9 to 6."

"Are you crazy, frorleen?" ses I pityingly. "Shure the family ates at 7 P.M. at nite. Wud ye have me leeving the dishes over till marning?"

"That's a quischun for the mistresses to settle," ses the American girl, tossing up her chin as if she had a camio broach undher it also. "I move that moshun be passed."

"I'll be dummed if you do," ses I, litting the potato masher shtrike a turrible blow on the table. "Now," ses I, "I'm pressydint of this yunion. I've perlitely infarmed ye all that the babby is afther wanting his sereal at 7 A.M. in the marnin and dinner is sarved at the same hour at night. Are you thrying to confoose me figures. How do ye make eight hours of that?" ses I.

"But you must shange—shange!" cries the frorleen exsitedly. "Rayfoose to sarve sereal till 9."

"What's that ye're saying?" ses I, shtaring at her wid me mouth open. "And have the lamb go hungry?"

"Ah! Ah! Ah!" cries she, shaking hands first wid the American and then the Frinch and Swedish girl. "It is no use. She is impossible—impossible!"

"Am I or am I not Pressydint of this Yunion?" inquiries I.

"You are," ses she, promply, "but help us all to help our condishuns."

"The hours will remane oonchanged," ses I.

And thin a new quischun aroze.

"Mistresses," ses the American girl, "shud have more regard for the feelings of their sarvints. Why shud we be addressed by our Chrischun names?"

"And what wud ye have them calling you by?" inquiries I.

I seen her look exasperatedly at the frorleen.

"Why shud we be insoolted by the gift of there old clothes?" shrilly demanded the American girl.

"Are ye ixipicting the new wans?" inquires I, sarsarskulluly.

"No—no," ses she. "Let us not accipt charaty at all. Let us have wages which will enable us to buy new articuls."

Bridgay Fogarty aroze. She's the cook over at Dudleys and ways three hundred pounds. Shes after being cristened Bridget, but, being swate on Museer, she's changed the name to Bridgay and made it Frinch. Wance upon a time she shpoke wid sinse, letting loose anny dummed ward which sooted her tung. But now shes all simpers and titters.

"Can we not," ses she, "inthrajuice the Frinch methods into the houses? Let us say ———"

"For the luve of Mike sit down," ses Larry, whose the crachures own first cousin. Museer pulled the inds of his mustash, and toorned perlitely to me.

"Let us heer your opinyun of ze misthresses, mumsell," ses he. I beemed upon him.

"I'm glad for the opporchoonity to shpake," ses I, "if I'm alloud a ward in idgeways. There are misthresses and misthresses. The frorleen over there dishpises hers because she is foolish enuff to call her familyurly Frorleen. We all know what that meens," ses I wid contimp.

"It is a rayspictable term for miss," screems the frorleen exsitedly.

I nodded as if I didn't belave her, and wint on camly:

"The lady frum the South—at yere rite, museer—the wan also ankshiss to dishcuss the sex quischun, hates her mistresses because the lady wont call her frorleen in English. The Frinch musoo, who shpoke a moment sinse is mad clane throo because insted of rubbing her lady's face and body she'd like to be pinching it insted—Frinch fingers being fond of that exsisose. Excuse me, Museer," ses I perlitely. "Prisint company is always accepted. Minnie Carnavan dishpises all her misthress," I wint on, "for she's niver long enuff wid wan to get acquinted wid the puir crachure at all at all. The men have all been silint upon the paneful subject—all save wan—the gintleman frum Japan, who has so shmilingly explained to you why women fail as misthresses because of there sex; but, noon the less, all the men sarvints in this cuntry nearly who wark *oonder* these same ladies—mimbers of the aforesed dishpised sex—are almost intirely from the proud race proclaming the speeriarity of the mail sex. We cum at last to the reel quischun. Are misthresses, good, bad, or indiffrunt? They are! The quischun is ansered!"

There was silince after me iloquant wards. Then up rose the American girl again.

"Let us get down to bisiness," ses she. "Let us put several quischuns to the meeting and pass them. First shorter hours."

"That is desided," ses I, conthrolling the pertater masher.

"Sicond," ses she, ignoaring me. "The use of the parlor wance a week, already agytated by our frinds, the club ladies, to see our company in."

"What would ye be doing there?" asks I. "And sure how manny of you will occupy it at wance? Where will ye dance a quiet little jig, if ye've a mind to it, and where wud Mr. Moriarty or Bridgay Fogarty, or Minnie Carnavan there, be taking in peece her little nip of the crachure itsilf?"

Minnie shtood up.

"No gineral housewark!" she suddenly shouted at the top of her voyse.

The frorleen became histiricul. The Frinch musoo was weeping. The eyes of the American girl were flushing out of her hed. Up jumps the Frinch wan.

"Vunce," ses she, "ven ze nurse was seek, I mind zose awful leetle divils for tree hours by my vatch. Mon joor! Me—a mussoo!"

The cam voyse of the American girl indivvured to make itsilf hurd above the hubub of uther voyses.

"One wark only for each girl," ses she.

All over the room now, from the men as well as the wimmen the cries broke out.

"Yes—yes—yes. One wark only!"

"A cook," ses Bridgay Fogarty, "shall cook only."

"A waiter wait," pipes anuther.

"A nurse nurse."

"Miss Pressydint," ses the American girl; "may we ask that you kindly sit down these moshuns in ordher."

"Museer," ses I, toorning to him perlitely, "will ye kindly have the goodness to act as me suckercherry."

So Museer rote. Aich wan of us was to have a grand time indade, doing nothing all day but wan articul of wark, folding our hands betune times. Ivery family, rich or puir was to kape at leest five in hilp. "Whin," ses the frorleen, "the wark is properly devided and aich girl assined her proper wark—doing not a thing else—we shall have come to the mile-endium."

"Yes," ses the American girl fervently, "whin gineral housewarkers is an oonknown quolity."

"And what," finilly inquires the frorleen, looking at me cross-eyed, "shall we vote the fate of wan who brakes the rools?"

"The scab?" ses Minnie savugely, shnarling in me very face.

"She shall be torn to peeces—wiz our tungs!" whispers the Frinch musoo at the top of her voyse.

I shtood up. The trooth doned upon me. Here was I the Pressydint and fownder of the yunion, a victim of a base conspirissy—for, among the hole boonch of thim, I was the only gineral housewarker. The shtriking was to be dun by me aloan. I gripped titely hold of me faithful weppon, and shtarted for thim. I sloshed out rite and left.

Bridgay Fogarty faynted ded away in the arms of museer—and she waying three hundred pounds. The frorleen wint into vyillent histiricks as she run for her life frum the room, the hole lot of thim folering her leed, fleeing for there lives out of reech of me pertater masher, there preshus rools, resilations and moshuns moving wid thim.

I turned to Larry Mulvaney, the only wan of the boonch left.

"The meeting," ses I, "has broken up in dishorder."

"Delia, darlint," ses he, "wud ye mind calling the roll."

(*Saturday Evening Post,* August 22, 1908)

✳

ELSPETH

Elspeth was sixteen years old. She was pretty and temperamental, or, as an unkind friend once described her, "temperish". Her mother was exactly eighteen years older than Elspeth, and that fact the girl seized upon to "rub in" when the other woman attempted to prohibit the early association with youthful members of the opposite sex.

"You're a nice one to preach," cried Elspeth, her eyes dancing. "*You* must have had beaus when you were in short skirts. How old was father when you married him?"

"Your father was twenty-one", replied Mrs. Maitland, very rosy and flustered.

"Ah-*ha!* Well, *one* of you was of age anyway. That's enough, isn't it?" She added the last question with a certain artlessness that nevertheless perturbed her mother.

"But Ellie, dear, I wouldn't want you to make the mistake I did."

"Mistake!" Instantly Elspeth was on the warm defensive.

"Are you trying to say that your marriage to my father was a mistake then?" she demanded indignantly.

"Yes, it was a mistake, Ellie," affirmed her mother quietly, "for we were nothing but children, and I believe things might have been very different for your father. . . . And then his people might not. . . ."

"His people, uh?"

Elspeth seized the opportunity to demand information concerning "my father's people."

"Who were they, anyway? And why don't I know them? And where do they live? And why don't they like you mother? How is it you *never* talk about them?"

"Why, they are just ordinary people, Ellie. You don't know them because they live a great distance from here—in the east, and as for their liking or not liking me. . . ."

She hesitated, bit her lip and turned from her daughter. Instantly Elspeth sprang to her, excited, thrilled, and convinced that her "hunch" about her father and his people was correct. He had married beneath him! That was it. No doubt, he came of an illustrious and very wealthy family, while her mother . . . well, Elspeth's mother, as she once herself quaintly expressed it, had always been "Saturday's Child", who must work for her living.

"Mother, tell me the truth at once. You've kept it so long from me. *Isn't* there a great romance in your life about you and my dear dead father? Weren't his people multi-millionaires, or swells of some kind? Did they object to his marrying beneath him? Don't be hurt, muzzie. For my part I admire working girls, and if it wasn't for *other* plans already made, I might be one myself some day. But do tell me. . . ."

"Ellie, you foolish child, if you must know, your father's father was a plumber. My father was a college professor" . . .

"Oh-h-h!"

Ellie had turned pale. She was hard hit. Her eyes looked luminous and very large, as she took in this intensely humiliating information concerning her antecedents. Her pride was in the dust, and all of her fine castles tumbling about her. She felt that she never never could adjust herself to the thought of being a plumber's grandchild. After a long and painful silence, she said resentfully:

"Then I don't see why they objected to his marrying you."

"I never said that they did. You've been imagining things."

"Well, but they never speak to you."

"Yes, they do, when we see each other, but the years and distance are great separators, Ellie."

"And didn't you even elope then?"

"Now, Ellie, that's a foolish question. We came out here like a couple of foolish children to avoid the objections which our parents naturally were raising to our marriage on account of our extreme youth."

"Anyway", said Ellie triumphantly, "you *did* elope. You can't get away from that."

Mrs. Maitland sighed, and Elspeth, her attention already diverted by a group of young people passing the house added hastily:

"Poor old muzzie! Well, you should worry!" Then screamed to the passing girl without:

"Hi-yi, Dot! Wait for me, will you!" She was out of the house in a flash, and arms linked with her friend's was waltzing down the street to the strains of a whistled melody, which came from the background of youths who loitered, simpering, behind the girls.

Mrs. Maitland, looking after the dancing young figure disappearing down the pretty tree-ed street again sighed.

* * *

It was no easy matter to govern the headstrong passionate young creature that fate had confided to her care, and whom she was obliged to leave all of the week days. Ellie's wants grew like an ever rolling snow ball, and there were so many things she was obliged to ban, for the girl's own good, and neither Ellie's tears nor her defiance were comforting matters to face upon her return from work. She had solved the problem of the play, the dance, the movie and the joy rides with gay parties of young folk, and she no longer sat up for Elspeth, dancing till the small hours. They had come to a satisfactory arrangement. Elspeth was to have definite evenings out; she was to be home at a stated hour, and her mother would know exactly who was her escort and who constituted the party. On the other hand, she agreed to allow her child to invite her friends to the house on the evenings she was in. Indeed the little house rang with mirth and music and motion day as well as night. Upon her return from work, it was no uncommon thing to hear the gramophone bleating out some banging waltz or foxtrot, as the whirling young couples ranged over the entire lower floor. Rugs were pulled up, and furniture thrust back to the wall. Elspeth's lovely, flushed face and starry eyes somehow compensated the mother for the sacrifice of those peaceful hours which in her heart of hearts she craved above all things.

Ellie always broke like a flower from the midst of the merriest group, and rushing to her mother, she would cry breathlessly something like this:

"Oh Muzzie, isn't that just a pippin of a waltz song? Don't you just *love* it? Old thing dear, your supper's red hot in the oven. I've got it all fixed for you, angel."

Her mother often thought that she would have preferred to buy or make the cake herself rather than clean up after Elspeth, who thrust pans behind and under the stove, and piled pots and dishes and cups into pails and "any old place" where they could be hidden for the time being.

* * *

However, the noise and movement that seemed always somehow to be in the wake of Elspeth and the upset house, over which a trail of the girl's things were scattered were minor matters compared with a more serious menace to the peace of mind of her mother. The business woman was none the less mother enough to regard with indulgence mere matters of noise and sauciness, and all girls at that age, she believed, had a constitutional reluctance to housework. Girls of Elspeth's time, thought her mother sadly, literally jazzed their way through life, while their bewildered and befuddled parents prayed for that period to pass hastily, and sometimes wondered why God had cursed them. So she blamed not her daughter for what she believed was the inherent nature of a girl of her age, and she endured with a mother's patience the affliction of the innocuous company of immature youngsters continually in her house, and that atmosphere of careless disorder that pervaded the place. Then suddenly she found herself fronted by a new problem— one that aroused her alarm and concern and kept her up nights, hovering at the top of the stairs or the hall, leaning over the banister to peer down and listen, till Elspeth should come slowly and reluctantly to bed.

All the way up in the car, Mrs. Maitland had been thinking of Hal Holloway, and of that tumultuous hour the night before, when her daughter had flown into a passion at her attempt to curb an affair that was taking on serious proportions.

* * *

Holloway was a newcomer in Elspeth's "crowd", and was older than her other friends. His people belonged on the West side of the town. A McGill student, home for the summer vacation, he had in some way drifted into this younger set on the humbler side of the city and of which Elspeth was the leading spirit and magnet. There was something magnetic about Elspeth's personality, something that drew about her all the young people of the neighborhood, and made her highly popular wherever she went. She seemed to live and thrive upon excitement and thrills. Elspeth had no patience with the leisurely wayfarers along life's pretty pathways; she herself was breathlessly engaged in hurtling her way through. It seemed to her mother that this strange child of hers was always running, like one in a breathless race, and many a time she tried to check and hold the girl back in her headlong career.

"Ellie, Ellie, don't go through life as if you were in a race to catch a train. There's whole heaps of time. Walk, dear, or better still, sit down awhile by the wayside."

Elspeth, flushed, tense, sparkling laughed in her mother's face. "Old Sloweypokey" she called the woman who was doing a man's work in the world.

"Thrills and ripples, muzzie! That's all that's worth while in life. When the bubbles go, then what's left is stale and dull."

Yet the coming of young Holloway had wrought in a few days that change in Elspeth that all her mother's admonitions had failed to effect. All of a sudden, Elspeth had turned strangely still and sober. And with this subtle change in the girl's nature, the whole course of life in the business woman's house somehow altered also.

No longer Mrs. Maitland returned to a house shaking with music and mirth, with every light going brightly. Now the lights were always dim, or more often than not, the place was dark. No longer Elspeth burst from that bright bouquet of young friends surrounding her, and fell upon her mother with extravagant expressions of welcome, with kisses and cajolery. A new Elspeth came out of dim corners of the room, and followed by Hal Holloway, greeted her mother with the intensest seriousness and with unwonted tenderness and emotion.

Elspeth's confidence had always been reluctantly given to her mother. She was of that type of girl, who hesitate to confide the serious matters of life to their own mothers, but pour them in a flood into the sympathetic and appreciative ear of an exclaiming and understanding friend sworn to deadly secrecy by the symbol of crossing a neck and crossing a heart and hoping she "might die if I tell." However, she was so impulsive and transparent, that her mother knew she was incapable of holding a secret for long, and sooner or later it would be "let out."

Mrs. Maitland waited a week to learn something about her daughter's latest friend, he who had "cut out" all of her boy and girl friends, and who had the effect upon the spirits of the girl of what a resentful friend termed a "dampener". But if Elspeth's laughter and gay chatter no longer filled the house, nor the rush of her flying feet was heard, there was a light in her eyes that had a poignant beauty all of its own. If love does not make life joyful; if bliss is illusory, at least it gilds and transforms one's life with an exquisite touch of artistry that is hard to analyse.

* * *

That night, Elspeth had come slowly up to bed and in the dark undressed and got in silently beside her mother. For a long time that silence that does not always mean sleep reigned in the room, and then the mother discovered that her daughter was trying to smother her sobs in her pillow.

"Ellie, are you awake?"

Silence—Ellie frantically trying to control her voice. After a moment:

"No. What d'you want?"

"I just wanted to talk to you about this—er—young Holloway. Who is he, dear?"

A stiffening of the young creature beside her in bed, and then a little gasping cry, like a child's. Ellie and Hal Holloway had had their first "lover's quarrel", but not for worlds would she have admitted this to her mother, though, in fact, the quarrel had, in a way, been on her mother's account, for Ellie had refused nobly, as she believed, to listen to the pleading proposals of the boy who passionately had begged her to leave her mother and fare forth with him into the wonderful world that he pictured to her was without.

Mrs. Maitland leaned across, put her arms about her child and waited. After a while a muffled voice said:

"Muzzie, do go to sleep. Don't bother 'bout me. I I—j-j-just g-got a t-too—tooth-ache."

"Who is this young Holloway?" persisted her mother.

"Oh he's just—just Hal Holloway that's all. I don't want to talk about him."

Ellie's voice had an edge of rising irritation. After the sacrifice she had made on her mother's account, she felt that it was a shame to be repaid in this way.

"Why does he come here so often? You are too young. . . ."

"Now don't begin that. . . ."

"Well, but I must. I should like to know what he has said or done to make you change so. You are not yourself at all. I never saw such a change in a girl."

"I'm just the same as I always was, and I wish to goodness you'd stop quizzing me like this."

"Ellie", said her mother patiently, "you are really nothing but a little girl, when all's said and done, and if I were you I'd hold on to my youth as long as I could. You'll be a long time old, and such a little while young. You don't know how precious youth is. Do hold to it, darling, as long as you can."

"Do pity's sake don't start preaching at this hour of the night."

"I'm not preaching, dear. I just want you to understand. Now, I don't want you to tell stories about your age. I heard you to-night. You told Mr. Holloway you were going on to nineteen."

"So I am!" came swiftly from Elspeth.

"Yes, going on—three years off," said her mother dryly.

"Well, its going on just the same, and I don't see why you need to rub it in. It isn't *my* fault I'm only sixteen. I *loathe* being so young!"

"Don't be foolish, Ellie. You'll be old soon enough and. . . ."

"I wish you wouldn't nag me all the time. Can't you let a fellow alone a minute?"

"That's not a nice way to talk to your mother, Elspeth."

"I don't care. You started it. I wish you'd leave me alone and not ask questions about things that—that arn't any one's business but mine. I guess I know how to take care of myself."

"You don't," said her mother quickly, "or you wouldn't sit in a darkened room with a young man, and you wouldn't let a stranger hold your hand. It was all I could do to keep from walking in and ordering him out of my house."

Elspeth had leaped up in bed, pulling the covers half off her mother.

"You wouldn't dare do such a thing."

"Yes, I would dare, Elspeth. I'd dare anything for your good."

"It wouldn't be for my good. It would *kill* me. I'd be so—so mortified I'd want to crawl into the smallest hole in the earth. I could never never look him or anyone else in the face after a thing like that."

"Lie down, Elspeth."

Even mothers are only human, and subject to irritation when exasperated beyond measure.

Elspeth subsided to the bed, but she still flung forth her defiance to her mother.

"Well, if you talk like that, I won't listen to you."

"You *must* listen to me, Elspeth. Now that we've started upon this subject, I have something to say to you, and questions I must ask you."

"I've got my two hands over my ears and I can't hear a word you say," cried the young rebel, while the older woman's hands itched to box those allegedly hidden ears. If her daughter lacked self control, she at least prayed for patience to endure this unwarranted defiance and gratuitous impudence. The long silence that followed was broken by a loud sob from the now secretly remorseful Elspeth, convinced that she had alienated her mother forever more. That sob however was sternly ignored by the indignant Mrs. Maitland, and the girl too proud to make the desired overtures, added fuel to the flame by bursting out with passionate abandon:

"All right, then, I will tell you, since you want to know so much about us. I'm head over hands and heels in love with Hal Holloway, and so is he with me, and we *adore* the very ground he—I mean we—stand upon, and its all on account of *you* that we quarrelled to-night; but I'm going to make up with him the first thing to-morrow, and you'll see what we'll do. We're going to get married, that's what we are. You just wait and see if we don't."

"Don't be foolish, Ellie. You can't get married at your age. It's against the law. It can't be done, without my consent."

"We can too. He's of age already and I could easily pass for nineteen, and he knows a man that. . . . So you see."

"All I see is that you are a very silly girl. I see too that I've been far too lenient with you, and it's just about time that I took some steps to restrain you. You've two more years to finish at High school. The reason you didn't pass last year is because you were fooling around with boys. If you had any sense you'd soon see that you cannot take anything they say seriously. They don't mean half the foolish stuff they talk about."

"I *know* the *average* boy doesn't, but Hal's different. He means every last word he says. He doesn't even know what it *means* to pretend that he cares for a girl when he doesn't. He told me that I was the only girl he'd ever known that he cared a button about. Those are his very words."

"All the same, I think I'll have to curtail his visits if it is going to upset you like this."

"Who's upset? What are you talking about now?"

"You are, and so am I. You will never make your grade at school if you don't get this boy nonsense out of your head."

Again Ellie jerked up in bed, wild and furious again.

"Thousands—*millions* of girls don't go through High school, and why should I, who hate it? I *see* myself going through."

"That's enough of that sort of talk. I'll send you to boarding school."

"Me? Boarding school?" Her voice rose shrilly. "I see myself going to prison. Oh yes, I'll go like a tame lamb, won't I though? Don't you see me?"

Her impudence was intolerable. Her mother had the impulse to whip her as she had done when Elspeth was a little girl, and in a tantrum would throw herself upon the floor and kick and scream with rage.

"Lie down. I've had enough of this."

"I want to know what. . . ."

"Never mind that. The important thing is that we must have our sleep. I, because I must go to work in the morning, and you because you are working yourself up to a senseless state of excitement about literally nothing."

"Is it *nothing* that for the first time in my whole life I should be madly in love with the only man I. . . ."

"I don't want to hear any more of that ridiculous nonsense. You are too young to know your own mind and. . . ."

Recklessly, passionately Elspeth flung her last bomb:

"What of you then? You didn't think *you* were too young to marry at my age. *You* went ahead and did as *you* liked, and I can do the same."

"Ellie, I want to go to sleep. You forget that I am a working woman."

"Who started this anyway?"

"Never mind that. Lie down there. We'll talk this over to-morrow."

* * *

But when to-morrow came, the clock pointed to 8:30 when Mrs. Maitland awoke, after a few hours sleep snatched toward morning. Elspeth lay with her flushed cheek turned into the pillow. The turbulent emotions of the night were all sunk into the deep sleep of health and youth, and her mother, with a sigh that had in it an element of compunction—after all, she should not have taken the child seriously she told herself—bent above her to drop a kiss upon the petulant young lips, ere, too late for breakfast, she hurried out for her day's work.

That day was long and hot. Part of the time her head ached and all day long she thought of Elspeth—Elspeth, sharp tongued and hot hearted. After all, her side to the question has to be considered. To her at least her love affair was a serious matter. She felt that she had handled the situation very badly. She should have kept her head and not allowed the child's extravagant expressions to offend or hurt her. Her self reproach was followed by an attempt to formulate some plan by which she might bring about a change in their mode of living. That was it—a change. They both needed it. They needed to break away from the habits and ties that chained them down like galley slaves. Elspeth was entitled to a real home, such as other girls had, and not the makeshift careless establishment over which there was no real head, and which floundered like a crazy derelict perilously near to the rocks. And Elspeth was entitled to a real mother. Not this business machine that could only throw to her a few snatches of her time. No wonder they had drifted so far apart that the girl preferred to pour her confidences into the ears of a stranger rather than her mother's. It was her own attitude, not Ellie's, that was to blame for their estrangement. Her nature was the antithesis of her daughter's. Shy, guarded, reticent, she held everyone at arm's length. But her little daughter—that was not right! They should not be so far apart; she should have affected some of that buoyancy of spirit so peculiar to her child, and which she sadly lacked. She wondered if it was because of her long life of work. She had been working now for seventeen years. That was quite a record. She took the full blame for Elspeth's angry retorts, her insolence, even her outbursts of temper. Elspeth had never been properly "raised". Her mother excused or drew a veil over each and all of her defects. She told herself that it was a career in itself to be a mother. She had stolen the greater or part of herself from Elspeth to whom it rightfully belonged and given it to an office—a mechanical business that ran along from day to day and year to year, built up and cultivated and toiled over for just one purpose, the unlovely pursuit of the everlasting dollar.

* * *

"Of what are you thinking?"

The question came from the desk adjoining her own. For some time, her employer had been engaged in the pleasing study of Mrs. Maitland's lovely profile, pink ear and flushed cheek.

She came back to earth with a sigh, and met the quizzical glance with a troubled one.

"I was just thinking," she said, "that I'll have to quit."

He was moved enough to stare at her with dropped jaw. She had always been an enigma to him, this pretty woman content to labor along from year to year, without any of the pleasures or compensations that should have been the portion of one such as she. He knew of Elspeth, and surmised that "that girl" was the reason why her mother had never married, nor permitted herself even the friendship of a man. Once or twice Elspeth had come to the office, and there was that about her thorny little personality which apprised the employer of her mother that she was violently opposed to any one encroaching upon her mother's thought or time besides herself. Once he had escorted Mrs. Maitland home, after some night work at the office, and ascending the little steps to the house, he had made a slight motion to follow Mrs. Maitland into the house, when Elspeth, behind her mother's back, had deliberately closed the door in his face. It was such a quick act, so final and eloquent of the girl's opinion of him, or for that matter, any man who might be interested in her mother. Elspeth's attitude was similar to that she took about her mother's clothes and personal possessions. She had far more things than her mother, but she was utterly callous in the way she helped herself to what she chose of her mother's things, and even impudently justified this course, with one of the pretty, naughty tosses of her head:

"Muzzie, what's yours is mine, and what's mine's my own," she would say mischievously, and receive either a kiss or a reproving shake of the head, for Mrs. Maitland had a passion for keeping her things neatly and in order, and it was distracting to find all her possessions tossed over and hidden about in this or that drawer or lost. And so with men, or for that matter, women. Elspeth would have squelched any friendship of her mother's. "Muzzie" belonged to her and to her solely, and she didn't propose to share her with any other living soul in the world. She wanted "muzzie" to "mourn" a life time for that father whom she had so rosily colored in her imagination.

"Quit! You! That's a preposterous idea!"

"Even me!"

She was slightly smiling, and he noted that her eyes looked very tired. It occurred to him that she was not sleeping nights and he said gruffly:

"You need a vacation. Don't wait till August. Take it now."

"I need a permanent vacation," she said slowly. "I don't want to work any more. I'm tired out."

"Can you afford to quit?"

He studied her keenly, and with some anxiety. He knew little about her financial status. Her salary was a good one, for work of that sort. He would have liked to make it much larger, but there were three other partners in the concern, and they had to be considered. Her home, he knew was a modest one. Rent on that side of the city was low he had heard, but even so, it must cost considerable to maintain the place, even in the slap dash way in which "that girl" ran things. Elspeth, by the way, was the housekeeper of their peculiar menage. Furthermore, Elspeth he felt sure, must cost her mother a pretty penny for clothes and the thousand and one things he suspected she demanded and got from her mother. How, then, had it been possible for Mrs. Maitland to save enough out of her salary on which to retire. She took her time about replying to his query, as if she weighed the question in her mind and hesitated to reveal the meagreness of her resources even to this man whom she knew so well.

"It's true I havn't much."

She gave him a small wry smile, that somehow touched him:

"One can't save much on a Fairbanks-Ross salary." That was the name of the firm.

"Still, I've managed to keep up an endowment policy, and now its about due. I can go along on that for awhile at least."

"I see. You know your own business. If you feel that you can carry on with the Insurance money. . . ."

"Oh we couldn't live very high of course, but we'd manage somehow."

"Look here."

Her employer was leaning across the desk. He had grey curly hair and bushy eyebrows; otherwise his face was almost young, and he had a long lean body that stretched up like a young athlete's when he rose from his chair.

"Look here! What's the matter with you and I. . . ."

"I know what you are going to say, but you can stop right there. No. That's final."

"You don't know what I'm going to say."

"Yes, I do, because you've said it before."

"Hmph! So I have, doggone it."

She laughed suddenly, and the pink glowed in her cheeks. She stood up, and began pinning on her hat. He blurted out angrily:

"I know I'm a tough old nut, but I'm square, and you might do worse."

"I know I might, and you're not tough. If you say hard things about yourself, I'll be very cross with you. I—I—will say instead that its been fine to work for you, and in a way its been a compensation for other things—this—this fellowship and friendship. I don't want anything else. It wouldn't do."

She held out her hand, which was first sulkily ignored and then grasped in a rough, strong hold.

"Good-b . . . " she began.

"None of that goodbye business now," he growled. "You go on your holiday. I've a hunch you'll be back soon. Your job and I will be waiting for you, together or separately, just as you say."

"Thanks, thanks, very much."

She wished that the warm clasp of that strong hand over hers did not have such a strange effect upon her. It was ridiculous that her heart should be thumping like that. Whatever in the world was the matter with her? Why, she was almost as foolish as Elspeth. Elspeth! At the thought of her girl, she withdrew her hand, crimsoning under the strange look of the man beside her.

"Well, goodbye, then," she said.

"Not on your life, it's not goodbye."

She laughed, and her laugh had a silvery tinkle. She was very pretty with her flushed cheeks and bright eyes.

"Goodnight, then."

"That's better."

He smiled now, and she knew the warmth and comfort of that smile. It set her blood racing, and she went out from the office feeling well and young again.

* * *

As she stepped into the little hallway her first feeling was one of exasperation. Really, it was too bad of Elspeth not to have a single light going. She found and punched the button on the wall. The living room and hall were flooded with sudden light, but there was no one in even the farthest of corners, and not Ellie or young Holloway came from behind the folds of the portieres or from out the little sun room that adjoined the parlor. Elspeth had even omitted the pretense of a meal for her mother, and Mrs. Maitland found nothing better in the ice box than a cold mutton chop and a bit of wilted lettuce. She warmed over the chop and made herself some tea. The tea cleared her head, and when she went to her room, the dreariness of the day and the sense of exhaustion following her sleepless night pressed less heavily upon her. She even found herself smiling in a sort of absent way at her own face in the mirror.

After all, she was only thirty-five and in these days, women of thirty-five, dressed and felt and looked like "chickens". That was one of Ellie's terms, and she laughed girlishly at the thought. Many women of her age "fixed up" a lot. A bit of talcum powder was her only assistance to the smooth and clear complexion with which nature had so kindly endowed her. Even her hair was untouched, though it was the fashion of even young girls to "henna" or "brighten up" their hair. Mrs. Maitland's had that live young growing look. Its waves were smooth and natural, and it was the color of dark gold. She said to herself suddenly:

"It's perfectly ridiculous for me to stand here and admire myself in this way. It doesn't matter the least little bit whether I'm young or old, or pretty or ugly. I'm just Elspeth's mother—that's all. Elspeth!"

Everywhere about that room Elspeth had left her mark. Even all around the edges of that mirror, photographs of the girl's friends had been stuck into the ridge. On the left side, quite prominently stuck out, there was a piece of white paper, and presently Mrs. Maitland saw it. Idly she pulled it out and unfolded it. Elspeth's childish handwriting was sprawled across either side of the sheet, and right in the middle of the note there was an unmistakable smudge.

"Dearest Muzzie:

Now I know you're going to be awfully mad with me, but I just had to do it or bust. Hal and I adore each other, and we couldn't live another single day apart. So we are going to" Here a word had been scratched out . . . "away, and we're going to get married, whether the old law says we can or not. I know you'll say I'm too young and all the rest of that guff, but if you only knew how I fairly loathed that word—*young* you'd never use it again. Besides, I always remind myself that you were almost as young as I when you ran away and got married too, and Hal says what one person can do, so can another. So, Muzzie dear, do forgive me, and won't you like an old love, break the news to Hal's people. They'll be awful mad too, but we should worry. He's of age, and his parents can't do a thing about it, and he says he doesn't mind giving up college so long as he has me—he says I'm worth ten colleges and more—and as for me, Oh muzzie love, I know you won't do anything to hurt your own and only daughter.

Elspeth."

Mrs. Maitland's hands shook. The paper fluttered from her fingers—drifted to the floor.

"Oh Ellie, Ellie!" she cried. "My *baby!*"

* * *

After a long interval she picked up the letter, and read it through again. A smile forced its way to her lips, and her eyes were moist. How characteristic that letter was of Elspeth—poor, impulsive, hot-hearted, hot-headed child! Elspeth, who loathed Youth! Ah! If she but knew!

Holloway! That was the boy's name. Ellie had asked her to break the news to his people. But who were his people and how was she to find them. Calgary was a big city now—80,000 population, and more and more people were coming in with every year. Still, the name was not a common one; indeed it was the name of the biggest man in the country so far as that went. It was plainly her duty, at all events to discover who were Hal Holloway's people, and, as Ellie had required, acquaint them with the fact of their son's marriage.

She went slowly down to the little hall again, and sat by the telephone table, turning over the leaves till she came to the H's, and then running her finger down till she came to the clan of Holloway. Five of them had telephones, and these one by one she called, and to each query whether they had a son named Harold or Hal, came back the clear response. No, they had not.

There remained then merely the one name, Senator T. Beveridge Holloway, the big man of Alberta. She became flustered at the thought that he could possibly be the father of Ellie's young man. In her little world of work and Elspeth, she had learned very little concerning the families of any of the handful of Alberta magnates, as she lacked that feminine quality of curiosity that caused people to pry into the intimate secrets of their neighbors and fellow townspeople. She was indifferent to and most incapable of gossip.

She put her finger in the circle that caused the little automatic disc to ring, and the number W 4839 revolved around. A gruff voice at the other end admitted he was Senator Holloway, and a moment later, yes, he had a son named or known as Hal, though, shouted the senator, the lad's name was Harold Beveridge Holloway.

Then she broke the news to him, a bit tremulously, without awe of the magnate, but with a sympathetic thrill as she realized the power of the man who was now her Elspeth's father-in-law.

"Your son and my daughter have eloped and. . . ."

"What's that you say? What are you talking about?"

She replied:

"I said your son and my daughter have eloped. They are married now."

There was a silence, bristling with explosive energy, and presently a voice shot back through the 'phone.

"Who are you?"

"You mean my name? It's Maitland."

"Never heard it before. Who are you, and what the blazes do you mean by coming with a story like that. Who are you? What do you do?"

"Why I—I'm a stenographer in the Fairbanks-Ross company's office, and I. . . ."

"A stenographer!"

He shouted the word as if it were something offensive and damnable.

"And you're trying to tell me you've hooked my boy, are you?"

"I don't know what you mean. I'm trying to tell you that your son is married to my daughter."

"Like hell he is!"

Words were sizzling at the other end, and somehow the fury reminded her strangely of Ellie when Ellie was in one of her tantrums. This Senator Holloway was barely able to stutter, and the oaths he was using were unbelievably grotesque and strange. A string of them followed one after another in a long stream, and words were cut in half for oaths to be slipped in between.

Mrs. Maitland stared at that telephone, the color ebbing and flowing from her cheeks. That she should be called such names, and spoken to in this dreadful fashion. That she should be accused of conspiring to. . . .

She let the telephone receiver lie on the table, but the shouting, fearfully swearing voice issued from its end no longer at her ear.

". . . . . . not a G . . . d . . . penny! Two more years at college. . . . cut him off. . . . young cub. . . . blanketty blank fool. . . . . couple of adventuresses and cheat swindlers, blackmailers . . . I'll show you . . . an."

After a while she gingerly lifted the telephone receiver and hung it back upon the hook. Then her finger slowly picked out another number, and whirled the disc around.

"Mr. Fairbanks?"

"The same."

"Mrs. Maitland speaking. About our conversation to-day. I've changed my mind."

"Told you you would. What's the reason?"

"Well, I've just changed my mind, that's all."

"Glad to hear it. What about that Insurance?"

"I—I've got to use it for something else. You see I—I've got another person to support now and. . . ."

"What? Say that again."

"Yes, another person—a boy at college. I want him to go on. He—He's
my son-in-law you see!"

"Well, for the love of Pete. Has that girl gone and done it?"

"Oh yes, and I think it's my duty to take care of them both, and that's
why I have to keep my—my job. I hope you havn't advertised yet—have
you?"

"Not yet, but I will unless you'll do something for me."

"What?"

"Got your hat on. I'm coming over with my car. You're going for a ride
with me."

Her voice was vibrant, a young treble voice, quite as sweet as a girl's and
with even the little thrill of laughter to it that somehow was characteristic
rather of Elspeth.

"I don't mind," she said.

(*Quill*, January 1923)

PART 2

NONFICTION

THE HALF CASTE

Perhaps one of the most pitiful and undesirable positions in society in Japan is that held by the half breed. I mean the half breed whose blood is a mixture of the Caucasian and Japanese. It is usually the mother who is a Japanese, the father being a foreigner. Born in Japan, and entered on the registers of that country as Japanese citizens, they live strangely isolated both from their mother's people and from their father's. If they at all resemble their father, or act or live different from those about them, the Japanese look down on them, alluding to them half contemptuously, as "half castes." On the other hand, Westerners are inclined to regard them with interest, strongly mixed perhaps with a pity that the proud sensitive heart of the half breed resents.

Their Disposition

The Japanese half breeds are wonderfully precocious, their sharpness and brightness being almost abnormal, though as a rule they are so versatile that their cleverness is too general for them to accomplish much in any one direction. Furthermore they are extremely erratic and moody, made happy by the smallest things, and plunged into the depths of despair at trifles.

Some one once said to me that they considered half breeds as a rule hard and heartless. I have found it to be the reverse. It is true that they are reticent and slow to make friends, and even where they make them, it is observed no one ever gets really close to them, yet when it comes to an act of wonderful heroism or unselfishness, I am never surprised to find a half breed the one who has done it. They are generous to a fault to those they love, and bitter as death to those they dislike.

From their earliest childhood, whether in this country, Europe or Japan, they are made to feel that they are different from those about them. Children are very often the cruelest of torturers as well as the keenest sufferers. The sufferings of half breeds while in their childhood from the hands of unscrupulous, thoughtless children, can never perhaps be understood or appreciated by any one.

Always Despised

Should they be educated in Japan, the Japanese children will despise them because their fathers were Kirishitans (Christians). In this country or in England they are accused of being "niggers," "Chinese," etc. Such methods of torture are administered to these children under the very noses of the teachers both in Japan and other countries, though it is less common here in America. When it is brought to the notice of the teachers, they will perhaps administer some slight punishment, and the incident passes from their minds. How many acts of cruelty are daily performed by thoughtless children unknown by parents or teachers. To a supersensitive nature such as is that of the half breed, the smallest cut or slight is felt. This is how cynics are made. Half breeds are either cynics, or they are philosophers or geniuses. They are seldom ordinary—seldom normal.

I knew a little half breed Japanese girl of twelve years who used to say that she loved and hated every country in the world. It made her angry to find people patriotic, because patriotism seemed to her so selfish—an exalted sort of conceit. This is how patriotism appeared to a little girl who had no real country to be proud of. Perhaps both of the countries she might have called home, had bruised her so that in the midst of her yearning and love for them, she resented the fact that she herself belonged to neither of them, inasmuch as she was an alien on both soils—entirely different from those about her.

Not Demonstrative

Japanese half breeds are not demonstrative, nor do they love a great many people. When, however, their deeper feelings are touched, then the passion and trust with them is such that its very strength becomes a weakness. They are not lukewarm in their affections, hating fiercely or loving passionately; their lives are consumed with the intensity of their feelings, and the inevitable crosses they are bound to encounter.

The hardest, most cynical, careless and pessimistic person I have ever known was a Japanese half breed; the tenderest, truest, most generous and unselfish person I have ever met was a Japanese half breed. They give all, or they give nothing. Can you get beyond the harsh, cold wall by which they surround themselves, forget their skepticism, their egotism and cynicism and reach the real warm, pulsating heart? Surely no heart beats more truly. You have discovered a new country. That being you have always considered so hard and proud has suddenly changed; he has melted into a yearning, hungry, human being. Pride, sensitiveness—these are the garments in which the half breed enwraps himself. We say, "A shadow passes by," but pull the garments aside even for a minute, and like Columbus in discovering the new world, your heart will beat with a rapture that is almost akin to pain. It is the revelation of your discovery. It is the pleasure that one might experience in discovering that something we had always considered the commonest brass was the brightest and best of gold, which wanted only the outside coating, that the rough handling of many had left on it, to be removed in order to show its genuineness. But alas! these qualities are so seldom discovered, and often the hungry heart of the half breed becomes so hardened from enforced isolation that in a rash despair he plunges into a life of excitement and pleasure where he is forgotten of all the world.

Lack Veneration

The Japanese half breeds seldom make good sons or daughters, nor do they have that great reverence and love for the parents which is common among children of ordinary parentage. I do not know why this is so, unless it lies in the fact that the same love and care that are given by most good parents to their children are withheld from them. Their educations are spasmodic; they are taught the smarter tricks of their father's country, and those of their mother's. Very often their parents do not live together and then they have merely the guidance of a parent who is embittered perhaps. Of course, there are exceptional cases, where the children are brought up entirely as their father's people, or as their mother's, but this is only in rare instances, and usually the Japanese half breed does not know the counsel, and the dearly-to-be-desired strict guidance of a father, or the watchful, tender loving care of a mother.

Childhood

It must not be imagined, however, that the half breed's life is altogether devoid of happiness. It is generally in their childhood that they really suffer the most. After that period is passed, they go out into the world prepared to encounter sorrows. It is noticeable that people who have suffered an isolated childhood, who in their early youth have been ridiculed and tortured by companions, for no other reason perhaps than that they were different from them, usually make the very best or the very worst of men and women. Some of them become quite philosophic, and it is natural for them to weigh everything that comes their way. They look back on their childhood with amazement, wondering how they could have let such trifles cause them so much misery. These ones doubtless even in childhood fought their ways among their school mates and demanded and got all their rights. On the other hand the over-sensitive ones are spoilt from childhood for any sort of a higher life. From constantly being called names and shunned, they become morose, bitter and harsh in their judgments.

Characteristics

Half breed Japanese children are as a rule very pretty. They have dark hair and eyes, and in that way resemble more the Japanese; in fact, they are in childhood decidedly of a Japanese type. As they grow older, however, their features assume rather the cast of a Western face, their features being very regular and finely formed. Their eyes are larger than the Japanese eye but smaller than a Westerner's, though brighter than an eye three times their size. They generally enjoy fine physical constitutions, though they are nervous, highly strung, jealous, conceited, yet humble and self-depreciating and overly modest at times, sarcastic, skeptical, generous and impulsive. It is hard to analyze their natures, because they are so changeable. They are born artists. Maybe they inherit this from the Japanese, and being born in that home of beauty their passionate love of nature can be understood. Although they seem to have very little love for any particular country, yet I believe had they a country of their own they would be the most patriotic people in the world, though some of them would likely disclaim this, as they so often boast that patriotism is merely an exalted form of narrowness.

They are extremely ambitious, but generally meet with so many disappointments and hamperments that it is not a common thing for any of them to be more than ordinarily successful in life. Often the greatest impediment to their success is their own erratic, proud natures. One does not often find a Japanese half breed criminal, however, though suicide among them is more common.

Possible Exceptions

There are a great number of Japanese half breeds, though they are scattered so much that it is not often one comes into contact with them. I wonder whether the sadness of their youth ever leaves them, or whether it leaves its mark on them forever. We hear of few, if any, instances of their distinguishing themselves before the world. Perhaps the children of Lafcadio Hearn, the American writer, and those of Sir Edwin Arnold, the English writer, whose mothers are Japanese women, will prove exceptions, as they will doubtless have the protection and love of these great men. There are many Japanese men, too, in this country who have married American or English women, and whose children receive every opportunity, but alas! for the hundreds of pitiful little ones who are born in Japan every year, and whose fathers they seldom know.

(*Conkey's Home Journal*, November 1898)

THE JAPANESE DRAMA AND THE ACTOR

Even in the primitive times singing, dancing, and playing on musical instruments were not uncommon in Japan. The old histories record that verses were sung and musical instruments played on.

A variety of Chinese music found its way into Japan in the twentieth reign of the Empress Suiko (612), and continued in favor for two hundred years. It was chiefly used in the Buddhist courts and temples. Mimashi, a native of Corea, became nationalized in Japan and set forth a claim that he had mastered the art of Kushimo, a certain kind of dancing. He thereupon was established in Sakurai, where he taught his art extensively. This is said to be the first notice of Chinese music being introduced into Japan. From that time it rose, and to this day the Yamatogaku has been handed down as the refined and unmixed music of Japan. It includes both musical tunes and dances, and is distinguished by these terms: on-gaku, meaning sound-gaku, and bugaku, or dance-gaku. The Chinese music, however, cannot be said to have been altogether popular with the Japanese. In fact, while it was the fashion of the Buddhist temples and the court, where it found high favor with the priests and nobles, nevertheless the Japanese public at large was not particularly interested in the form of the dancing or the tone of the music.

The rise of the Japanese drama itself did not actually occur till about the sixteenth century, and neither Chinese nor Corean music had aught to do with it.

The earliest dramatic productions were called the "Joruri," having derived their title from the heroine of the plays which dealt with the love affairs of the Lady Joruri, daughter of a wealthy countryman, and Yoshitsuné, brother of the founder of the feudal system, and one of the favorite idols of Old Japan. The author of this play was said to be a talented woman, by name Ono O-Tsu, a waiting-woman in the house of Ota Nobunaga, the Taiko's master.

Katari (narrative or recitation) dates from the most remote past. The production from the Joruri was first given out in Katari form by a blind priest, accompanied by the koto. It met with almost instantaneous success. The samisen had also about this time made its appearance and was used with effect in the recitation of the Joruri. This instrument came originally from the Loochoo Islands, and is now considered the national musical instrument in Japan. Some hold that the Spanish adventurers, the first of whom, Magellan, discovered the Philippines in 1520, introduced it into the archipelago, but there are many who strongly oppose this, denying that the instrument at all resembles the Spanish guitar. Another version of the origin is that the Loochooans used to play on an instrument with a long body made of snakeskin, which emitted a sound resembling the cry of an animal which preyed on the snake, and thus were able to ward off the snakes and reptiles with which their islands were infested. However the instrument found its way into Japan in 1558 and cat-skin was substituted for snake-skin, while the strings were tuned to the first, second, and fourth strings of the biwa. It was changed and improved in other ways, and became a necessary adjunct to the Joruri. From the time of the production of the Joruri, men of distinct talent began to arise all over the country and, following the example of O-Tsu, gave to their country excellent dramas and plays.

Puppets were made to act in accord with the narrative. Later Takemoto Gidayu, whose gifts as a musician seemed phenomenal, appeared in Osaka, and at the same time also came Chickamatsu Monzayemon, the Japanese Shakespeare. These two men formed a unique partnership and worked in unison together, for, while Chickamatsu, who was a year younger than Takemoto, wrote his magnificent plays, Takemoto would simultaneously recite and sing them with his wonted skill, and make his puppets perform in accordance with the narrative.

Chickamatsu wrote about sixty plays for Takemoto during the twenty-eight years of their acquaintance, and only two of his plays were not written for Takemoto, but for a pupil. This unique partnership between two men of such remarkable talent established the lyrical drama of Japan. Newspapers were unknown in those days, and every item of news was eagerly devoured. Takemoto would keep his eyes and ears alert and open for sensational occurrences. As soon as he heard of one that pleased him, he forthwith went to Chickamatsu, who used the subject before it became commonly known, and thus it was presented to the people as something fresh and novel. Chickamatsu excelled in his domestic plays rather than in historical, as in the latter he was forced to subordinate his genius to the popular traditions of historical characters, and also to regard the mental capacity of his audience. In 1687 Takemoto opened his first puppet show in Osaka, where he sang and recited himself. At this time he was thirty-five years of age. His fame eclipsed any and all of his rivals.

Chickamatsu Monzayemon, who was born in 1653, had been brought up in the temple, and was in the service of a court noble for some time. He began writing libretti for puppet shows. He wrote eight plays before he produced the first of his great plays for Takemoto. These first plays had no particular merit and are extinct in literature to-day.

Takemoto died in 1714, and ten years later his then celebrated collaborator followed him.

The beauty and diction of the plays of Chickamatsu are almost unsurpassed in Japanese literature, and his mastery of language was such that even the scholars of the classical and Chinese schools gave him their sympathy and admiration. His greatest play is the Tenno-Amijima. It describes the suicide of two lovers, a paper dealer, and a courtesan. It was written while he was in his sixty-eighth year. After the death of Chickamatsu, joint authorship in writing dramas came into fashion, and a number of talented writers collaborated with each other in the production of celebrated plays. Each one would be assigned a certain portion to write. Then they would meet together and the whole would be thoroughly revised and gone over.

"The Chushengura," by Tukeda Izuama, is supposed to be the best of these dramas. It is to-day the stock play, and will draw full houses when all others fail. Danjuro, the leading actor in Tokyo to-day, has played the rôle of hero no less than forty-eight times. Chickamatsu Monzayemon, Chickamatsu Hayi (1725–1783), and Takeda Izuma form the great trio of lyrical dramatists; but after their death the school declined. Few plays of any great note or merit have been produced since; and with the decline of this school the puppet shows fell out of favor. They are still held regularly in Osaka and Tokyo, but the theatre has practically superseded them.

These dramas, formerly produced with puppets and narrative and singing, now are produced on the stage, though the lyrical drama is not the only form to-day. Crude plays were written in the seventeenth century by actors owning their own theatres, who thus added original plots and situations to their repertoire of lyrical plays. And in the following century, even while the dramas of Chickamatsu Monzayemon and his successors were still at the zenith of power, the prose drama took a high literary form under Tsuuchi Jihei, who was succeeded by many talented writers, the last of whom was Kawalake Mokuami (1816–1893). But even the high standard of the literary excellence of their plays could not diminish the popularity of the lyrical dramas of Chickamatsu Monzayemon and his successors. The Restoration even has not yet given rise to a new form of drama.

In 1564 O-Kuni, a priestess of Izuma, appeared among the dancing girls, and by her improvement in the art added to the excellence of even the drama itself. At first she went from city to city and danced to collect funds to repair the great shrine of that province. In Kyoto she danced before the Shogun himself, and pleased him so much that he at once ordered the shrine to be repaired out of the public fund. The girl, who was beautiful, young, witty, and talented, remained in the capital and soon captured the heart of a young noble, a retainer in the Shogun's household named Nagoya Sanza-yemon. He wrote simple dramatic pieces for her, and they were privately married. When the Shogun heard of it he was very wroth and immediately discharged the young man from his service, and the couple set out together in their profession, playing in open air or in booths. They met with great success and had a large following. The plays of O-Kuni are known as "O-Kuni-Kabuki." O-Kuni is represented in old prints and picture books as being dressed in the most dazzling attire, her wealth of hair in the wildest confusion about her, a golden crown on her head, her face and form of an almost unearthly beauty. She carried all by storm before her, and became the mad fashion of the hour in despite of the displeasure of the Shogun himself, who, however, subsequently forgave the young couple.

In the era of Seiho and Keian (A. D. 1644–1881) women were forbidden to appear on the stage and men were substituted.

The first theatre of Japan was constructed in 1624 in Yedo (Tokyo). It has been burnt down frequently or destroyed by the authorities. It was built by Suruwaka Kanzaburo and was owned by his hereditary descendants. To-day semi-European theatres are now built with high brick walls. There are, I believe, six large and twelve small theatres in Tokyo.

While, of course, the truly remarkable performance of Takemoto and his puppets was never questioned, still the first really great actor to perform on the Japanese stage bore the stage name of Ichikawa Danjuro. He was born in 1660, and was acknowledged as the leading actor. He began his career as an actor at the age of thirteen. In 1704 he was murdered by a fellow player. His son, Kuzo Danjuro succeeded to the stage name and maintained its high repute till his death.

Strange as it may seem to westerners who flock to see an individual actor or actress who have made their names through their own personal merit and genius, yet in Japan an actor's popularity depends largely on the name he has *inherited,* either from his ancestors or as a gift from a master. Thus, for instance, the name Danjuro, which is to-day borne by the greatest Japanese actor, has also been the name borne by the great Japanese actors before him. The son of a great actor will inherit his father's stage name, and will endeavor to uphold it. Should he prove unworthy of it, it is a source of regret to every one, who, however, will go to see him rather because he bears the name than from any knowledge of his ability. Fortunately, it became legal for a great actor to bestow his stage name on a clever pupil whom he would adopt. So the excellency of the art was maintained with the high name borne. Several actors may bear the same stage surname, and while the one who is the most efficient and pleases most may not be at all a descendant of the illustrious man who established the name, nevertheless it is a high honor for him to bear it. To be a Danjuro, for instance, means that one has either proved by one's talent and genius the right to so high a title, or else is a natural descendant of the name. In the latter case, where talent in this direction is plainly absent, the individual generally prefers to drop the stage name of his forefathers, and while retaining his rightful name takes up another calling, leaving others more competent to add to the glory established by his ancestor.

The Danjuro name has been handed down thus: The first Danjuro was murdered. His son Kuzo, succeeding, had no son of his own. He adopted one, on whom he bestowed his name. This young man died at an early age, and Danjuro Kuzo adopted another. This, the fourth Danjuro (1711–1788), was succeeded by his son, fifth of that name (1741–1806). The sixth died before his father, and the coveted name was transmitted to a nephew. He was the ablest of the seven Danjuros. His son committed honorable suicide in order to save his father from disgrace and reproach, and for nineteen years the name remained in abeyance. In 1874 his half-brother assumed it. This, the ninth Danjuro, is acknowledged as the greatest living actor in Japan.

Thus it will be seen that it is not an easy matter to succeed as an actor in Japan unless one can begin with some great hereditary stage name. Of course, there is a strict law which prevents any one adopting these names unless legally entitled to do so, either by descent, adoption, or gift of the former holder of the name. So an actor, bearing a great name, may bestow it on whomsoever he chooses in the profession. However, many actors who have no great stage name to back them do succeed in their profession entirely through their wonderful efforts and talent.

In the old days a square cage rested on the front roof of a theatre, wrapped about with a curtain. Here a drum was beaten morning and night. Modern theatres have done away with this, however.

The interior of a Japanese theatre is square, and is partitioned into little compartments. These compartments will hold four or five persons each. An entrance way level with the top of the compartments runs down each side of the pit. These were formerly adorned with flowers and called "The Flowery Way." Thus when one has descended to the little compartment his head and shoulders reach this level, and when bordered with flowers the effect is surely delightful and grateful. The stage faces south. Outside "The Flowery Way" are two or three more rows of compartments a little higher than the pit. These are the better seats. There is a second story of compartments facing the stage and rising one above the other, until bounded by a long window with iron bars. Outside this window runs a passage. Here a spectator is admitted for one single act. Should he desire to see more, he is obliged to pay extra.

The stage curtain draws from side to side. In the centre of the stage is the large turn-table or revolving stage. By this revolving stage scenes can be changed and shifted without the curtain having to be drawn. Thus a whole scene revolves to present a new one on a new semicircle. This is managed adroitly by men who work in a space underneath the boards aptly called "Hell."

A theatre is to be open not more than eight hours per day; this rule being set by the Metropolitan Police Board. Previously, the theatre would remain open from dawn until midnight. Parties of four or five will occupy a compartment and enjoy the performance together, spending an entire day there. Adjoining the theatres are tea-houses and gardens, the proprietors of which agree to furnish the patrons of the theatre with whatever they desire between the acts. Thus one can spend an entire day in a theatre and not find it necessary to return home for his meals or other requisites. By this means also the tea-houses are enabled to profit largely. Meals are even served in the compartments, and while the play is in progress some of the men insist on having their "sake" at their elbows, and it is not an uncommon thing in consequence for some to grow drunk and unruly and so have to be ejected.

A play generally lasts thirty-five days, each act seeming like a new chapter in the history of the plot. Of course one can go and see but an act of the play and find enjoyment, to say nothing of the small one- or two-act plays, but an average good Japanese historical or domestic play will occupy this time.

The prompters are called blackamoors. They wear black veils and are on the stage visible to every one. They glide lightly about, keeping the stage in order, and prompting the "lines." The audience, strange to say, is supposed to be altogether blind to these figures; however, when interested in the play and the actors, one scarcely casts a thought to the dark figures at the back.

Where in the old days the actor was despised and held in low esteem, to-day he is respected of all, and the idol of the young particularly. The private life of the actor is said to be loose, his morality anything but of the purest, but however this may be the theatre is certainly the most pleasant diversion in which the Japanese indulge.

(*Critic,* September 1902)

✳

THE MARVELOUS MINIATURE TREES
OF JAPAN:
THESE CURIOUS EFFECTS ARE ONLY
ATTAINED AFTER GENERATIONS
OF PATIENT TOIL

Among the many delightful arts and studies of the Japanese none is more strange, unique and ancient than that of their training, cultivating and dwarfing of certain varieties of their flower-bearing trees. They seize upon certain peculiarities of the tree, and emphasize or exaggerate this trait even to the point of caricature. They aim to express delicate meanings which a Western imagination could scarcely grasp; as, for instance, laboriously training certain types of trees to convey the ideas of peace, chastity, quiet old age, connubial happiness, and the sweetness of solitude.

While essentially artistic, Japanese gardeners do not seek for rare flowers or trees, however beautiful they may be, but rather cultivate the cherry, the plum, azalea, japonica and other common flowering trees, and train these into the rarest of shapes, making festivals of their blossoming-time, and placing fairy plum and cherry trees in pots in the guest-chamber as a token of hospitality. The cultivated flowers of Japan are the wild flowers, and the cultivated trees are those most commonly known and understood.

It would seem that the same perverse order of things obtains in their culture of dwarf trees as in everything else Japanese. Where Westerners would train their trees to grow tall and straight and symmetrical, the Japanese fix upon a motif, and laboriously, patiently and systematically adapt Nature to their own design, until the tree is twisted and distorted from its original plan, and slowly follows their conception to perfection. The process sometimes covers hundreds of years, being handed down from generation to generation, for this precious labor cannot be accomplished by one man or one generation. When the design is developed by the exposure of the root it can only be done at the rate of a quarter of an inch a year. Many of the designs are developed by grafting various kinds of trees upon one root, or planting more than one tree in a garden and training the roots and branches together.

The Japanese exhibit the same exquisite veneration for age in trees as in people, and a favorite conceit is the training of the plum-tree, so rugged and gnarled and knotted with its slender shoots and sparse studded arrangement of flowers, that it typifies admirably the contrast of bent or crabbed age with fresh and vigorous youth, best displayed when the tree is in bud.

The plum-tree is, in fact, a favorite subject for their skill, and is trained in a variety of shapes, bent and curved, and with graftings of different-colored blossom-sprays, fresh, fragrant and long-lasting, form one of the most welcome and beautiful decorations during the early spring.

The plum-tree, originally the imperial favorite, was long since, however, supplanted by the cherry. A pretty story is told of the origin of the name "O-shu-ku-bai," meaning "Nightingale-dwelling-plum-tree," a variety with pink blossoms and a delicious odor: In the tenth century the plum-tree, which according to custom had been planted in front of the imperial palace, withered and died. In a search for a tree worthy to be placed in its stead, one was found in the garden of a well-known poet named Kino Tsurayuki, and was demanded by the court officials. The daughter of the poet was filled with grief at the loss of her tree, and wrote this verse, secretly pinning it to the tree:

> Claimed for our Sovereign's use,
> Blossoms I've loved so well,
> Can I in duty fail?
> But for the nightingale
> Seeking her home of song
> How shall I find excuse?

In some way the lines fell into the hands of the good emperor, and he straightway ordered the tree returned, hence the name "Nightingale-dwelling-plum-tree."

And in fact all the names of these curious trees have a poetic significance. One cannot visit Japan without hearing of the Recumbent Dragon plum-tree at Kameido, north of Tokio. This rare and curious tree of extreme old age and contorted shape, whose branches had bent plowing the soil, forming new roots in fourteen places, straggling over an extreme area, from its suggestive likeness was named the "Recumbent Dragon," and yearly clad with fresh shoots and white blossoms of fine perfume it attracted large crowds of visitors and pilgrims. The fruit of the tree was yearly sent to the shogun. But like everything else, it finally succumbed to extreme age, and was replaced by less imposing trees selected because of their likeness to its crawling shape.

The pine is indispensable to the true Japanese, and is found wherever he resides. It surrounds the chapel of the sun-god and that of the saints and patrons. The dwarf variety called Fine Gojo Matsu meaning "dwarf pine with five leaves," is much sought after, as it is a symbol of happiness and prolonged life. Sometimes a dwarf pine has its branches wide-spread and the top literally covered with snowy blossoms, a fitting symbol of winter in the home of the rich.

In this artificial culture of the pine, extremes meet; specimens of immense size and those reduced to minute proportions are placed side by side. At Okosaka is the celebrated pine-tree whose artificially extended branches have a circuit of one hundred and thirty-five feet, while at Yedo one sees a dwarf pine in a lacquered box not occupying more than two square inches.

The peach-tree has a mystic value derived from ancient Chinese legends. The peach-tree of the Taoists, said to grow within the gardens of the fairy Si-Wang-Mu, blossoms but once in three thousand years, but each peach is believed to confer three thousand years of life upon the fortunate or unfortunate mortal who consumes it. The peach-tree is seldom employed as an art motif except in association with the emblematic significance which links it to the pine. The pine forms the chief element of the Sho-chiku-bai, the triple emblem of old age, dwarfed by the horticulturist by compression of its roots and tortured and twisted into simulated antiquity by cords and training, and is in strange contrast to the noble forest-tree, permitted to grow unrestrained by artifice in its native soil. The dwarf pines are often trained out over the surface of the water in spherical form, or trailed upon the ground. Again, they are cultivated in the tama-tusukuri style, a method by which each tuft of foliage is cut into a disk-like form.

One specimen of tree, a larch, has been trained in a hoop to represent a moon, with branches trimmed to represent clouds across its face. Often trees are trained around a rock or grow from a mountain sponge. Some represent insects, grasshoppers, spiders, or the Japanese legend of the long and short armed man.

Two trunks are sometimes trained to represent the stork, with a low branch for a tortoise at its feet. Again, a tree is supposed to be growing under a waterfall, that washes away the earth from the roots; these are gradually uncovered in training, and the branches trimmed so that they seem to be blown back by the wind and the water from the fall.

Admiration deepens as one studies these gardens, never better shown than in the imperial gardens, where each carefully calculated hillock bears a poetical resemblance to Mount Fuji, each pond or row of stones has some philosophical meaning, not to be fathomed by a hasty glance.

(*Woman's Home Companion,* June 1904)

EVERY-DAY LIFE IN JAPAN

"All waters and women look the same under the light of the moon," but all nations do not appear the same in the light of civilization. The West speaks of the "heathen" East, and the East with equal contempt calls the Westerner a barbarian. Each complains that the other is uncivilized. It depends on what constitutes civilization. Progression and a certain religion does not necessarily spell it.

Convention walks hand in hand with any civilization. No nation is uncivilized which in the actual every-day living practices the little niceties and politenesses of convention. Do not deem a land uncivilized because the natives squat on their heels as they eat their dinners. Daintier and less barbarous the tiny bits of china and the long slim chopsticks of the Orient than the heavy carved gorgeous silver of the West.

The ancient practice of arising with the sun is still kept up by many of the Japanese outside the big cities. Tokyo, Yokohama, even Osaka, have become too commercial and cosmopolitan for the inhabitants to observe the mode of life practiced by their ancestors. The city people rush about with the eager breathlessness of the Yankee. At night they often dissipate, and sunrise finds them sleeping hard.

A man may not drink sake till past the last hour of the night and awaken to smile at the morning sun. The inhabitants outside of the big cities, however, make up the backbone of the nation, and these are the ones who arise with the sun.

At five in the morning shojis are pushed slightly apart and bright faces look toward the East. "Ohayo! Ohayo!" (Good morning—or more literally, "It is morning!") says the polite Japanese, and bows with great friendliness and appreciation to the big yellow globe pushing its way upward in the sky. A murmuring of voices runs through the house. Down in the kitchen the noisy maid-servant makes herself heard. She is scolding her little army of assistants, for she, the chief servant and cook, has an assistant, a boy of seventeen, who in turn has a small boy assistant, who in turn likewise has an assistant, a still smaller boy. The chief servant scolds them all thoroughly. She would like to shake more energy into their lazy, sleepy bodies. "Hurry! for the Okusama (august lady of the house) will be down presently." She sends them hurrying this way and that, one to draw and carry water, one to prepare the dining-room, one to sweep the verandas, open the shojis and let in the morning sunlight and air, and she herself sets to work upon the cooking. Thus in the hours when the average Western servant is sleeping the Japanese servants do all the housework for the day. Before breakfast the housework is done. When the honorable lady of the house descends to the honorable down-stairs the rooms shine in cheerful morning welcome to her; breakfast is on the lacquered trays which stand on feet a few inches in height. Before she breakfasts, however, the Okusama looks into the various rooms with the searching eye of the experienced housekeeper. If all is well she sweetly enters the dining-room, and herself waits upon her husband and parents, and pours for them the morning tea.

The family may have been up as early as the servants, but they have engaged themselves in bathing, dressing, and, for a short spell, in simply enjoying the rising sun and the early morning. Breakfast is ready by seven. Of course where the family cannot afford servants the mistress of the house, or, if she is old, her daughter-in-law or her daughters must do the housework, but even quite poor people keep at least one scullery maid.

Morning conversation must always be pleasant. How sad to begin the day with harsh words! The wife, if she is highly bred and fond of the politenesses of speech, will say to her husband,

"O shikkei itashmashita," which means, "I beg you to pardon me for my rudeness last time we met." She may not have been in the slightest rude, but she hastens thus to apologize for what might have been. The husband accepts her apology with graciousness, and observing that he too was augustly rude, he turns to the subject of the day. "The sun is honorably deigning to shine," or, "The honorable rain still falls. The earth must indeed be thirsty." There is no complaint made against the weather. In addressing each other the Japanese usually preface a name with the term "honorable"—in Japanese "O," "Go," or "On." The term "san" is usually applied after the name. "Sama," a more respectful and less familiar term, is used to strangers. Both words mean about the same as "Mr., Mrs., or Miss," though "san" in the family is affectionate. "O-Haru-san" will say the husband, "please, another cup of tea for O-Bankurpsama," the latter being a friend or guest.

In many families the son of the house has brought home to his parents a young bride. At this time she is undergoing the severe strain of attempting to win the most desired approval of her parents-in-law. The son on attaining his majority becomes superior to his mother, but she is the absolute ruler of her daughter-in-law. Hence it often happens that the young wife waits upon the older woman. When breakfast is finished the son takes the morning paper, a social rather than a news sheet, and glances through it hurriedly before leaving for his work. When he has finished he passes it to his wife, and then it becomes her duty to read it aloud to her mother-in-law, a task very often tedious and trying. But she is very anxious to please the powerful lady, for she knows that her happiness is entirely in the hands of her mother-in-law. Such is the latter's power, indeed, that if she deems it desirable, she can even divorce her son's wife, whether the son desires it or not. Taught to think more of the parent than the wife, he bows to the often unhappy inevitable. Indeed, many a man has gone away from home on some mission and returned to find himself wifeless, his mother having sent home and divorced his wife in his absence. I believe, however, that the power of the mother-in-law is on the wane. The life of the bride even under the dominion of an exacting mother-in-law is always gilded with hope. She prays daily and fervently that she may become a mother, for then she may, as a rule, have an establishment of her own, and her position becomes immensely elevated. Indeed, she immediately begins to speculate upon her own chances of becoming a mother-in-law. Foreigners have expressed surprise and amusement at the ambition of Japanese girls to grow old. This is one of the reasons. Age brings freedom, power.

When the men have taken themselves off to their various occupations the women, in turn, begin their daily tasks. Even rich women find something to do. There are always children in the family. The children are bathed and dressed, often altogether in the family pond. Clean linen clothes are put upon them. The babies are sent away with their nurses, the older children to school, and the little tots that come between are usually taken in hand by the mother or an elder sister. The Japanese women begin to teach their children manners when they are as young as three and four years. They will show them how to sit politely on the floor, how to bow gracefully, how to hold the chop-sticks, the proper and refined way to eat; they teach them words and greetings of politeness, and finally, but not least, they instruct them in the first principles of patriotism and loyalty. Everything they are told comes from Tenshi-sama (the Emperor), and when the final question, "If Tenshi-sama needs you, what will you do for him?" is put, the answer comes quickly,

"I will die for Tenshi-sama." One hour at least is given to this first home instruction, then the little ones are sent out into the gardens, where they play joyfully together.

The morning is the busy time for the Okusama. When the children have been sent out into the gardens she finds a few moments to give to her young daughter. The young girl will assist her at the tokonona, and while thus pleasantly engaged the mother imparts some good advice. The girl finds a moment, perhaps, to make some shy confidence. Often she confesses to the mother what she would not breathe to her father or any one else—her love affairs. For watched and guarded as is the young girl of good family, still she is a girl, and hence romantic. She is not permitted any familiar association with young men, but she has a chance to see, and sometimes even speak to young men in her own circle of family friends. But even if she is not given the opportunity to meet and speak to a young man, there is nothing to prevent her casting shy glances toward a prepossessing youth whom she may encounter when driving or walking abroad. Her "love affairs" are not like those of the American girl. She cannot tell her mother of words of passion and love poured into her ears, of tender hand-clasps and embraces. Such things are unknown to her. But she will tell of one who passes and repasses their house, of a flower placed upon her window-ledge, and sometimes of a little love-letter found in her sleeve. How it got there she cannot imagine, but the lover could tell of an obliging maid or even a small brother. There are few mothers who can find it in them to scold the daughter for such confidences. She will urge upon the girl the virtue of becoming modesty, and warn her against making any display of her feeling, but she is fully in sympathy with the young girl, and secretly she plans to do her utmost to bring the young couple together, to use her influence with the father to approach the boy's father with a view to making a proposal—or obtaining a proposal—either way. Matches are made for the young people by the parents of the youth and maiden. Some people employ the services of a Nakoda (marriage agent) where they are not acquainted with the family with whom they desire an alliance. Such marriages are not necessarily unhappy. The girls and boys expect it to happen this way, and parents, if they are the right sort, endeavor to choose wisely. Even if a girl is married to a man she has never seen till the time of the betrothal it may be that she has looked forward to the time when her hero is to come and claim her. The first man she is thus thrown in close contact with she naturally becomes interested in, particularly so in view of the fact that both of them are conscious of the relation they will soon occupy to each other. I do not believe in such marriages—still they are not so unhappy.

There are two tasks the lady of the house nearly always reserves for herself—the instruction and counselling of her children and the arrangement of the tokonona (place of honor in the guest-room). What servant could undertake properly either of these tasks? The Okusama does not fill the beautiful vases with flowers. She sets in it one branch, one flower, or a twig from a beautiful tree. It is placed just as it should be, so that all its graceful lines may show to the best effect. We have only two eyes with which to see. We cannot properly admire a great many beautiful things at once. Better admire to the full one little flower than surfeit oneself with a huge mass of them. And so it is with the other decoration in the tokonona. It is not a cabinet full of beautiful curios. The Japanese people of means and refinement keep their treasures in a storeroom. Each day they bring out one of them, and this is set in the tokonona. Every day there is a new scroll or ornament and flower to admire. It serves, too, as an excellent subject of conversation for a chance visitor, for all these ornaments have a history of some kind, hence their value. The visitor will politely ask questions concerning it, and thus a subject of conversation more interesting than the weather is afforded.

By the time the house has been thoroughly put in order the meat, fish, and vegetable men have come and gone; noon is at hand. All the members of the family are at dinner together. If there is one absent from home, still his place is set and served. His spirit, they say, still dines and abides with them.

The noon meal is a merry one—such good things to eat, such a buzz of joyful chatter! A little boy of twelve honorable years talks with his mother. His father is gone to the war. He is the head of the family, his mother's adviser, confidant, and protector. Or sometimes the soft-speaking young daughter-in-law moves gracefully about the room, waiting with solicitude upon the mother-in-law, preparing with her own hands the amber tea for the older woman, and when the latter condescends a word of commendation she appears very grateful. The mother-in-law tells her to be seated and eat her own meal, and finally, making sure that her mother-in-law is thoroughly served, she modestly takes her seat.

"A good, dutiful, modest, and gentle daughter, my son," the older woman will later assert, and the bride is rewarded, after all, since she has pleased her husband.

The afternoon is given up to social pleasures. Often the ladies of the house, attired in soft, silken omeshi, drive abroad in their jinrikishas and spend the afternoon in making calls upon friends. Sometimes they go to the city on a shopping trip and come back with their vehicle quite loaded down with the pretty things dear to the heart of a woman.

The Japanese wife and mother prefers to spend her afternoons at home with her children. They all go out together, if only into the tiny garden. Nothing in the house can compare with the outdoors. In spring and summer they are out nearly all day. The women sew and embroider under some pretty tree—a cherry, camphor, or plum-tree. Here, their hands employed sewing, their eyes and senses delighted by their surroundings, watching the children playing, is it any wonder that the Japanese woman is calm of soul? Nature is the greatest distraction from care, they believe. Live close to nature and you will forget the little bitternesses of life. How happy seem the little children—even the bare-legged ragged rascals of the poor. They twist like natural acrobats about the bamboo poles; they climb to inconceivable heights up the trees, and cling to swaying boughs with the agility of monkeys. The child in the garden, with the watching mother, flies his kite, while his sisters play battledore and shuttlecock. A favorite game for indoors is called sugoroku. On a large sheet of paper various little pictures are printed—portraits of eminent warriors or views of noted places. It is played with a dice. It is a simple game, and it teaches the little ones the names of historical characters and places.

Every month in Japan has its particular significance to the Japanese, January, the month of the New-year; February, the inari (fox festival); March, the doll festival; April, the birthday of Buddha, the month when people stroll out for hanami (flower picnic), and fields and hills are tinted with clouds of cherry blossoms; May, when the azaleas are ablaze and the picnickers flock to the beautiful gardens; June, the Temple festivals; July, the celebration of the "Milky Way"; August, moonlight banquets; September, the month of the kikuzuki (chrysanthemum) shows; October is a desolate month, for the gods are said to be absent. In November the parents celebrate the third, fifth, or seventh anniversary of their children, and entertain their friends; December, a month of work in preparation for the New-year.

Thus every month has its distractions to break the monotony of the everyday life.

It is said that the Japanese woman is a slave to her husband, an upper servant of his household. She is a very happy slave and her lot is an enviable one. The husband takes upon his shoulders the burden of business and leaves her with the children. She shares in their joys and is as innocent as they. But one does not confide one's deepest thoughts, one's dearest hopes and ambitions to one's slave. One does not earnestly listen to and heed the advice of one's slave; one does not unquestioningly give one's children into the hands of one's slave, nor does one cherish one's slave as a pearl. So the Japanese woman is a very happy "slave."

Before the Restoration the better-class Japanese esteemed it a degradation to work. A tradesman was despised. To-day there is hardly a man of Japan who does not follow some calling. The older men, the grandfathers, may stay at home, but the sons—the restless, modern, progressive sons of the New Japan—are not happy unless employed. The spirit of modern Japan is in them. They are as devoted to their business as to their homes. But they keep them well separated and apart. The Japanese who can afford it has his office in the big city, but his home in the suburbs. During the day he is in the midst of the busy stir and whirl of the city, but about four in the afternoon he is hurrying toward the grateful peace and beauty of his country home. The first thing he does on reaching home is to bathe and remove all the clothes he has worn at his office or store. With the changing of his business clothes he lays aside all thought of business. In his home he finds desired rest and recreation. He is by nature a lover of leisure. Few business men in America would leave their offices so early or would take so many holidays. The Japanese business man takes all the holidays he can afford. He is at home most of the fête-days. He goes with the family to see the carnivals, the temple, and flower festivals.

In the evening when the little ones are snugly sleeping the wife and husband enjoy each other's company. Each tells the other of the various happenings of the day. He gives her advice concerning the children, and she in turn advises him in matters she understands. Often they take little moonlight strolls together, or seek some pleasure-booth on a charming river, where they sip their sake or tea and listen to the music of the geishas. Often they entertain friends at a tea ceremony, and often are in turn entertained. Clad in her most charming dress the wife goes with her husband to visit their friends or relatives. Always they carry little lacquer boxes, for to show proper appreciation of the host and hostess the guests must either eat all placed before them or carry home with them what they cannot eat.

I have written chiefly of the daily life of the average Japanese of average means and education. There are the poorer people, whose lives are melancholy indeed. Yet if an American wrote on the home life of the Americans he would not describe the life of the slums. So I refrain from describing the pitiful ones. In the big cities of Japan people work rather than live. Many there be who from force of circumstances cannot afford a home in the suburbs. They are chiefly of the laboring class—pleasure women, such as geishas in tea-house establishments, shopkeepers, the families of factory hands, jinriki-men, and so forth. There are, too, many fairly well-off people who have city houses. The city has its attractions to many. It is not as healthful or as moral as the country, but it is exciting. Children play about in the open street; people use a common public bath; young men and women find their pleasures in tea houses and theatres and the story-teller's halls, and an occasional picnic in the country.

But a word regarding the farming people. They are the happy ones, rough and uncultivated as they seem. Ragged the farmer looks, and you will hear he is poor. But it is not truly so. The farmer has money in his ragged clothes; he is prosperous in comparison with the working-men in the big cities. He is proud too. His sons go out from home to make the brave army of the Emperor. Their homes are warm and comfortable. Look into one on a cold winter day. You will see the family gathered about an irori, a fireplace encircled by a wooden frame from which hangs a steaming kettle. The red-hot charcoal gleams warmly. The group seem to be enjoying themselves immensely. The features of these rurals are flat and coarse, but honest. It is hard to realize that the round-faced, snub-nosed woman with the baby on her back is of the same nationality as the lady of the Yamato type, pure and perfect of features, with white thin skin, small lips, dreamy eyes, straight nose, and exquisite hands. Yet the noisy rollicking laugh of the countrywoman seems almost as good to hear as the gentle, melodious voice of the lady, and within the countrywoman's heart as good and generous emotions stir.

(*Harper's Weekly,* October 20, 1904)

✳

THE JAPANESE IN AMERICA

Ever since the Japanese school trouble in San Francisco became acute I have read with interest and considerable sadness the various published articles and editorials upon the subject. A curious article by a special newspaper correspondent on the Pacific coast, impels me to take up my pen, not as a champion for the Japanese, but in appeal to the fair-minded, right-thinking Americans for ordinary justice and sane judgment for "the little brown man," as this correspondent terms him.

The writer of the article in question refers to the Japanese as "a race from which came our servants!" Repeated references are made to the fact that the Japanese stubbornly refuses to recognize the white man as his superior. "The white race every time," cries the writer, attempting to make a case from so poor an issue. Various mean characteristics of the Japanese race the writer enumerates, laying emphasis on his "conceit." Finally the writer makes the astonishing statement that the war correspondents who went to the front full of admiration and enthusiasm for the Japanese, returned voicing "eternal condemnation for everything Japanese."

Also the writer paints a ludicrous picture of the dowdy little Japanese woman as she appears in American dress. Such articles mislead and inflame.

What reflection upon the race can result through the failure of its women to dress in Western garb with style? The description of the Japanese woman given by the writer, however, must apply to the humblest among this race who live in America. The Japanese gentlewoman in America wears the foreign dress with far more smartness and ease than the foreign woman in Japan does the native garb there. The article against which I appeal appeared as a commentary upon the message of President Roosevelt dealing with the Japanese problem. The writer, "M. E. C.," a special correspondent of the New York "Times" in Oakland, Cal., had these things to say, among others:

"We recognize the grave import of the message, a message likely to be fraught with such consequences to the Pacific coast. And we hark back to the time when the Japanese first slipped quietly in among us. He was a demure little brown man, and we treated him well—we gave him a home and we educated him. We were the dominant Caucasian race, he was of the inferior Asiatic race—a race from which came our servants. The Japanese furnished only another phase of the intense cosmopolitanism of San Francisco—parts of which were distinctly of Europe and others of the Orient.

"The Japanese took up life quietly in many homes. He helped the mistress of the family before school, then went to school with the children. He aided in household tasks after school hours. He was well fed and had his own room and his evenings to himself. He was paid three or four dollars a week, as much as white servants were paid in the East. They were most kindly treated everywhere—in the home, in the schools. In the latter they received the greatest consideration, helped along by the children, and taught with exceeding patience by the teachers. Fancy the annoyance of having a Japanese man who cannot speak English in a class of fifty little children. The one man took up so much time that it was not always fair to the children.

*　*　*

"The Japanese do not come here to be our servants; that is only their stepping stone. They come to go into business, and that has been the experience also in Hawaii. The Japanese has not the responsibilities of the white man; he has not his traditions, his ideals. He lives on so little, in such squalid, meager surroundings, that he can lower business prices and business standards till the white man is driven out.

*　*　*

"San Francisco is a tremendous mass of debris—miles and miles of it. It is the great burden which the white laborer is bearing; it is his back bending to the load which one sees; he has no assistance from the Japanese laboring class."

Again "M. E. C." asserts that the war changed the Japanese.

"The great change in the Japanese, which seems to have precipitated all the trouble, dates from the late war. Sentiment was almost entirely with them. Here and there were a few who looked distrustfully at everything Oriental and said:

"'The white man every time—the white man against the field, right or wrong!'

"But most men got back to the principle involved and rejoiced with the Japanese as battles were won. It was only a few months ago that war correspondents from all over the United States and England passed through San Francisco on their way to the Orient. All was enthusiasm for the Japanese as they set sail for the land of the Mikado.

"But, oh! the difference when they returned to America some months later! They voiced eternal condemnation for everything Japanese. On one thing were they all agreed—on insincerity as a dominating Japanese characteristic. And they learned something else in their weary months of waiting among this alien people. They learned the hatred which these Oriental races have for the white race, a hatred well covered up ordinarily, but a hatred that exists. Any scheme for the settlement of the present question which fails to recognize this great race hatred fails in a very vital point."

Conceit Japan certainly has. What race has not? What of the conceit which makes the bland statement that because of its peculiar skin-color, a race is superior? Since when did the Oriental nations become the slaves or servants of the Caucasian race? To speak of the Oriental nations as inferior is to make an ignorant and stupid statement—dangerous, moreover. Is it desirable that the Oriental nations be goaded into proving they are not inferior? What constitutes civilization? A crossing of swords could actually prove nothing, but the Oriental knows it is the test of the Western nations and he may elect some day to be put to this test. With how tragic a result for the whole world! Why are the bigoted, stupid-tongued ones permitted to speak aloud? They awaken hatred, prejudice.

Are we no better to-day than in the time when the white-skinned Spaniard came all conquering to exterminate the darker-hued man of the New World? Do the Western nations, indeed, cherish the childish delusion that a race as proud and intelligent as the Japanese or the Chinese could be likewise subjected?

It is preposterous to name the Japanese as an inferior race—to wave a flag as red as that before the eyes of a people admittedly full of pride and pugnacity.

Yes. Japan is "bursting with conceit." So is every nation. Conceit, if such it can be called, is what makes one accomplish things. It is the assurance behind the hand that strikes which makes the blow the surer and severer. Why reproach Japan for an attribute common to every self-respecting nation on the earth? Of course, crowned with her new war laurels, Japan's vanity is more apparent at the present time. How was America after the war with Spain? At such a time would it have been well for another nation to speak sneeringly of it as an "inferior nation?"

The statement regarding the war correspondents is audaciously false. I read omnivorously all the books I could get written by these same correspondents after their return to America. With only one or two exceptions, they almost over-praised Japan. Indeed, Japan's conceit has been very much fed by the fulsome praise bestowed upon her by these very American writers who have lived among, known and sometimes loved the Japanese. Who will heed to-day the words of those who seek to decry the character of such a nation?

How foolish is the supposition that the Japanese immigrants will over-run this country, and in competition with the native crush him to the wall. Japan is a little nation at best. How many of her people would she spare to cause the terrible havoc here predicted? The closing paragraph of "M. E. C.'s" article follows:

"Now the wise men of the nation are studying a question full of important phases—the old question which always comes up when two alien races undertake to live out life together, under the same conditions. It is simplified to some extent when one is the dominant race and the other the definitely subjected one—the latter the servant class, and content to remain so. But when the alien race aims at equality it calls out the stubborn resistance of the stronger race, and an antagonism sets in, the end of which no man can see."

As for the school question itself, I cannot express an opinion. But I do not understand how the pupils in the schools are Japanese men; for education has been for long compulsory in Japan. Had these men not had a lower school education before they came to America? If they go merely to learn the English language, then, indeed, I sympathize with the Californians and believe that adult Japanese should be excluded. But as regards the little children, what a complication America would face, were it to supply separate schools for the children of every individual nationality!

The "social ostracism" of certain races is a sad thing, indeed; but when it strikes at a proud and noble people it is not only sad—it is foolhardy. The fact that California knows the individual Japanese as a domestic servant does not make of the Japanese a servile race.

The contempt with which the word "servant" is flung now at the Japanese awakes in me an understanding of the most important of all problems to American women—the servant problem. People are abandoning home life because of it. Race suicide is one of the direct results. And the reason? Because of the contemptuous term "servant."

Recently to your shores has come a new kind of servant—a self-respecting, clean, decent person, who in his very character has elevated the station of the servant. Would you discourage him also? He comes of a race which deems no employment degrading. In Japan a mistress does not despise her maid. She will make the simple statement: "Who knows but that I may come to this myself."

We are all servants—of various sorts. I serve you, for whom I write. You serve your customers, or your clients. Shall each one of us kick at the one below us? And why is the work of a home, the cooking, the ministering to our personal wants and needs, not to be esteemed? To be done properly it should bring out the best traits of our character.

I myself have had servants in America of nearly every sort and kind. I had best service from the Japanese, for the simple reason that I found them less dissatisfied with their thankless work than were the others. But even they were affected by the attitude of Americans toward the servant. I remember Dan, a cook and butler, whose surliness, independence and resentful looks I never understood until I questioned him. He said, "Mrs., in America to be servant is to be dog. Velly well—dog bark and bite. Me too." Later I obtained the services of a newer recruit—an optimistic, apple-faced newcomer, whose shining eyes beheld everything American with astonishment and delight. Him I regretfully dismissed because of his inability to understand morals—as viewed by a Westerner. Taku was wont to take his daily bath in a tub, openly set out in the center of my kitchen floor, and when a scandalized Irish maid would walk into the kitchen, he would arise politely and bow to her from his watery retreat.

Yes. The Japanese of the poorer class will work for you as servants—but not for long—for some day you will teach them the opprobrium of the term "servant," and the meanest Japanese has pride.

"M. E. C." avers that the Japanese hates the white man. He does not. I have never known one to do so yet. What race is engaged in the thankless employment of hating any other nation, save its oppressor or enemy.

I am not Oriental or Occidental either, but Eurasian. I must bleed for both my nations. I am Irish more than English—Chinese as well as Japanese. Both my fatherland and my motherland have been the victims of injustice and oppression. Sometimes I dream of the day when all of us will be world citizens—not citizens merely of petty portions of the earth, showing our teeth at each other, snarling, sneering, biting, and with the ambition of the murderer at our heart's core—every man with the savage instinct of the wild beast to get the better of his brother—to prove his greater strength—his mightier mind—the superiority of his color.

(*Eclectic Magazine*, February 1907)

PREFACE TO *CHINESE-JAPANESE COOK BOOK*

Chinese cooking in recent years has become very popular in America, and certain Japanese dishes are also in high favor. The restaurants are no longer merely the resort of curious idlers, intent upon studying types peculiar to Chinatown, for the Chinese restaurants have pushed their way out of Chinatown and are now found in all parts of the large cities of America. In New York they rub elbows with and challenge competition with the finest eating palaces. Their patronage to-day is of the very best, and many of their dishes are justly famous.

There is no reason why these same dishes should not be cooked and served in any American home. When it is known how simple and clean are the ingredients used to make up these Oriental dishes, the Westerner will cease to feel that natural repugnance which assails one when about to taste a strange dish of a new and strange land.

Bread, butter, and potatoes are never used by the Chinese or Japanese. Tea is drunk plain, with neither cream nor sugar, but great care should be used in its brewing. Rice is indispensable, and should be cooked in that peculiarly delectable fashion of which the Oriental peoples alone are past masters. The secret of the solid, flaky, almost dry, yet thoroughly cooked rice lies in the fact that it is never boiled more than thirty minutes, is covered twenty minutes, never stirred nor disturbed, and set to dry on back of range when cooked, covered with a cloth. Mushy, wet, slimy, overcooked rice is unknown to the Chinese and Japanese. Sweetened rice, as in rice pudding and similar dishes, is unknown. Rice takes the place of such staples as bread and potatoes. Syou, sometimes called Soye, is similar to Worcestershire and similar European sauces. In fact, the latter are all said to be adaptations of the original Chinese syou, and most of these European sauces contain syou in their makeup. It lends a flavor to any meat dish, and is greatly esteemed by the Oriental peoples.

In China, with the exception of rice, bonbons, and so on, food is served in one large dish or bowl, out of which all eat, using the chopsticks. Considerable etiquette governs the manner of picking desired morsels from the main bowls. In high-caste or mandarin families a servant has his place at the foot of the table, but he stands throughout the meal. It is his duty to serve at the table the portions from the main dishes to each individual, and to do what the host generally does for the comfort of those at table. The other servants waiting on table take their orders from him, and he is really there as a sort of proxy for the host.

In Japan, individual meals are brought in on separate trays to each person. All sit cross-legged upon the floor before their trays. The Japanese consider it gross and vulgar to put food in quantity upon the plate. The portions are very small, the largest being about the size of an egg. There is a striving for daintiness and simplicity.

For this book only such Chinese and Japanese dishes have been selected as would appeal to the Western palate, and which can be prepared with the kitchen utensils of Western civilization. Many dishes prepared by the Chinese cooks in this country are only modifications of their native dishes. Recipes for the same dish, obtained from different parts of China, vary considerably. The combinations here given are those which experience has proved most easily prepared and most palatable.

The authors advise any one who intends to cook "Chinese" to go to some Chinese restaurant and taste the various dishes he desires to cook. A good cook always should know what a dish tastes like before he tries to cook it. All cooks can tell how the taste of a strange dish reveals to him many things, and it is often possible to guess of what the dish is composed.

No cookbooks, so far as the authors know, have ever been published in China. Recipes descend like heirlooms from one generation of cooks to another. The recipes included in this book (the Chinese ones, that is) have been handed down from Vo Ling, a worthy descendant of a long line of noted Chinese cooks, and himself head cook to Gow Gai, one time highest mandarin of Shanghai. They are all genuine, and were given as an especial expression of respect by a near relative of the famous family of Chinese cooks.

Rules for Cooking

General

The first and the most important rule for Chinese cooking is cleanliness, first of the hands, second of the utensils, and third of the food.

Meat should not be washed, but should be rinsed in cold or lukewarm water and, if necessary, singed over a hot flame and scraped with a sharp knife.

All vegetables and fruit should be washed in cold water,—if necessary, in fifty different waters.

Never use soap to wash saucepans. Use washing soda or sand.

All cloths and dish towels should be boiled and rinsed thoroughly.

Care must be taken to measure accurately the ingredients of recipes, for the spices and relishes used in Chinese kitchens are exceedingly hot and pronounced in flavor.

To make rich stock for soup use only a quart of water to every pound of veal, mutton, or beef bone.

To determine whether a fish is fresh, watch that its flesh is firm and thick, its scales glistening, and its eyes prominent.

When dropped into a bowl or pan containing cold water, eggs that are absolutely fresh will immediately sink to the bottom and rest there; eggs which are not perfectly fresh will stand on end or rise a little.

Delicious dishes can be obtained only from the use of the purest and best quality of ingredients. A good cook needs to be as well a discriminating purchaser.

Glass measures recording pints and quarts of liquid and ounces and pounds of solids (like sugar), with the fractions thereof, are handy and sanitary.

(*Chinese-Japanese Cook Book*, with Sara Bosse, 1914)

ONOTO WATANNA (Winnifred Eaton Babcock Reeve) was the first novelist of Asian ancestry to be published in the United States. Born in Montreal, Canada, in 1875 to a Chinese mother and an English father, Watanna earned fame and notoriety as a romance writer. Capitalizing on American interest in Asia, most of her works feature Japanese heroines who fall in love with Western men. In an era when fictional depictions of passive "lotus blossoms" were the norm, Watanna presented Asian women as smart, strong, and self-reliant.

LINDA TRINH MOSER is an associate professor of English at Southwest Missouri State University, where she teaches courses on women's, ethnic American, and non-European literature. She has published articles on Pardee Lowe, Jean Wakatsuki Houston, Sadakichi Hartmann, and Onoto Watanna.

ELIZABETH ROONEY is the great-granddaughter of Onoto Watanna/Winnifred Eaton. A library technician at the Women's Health Resource Centre in Toronto, she has a B.A. from the University of Toronto and a diploma in library and information technology from Seneca College of Applied Arts and Technology. Her longtime interest in topics related to the Far East has taken her to China as well as Japan, where she spent a year teaching English in Osaka.

The University of Illinois Press
is a founding member of the
Association of American University Presses.

———————————————————————

Composed in 10/13 Sabon
with Sabon display
by Celia Shapland
for the University of Illinois Press
Designed by Dennis Roberts
Manufactured by Thomson-Shore, Inc.

University of Illinois Press
1325 South Oak Street
Champaign, IL 61820-6903
www.press.uillinois.edu